GW00726934

THE
PROMISED LAND

Recent Titles by Caroline Gray from Severn House

BLUE WATERS, BLACK DEPTHS
CROSSBOW
THE DAUGHTER
GOLDEN GIRL
MASQUERADE
SHADOW OF DEATH
SPARES
A WOMAN OF HER TIME
A CHILD OF FORTUNE

THE
PROMISED LAND

Caroline Gray

SEVERN SH HOUSE

This first world edition published in Great Britain 1997 by
SEVERN HOUSE PUBLISHERS LTD of
9–15 High Street, Sutton, Surrey SM1 1DF.
This title first published in the U.S.A. 1998 by
SEVERN HOUSE PUBLISHERS INC of
595 Madison Avenue, New York, N.Y. 10022.

Copyright © 1997 by Caroline Gray

All rights reserved.
The moral right of the author has been asserted.

British Library Cataloguing in Publication Data

Gray, Caroline, 1930-

    The promised land
    I.   Title
    823.9'14 [F]

    ISBN 0 7278 5294 9

This is a novel. All situations in this publication are fictitious and
the characters are invented and are not intended to portray real people,
living or dead. The events have not yet happened.

Typeset by Palimpsest Book Production Limited,
Polmont, Stirlingshire, Scotland.
Printed and bound in Great Britain by
MPG Books Ltd, Bodmin, Cornwall.

Prologue

"Oh!" Miriam Grain gasped, as the ship seemed to fall away from beneath her. "Oh, my God!" she screamed, as the bunk came back up and slammed into her body. "We should have flown. Oh, we should have flown."

"Now, Mums," Matilda said severely. "You know we couldn't afford to fly."

Miriam groaned as the ship hit another wave with a shuddering jar. "If we were on a bigger ship . . ." William ventured.

"We'd be in second class," Matilda reminded her brother, brutally. "Gosh, that was a big one."

Once again the ship came to a shuddering stop, and spray splattered across the cabin windows. Joanna rolled out of bed, reached for her robe, and staggered to the door. She didn't think she was going to be sick; she just didn't want to hear them wailing and complaining any more.

She dragged the door open, lost her footing as the ship rolled, and landed on her hands and knees. Gathering her nightdress almost to her thighs she pushed herself back up. The cabins on board the *Caribee Queen* opened directly in to the saloon, and there were lights on in here, although thankfully at two in the morning it was empty of people; Joanna staggered across the heaving deck and reached an armchair, into which she collapsed, gasping. It was bolted to the deck.

It was remarkable, she thought, how small the ship suddenly felt. The *Caribee Queen* was eight thousand tons, one of a line of freighters that traded between England and the Caribbean, which took twelve passengers; she had seemed quite large enough when they had boarded her in Georgetown, five days before. Now she seemed just a plaything, her engines racing as her propellers cavitated, more spray rattling across her windows.

1

Joanna wondered if she was going to die, was surprised at being less afraid than curious, and somewhat disappointed. She was sixteen, but big for her age, both in height and body; William, two years younger but a keen student of the female anatomy, used to annoy his older sister Matilda by telling her that Jo's boobs were as big as hers. Matilda, at eighteen very much the grown-up, had no sense of humour where figures were concerned; hers was the best.

The door to the deck opened, and Joanna hastily sat up, scooping her long yellow hair back from her face, dragging the robe over her shoulders. The man who came in didn't notice her for a moment as he took off his oilskins, draping them across the bar. Then he turned towards her, and grinned. "Good morning."

Joanna nodded, unable to frame an adequate reply. He came across the deck towards her, apparently able to maintain his balance with perfect ease. "Not scared, are you?"

Joanna pulled the robe tighter around her shoulders. He sat in a chair beside her.

"You're Joanna Grain," he remarked. Well, he would know who she was, as all the passengers ate together at the big table at the far end of the saloon. He had not taken any notice of her before, though, apart from smiling at her when they had been introduced the previous day; he had joined the ship in Barbados.

It had been an impressive occasion, the officers standing to attention and several of the crew, too, as he had come up the companion ladder from the launch. He was not a big man, hardly taller than herself, with slim build and strong features to go with his black hair. But he was the owner of the Shipping Line. His name was Howard Edge. Now he was frowning at her. "There really is no need to be afraid," he said. "This ship could drive through a hurricane."

"Isn't this a hurricane?" she asked, faintly.

"Good lord, no. This is a gale. We'll be out the other side in a couple of hours. You go back to bed and sleep sound; when you awake, it'll all be done."

"I'd rather stay here," Joanna muttered.

"Bit crowded in there, eh? I'm sorry about the accommodation. Especially having your brother in there with you."

"Oh, we want him there," Joanna protested.

"I know," he said sympathetically. "You need to be together." She glanced at him, suspiciously; how much did he know?

"You're going home to relatives?" he asked.

She nodded, and he held her hand. Her instinct was to withdraw it, then she let it lie. How old was he? There were little touches of grey at his temples, but his hands and eyes were young. Forty, perhaps. Old enough to be her father. "What's it like, to own a shipping company?" she asked, desperate to make conversation.

He grinned. "In the middle of a gale, concerned."

"You said there was nothing to be afraid of."

"There isn't. But there's always the possibility of damage to the ship, and that costs money."

"Do you sail on every voyage?"

"Chance would be a fine thing. I love the sea. But I can only sail when I can spare the time. Would you like to sail all the time?"

"Oh, yes," she said without thinking.

"Who knows, maybe one day, you will." And to her consternation he kissed her.

Part One

The Man

'England – a happy land we know,
Where follies naturally grow.'
                              Charles Churchill

Chapter One

Coming Home

"There!" Mother pointed. Like most of the passengers, the Grains had been on deck since dawn. It was a fine summer's day, with little wind and calm seas through which the freighter was ploughing at full speed, her wash creaming away from her bows to meld with the wake that drifted astern and out of sight; the mid-Atlantic storm was, as Mr Edge had promised, nothing more than a bad memory. Because of the calm weather there was mist.

But the sun was up, and the mist was burning off. And in front of them, suddenly, were low green hills. "Could be Barbados," William said.

Matilda squeezed Joanna's hand. "The Promised Land," she whispered.

The three siblings were remarkably alike, given the difference in their ages. Matilda was tall and willowy, small-breasted and slim-hipped. Her face was too aquiline to be pretty, but was certainly handsome. Her hair was a pale gold; unrestrained this morning by her habitual Alice band, it floated in yellow profusion about her head in the wind created by the ship's speed. Joanna was an improved model, as if the Creator, having considered Matilda, had determined that He could make some advantageous improvements. Joanna had the same blonde hair, but hers was a deeper yellow and more thickly stranded; it moved together instead of scattering. Her features were more rounded than her sister's, and promised genuine beauty. She was somewhat shorter than Matilda, but was still growing, as was her figure, equally more rounded and promising – but she had the same long legs.

In her more intense moods, which were common enough, Matilda was jealous of her baby sister. But recently, since the tragedy, they had grown closer together. Mother was sometimes a most practical, capable person, but she needed protecting, in their opinion. And they both adored William. He was already as tall as Joanna. He had the sharp features of Matilda, but the thick yellow hair of the younger sister. His body was muscular – until recently he had attended a school in which he had been one of only twelve white boys in six hundred blacks, Indians and Chinese, he had needed early to cultivate a self-assurance, an assumption of inherent superiority, which was all the white races had really possessed for so long, in their dominance of the dark.

But those days were surely behind him, now.

"Good morning, ladies." Howard Edge came down the ladder from the bridge. "At last, eh?"

"Good morning, Mr Edge," Mother said, effusively.

He smiled at Joanna, and passed on.

"He fancies you," Matilda whispered, enviously.

"Rubbish," Joanna said, remembering that kiss. But it had been a quick, chaste kiss, and nobody else knew of it. And since then he had treated her like any of the other passengers. Except that when he looked at her . . . "He's old enough to be my father."

"They're the worst," Matilda said. "Middle-aged men with ants in their pants for young girls. He should be locked up."

Joanna stuck out her tongue at her. Wouldn't it be marvellous, she thought, if he were to ask for my address in England. That would drive Tilly out of her mind.

"Aunt Ethel said she'd drive down to meet us," Mother said. This was important. Miriam Grain had no idea what her children were going to make of this country they had all been brought up to regard as 'home', but which none of them had ever visited before.

8

Even she had not been home – and it *was* her home – for twenty-two years. When, in the summer of 1938, she had accompanied her husband back to British Guiana, where he had been a police inspector, she had been assured that there would be 'long leave' every four years; his terms of contract were in four year tours, renewed, except in exceptional circumstances, after each tour. The war had put an end to that. Together with her pregnancies. They had enjoyed a long honeymoon for the first four years, preferring to consider a family as a distant prospect. But when it had become obvious that the War was there to stay, and thus long leave gone for the foreseeable future, the condoms had been thrown away, and Matilda had duly appeared in the spring of 1942. Joanna had come a year and a half later, and William two years after that.

By then the War had been over, but long leave remained a distant prospect. England had not seemed very attractive in those grimly austere days, money had been tight, and there had been a lot to do in the colonies, with talk of independence filling the air, and civil unrest filling the streets. Leave had been postponed again and again, and she had been resigned to watching her children grow up as total colonials, to whom England was a myth, perhaps to become reality in adulthood. That had been before a vengeful Indian, arrested and charged with murder by Superintendent Grain, but acquitted by the courts, had crept up to the window beyond which the police officer had sat at his desk, and blown away his head with a single shotgun blast. This time the assassin *had* been convicted of murder, and had been hanged. But that had meant an abrupt change of status for the policeman's widow and family.

There was a widow's pension, but it was not very great. There had been nothing else; police officers lived in houses owned by the Government, as they were regularly moved from one post to another in the huge colony, itself the size of England. England had beckoned, in circumstances Miriam Grain had never envisaged. At least, in England, William would be able to complete his schooling, free from racial tensions, and with perhaps more congenial companions. And the girls should be able to find jobs which would not entail possibly having to work beneath bosses of different races and creeds. Miriam Grain would have angrily rejected the suggestion that she was a racist; she had merely been re-educated, during her years in Guiana, to the belief that the white man, or to be more accurate, the British white man, was the superior of any other living creature. This belief was an absolute necessity where an officer like Gordon Grain, with the assistance of perhaps one other junior white inspector, had to rule a district the size of Yorkshire, containing to be sure another score of white men, perhaps, overseers on the sugar plantations, but which also contained more than fifty thousand blacks and East Indians – even his policemen were nearly all black men. It was an assumption that had ultimately cost Gordon Grain his life.

England also meant that she would be back with her family, in the person of her sister Ethel. Ethel, some years older, was also a widow, but a relatively wealthy one, and, herself childless, she had written suggesting that she would welcome a ready-made family – Ethel had never really cared for Gordon, and even less for the concept that her baby sister should be swept away into the wilds of South America. Most important of all, removing the children to England meant that she would be relieved from the greatest fear that any English mother in the colonies could have – that one of her children might marry 'colour'. Miriam had seen this happen to other families, and had thus watched over hers with especial care, but she could not be with them twenty-four hours a day. They were naturally gregarious. They went to school with black boys and girls, and Indian boys and girls. They made friends. Gordon had never allowed them to bring their dark friends home, but they had been to their friends' houses. And they appeared to be totally unaware of the colour question; if they paid lip service to it when at home, Mirian knew it was with the mental reservation that 'Mummy and Dad were always going on about these things'. That too was a problem now behind her.

"Plymouth Hoe," William said, as the ship nosed her way up the

Sound to her berth. "Where Drake played bowls before beating the Armada." William prided himself on his knowledge of history, as was to be expected in the son of a man who had been so history-minded that he had named his three children after medieval kings and queens.

The women were less interested in Drake's feats than in the land on which they would be setting foot after ten days at sea. And in the people who would be there. Miriam shaded her eyes and looked for Ethel in the crowd on the dock. Matilda studied the various women, considering fashions, and was amazed, but excited, at the shortness of the skirts.

Joanna just stared. Never before had she seen such a sea of white faces. Suddenly she felt concerned for the other passengers on the ship, most of whom were black. They were immigrants, seeking a new home, and perhaps prosperity as well. She was coming home! Then she saw three people standing apart, a woman, and two small children. The woman was short, slim and *svelte*; she wore a genuine fur coat and dark glasses. It was difficult to tell if she was good-looking or not, but she stood with an aura of permanent superiority. Suddenly Joanna knew who she was. She felt quite sick.

Getting through Customs and Immigration took a very long time, and it was nearly noon before the Grains were finally allowed into the huge exit hall, where, happily, Aunt Ethel was indeed waiting for them. Ethel was an older edition of Miriam, and had somewhat severe features, but these softened as she embraced her nieces and nephew. "What lovely children," she remarked, which didn't go down very well with Matilda. But they were all still trying to stop staggering about as their feet insisted on allowing for movement that was no longer there.

"We'll eat on the way," Ethel said. "It's a long drive. In fact, we won't make it today. But I know a neat little hotel where we can spend the night. I've booked us in."

11

Joanna hardly heard her. Howard Edge had said goodbye to them, as he had said goodbye to all the passengers, formally, before joining his wife and children for a huge hug and a kiss; he had then got into a waiting Rolls-Royce and driven off. He had kissed her that night on the ship. Matilda was right, after all; he was just a dirty old man.

Now she stared out of the window of the little car – they were very tightly packed in the back – as they left the city behind and drove into the Devon countryside. This was unlike anything she had ever seen before in her life. In Guiana, if one travelled several hundred miles inland, either by aircraft or river – there were no roads in the interior – one came to very high mountains; she had made two such trips. But the coastal strip, a couple of hundred miles wide and some four hundred deep, was flat alluvial plain. Once it had all been forest, but on the coast itself the trees had been felled to make way for the sugar estates and rice plantations. Outside of the capital city of Georgetown, one could go either east or west; there was only one road in either direction. And the road itself was composed mainly of burnt earth, liable to wash away or pothole in the wet season – which continued for most of the year. In places there were eighteen-inch-wide concrete strips, laid an average car width apart, which provided a smoother passage – providing one could keep the tyres on the strips. One drove endlessly past waving cane or flooded paddies, with the courida swamps which kept out the sea filling the other side, through scattered villages crowded with naked children, while the journey in each direction was punctuated by river crossings which involved driving across two planks laid over the rushing water, much narrower than the concrete strips, onto the deck of a ferry – and driving off again on the other side.

Joanna had looked forward to getting her licence in the coming year, before Daddy had been murdered. She had no doubt it would be easier to obtain over here, because driving was so much easier. The road was wide, and metalled, and smooth, and it was only one of a hundred roads which wound in every direction, intersecting and writhing to and fro. There were no animals. Occasionally there was a sign to beware of leaping deer, which she found entrancing, never having seen a deer before, whether leaping or still. In Guiana one was fortunate to drive ten miles without killing a chicken, or being halted by a herd of pigs or a flock of sheep, or a straying cow.

"It's so grand having you here," Aunt Ethel said. "Now we must talk about what you're going to do. I've spoken with the headmaster of our local school, and he is sure a place can be found for William. What form were you in in BG, William?"

"I was in the Fifth," William said, importantly.

"Oh, splendid. You'll have to take an entrance exam, of course, but there shouldn't be any trouble about that."

"I shouldn't think so," William agreed.

"Now, Joanna . . . you don't have to go back to school if you don't want to."

"I'd rather get a job," Joanna said.

"Are you trained in anything?"

"Well, I was doing secretarial . . ."

"That's the ticket. We'll get you into a secretarial college for a year, then you'll be ready to take on the world."

"Won't secretarial college be very expensive?" Miriam asked.

"We'll sort something out," Ethel said. "And what about you, Matilda. What is your special talent?"

"Dancing," Matilda said.

"Dancing?" Aunt Ethel took her eye off the road for a moment to look at her sister.

"Matilda's brilliant," Miriam said. "She won a competition, last year."

"In British Guiana," Ethel said, doubtfully. "You mean, ballet?"

"Oh, no," Matilda said. "Well, I've done ballet, of course. But my speciality is tap."

"Tap." Aunt Ethel was more doubtful yet. "I'm not sure there's much demand for tap dancing in England, at the moment. But we'll see," she added optimistically.

* * *

13

The small country hotel Aunt Ethel had chosen was a place of hushed voices and soft carpets. By the time they arrived they had already sampled English food, at the pub where they had stopped for lunch, and where Joanna and William had been forbidden to drink the beer. But they had enjoyed the pickled onions and hard-boiled eggs, again quite unlike anything they had encountered before. The food for dinner was thinly sliced and utterly tasteless beef, with carrots, beans and sautéd potatoes. None of them had much taste either. But Aunt Ethel pushed out the boat and ordered a carafe of house wine, and this time Joanna and William were allowed to join in. "When you say tap," Aunt Ethel returned to the subject, "what sort of music do you tap to?"

"Tilly can tap to anything," Joanna said enthusiastically. "Even Bill Haley."

"Bill who?"

Joanna looked at Matilda, desperately trying to stop bursting into giggles. But Matilda's eyes were drifting from the dining-room to the bar beyond, where a group of young men had just gathered. They were all dressed alike, with velvet collars to their jackets, ties which looked very like strings, sideburns, and very narrow trousers. "Teddy boys," Aunt Ethel remarked, disparagingly.

"What?" Mirian asked.

"That's what they're called. Teddy boys. They're a symptom of the degeneration of the country. Shocking. And now this business of Princess Margaret going to marry a commoner! Really. The country is going to the dogs."

"I thought he was rather good-looking," Matilda ventured, to be silenced by a glare from her aunt.

Aunt Ethel had only been able to secure three rooms, two doubles and a single. William had the single, and the two pairs of sisters shared. The bed was a double with a feather mattress, and Joanna and Matilda found themselves virtually in each others' arms, which meant a sleepless night so far as Joanna was concerned – Matilda

14

was very restless. "Do you think you will find a dancing job?" Joanna asked.

"I'm going to try. Are you really going to secretarial college?"

"I'd like to do what you do," Joanna said. She knew she would never be as good a dancer as Matilda – she wasn't sufficiently light on her feet – but she wanted them to be together.

"Did you see that louse Edge and his wife?" Matilda asked. "And the Rolls."

"I never noticed," Joanna lied. She was trying desperately never to think of Howard Edge again. But what had she expected, even if he hadn't been married and a father? That he would sweep her off her feet and carry her off to his castle, or whatever?

She felt such a fool. Even if only she knew she had been a fool.

"What did you think of the teddy boys?" Matilda asked.

"I thought they were rather cute." The sisters giggled. There had been nothing like that in BG.

Aunt Ethel lived in a northern suburb of London, but deliberately, she took the Great West Road into the West End before swinging up the Tottenham Court Road. The delay was only brief, and she wanted her nieces and nephew to see something of the city. They were predictably astonished, and not merely by Trafalgar Square and the traffic and the crowds of people. Georgetown, British Guiana's capital, had few houses or indeed shops and offices, taller than two stories, simply because the city was built on mud and any excess weight would cause the buildings to subside. Now they looked up and up and up.

"Wait till you go to New York," Aunt Ethel remarked.

Matilda and Joanna hugged each other.

After all the difference and excitement of the journey up from Plymouth, Aunt Ethel's house was disappointingly ordinary. It could indeed have been a Guianese house, except that it was situated in what was called a close, a cul-de-sac of identical buildings. The rooms were smaller, and of course it was not built on stilts, as were all Guianese houses to keep out the flood waters. But it had the same two floors, the same matching rooms up and down, the same staircase, and an almost identical bathroom, except that there was no shower.

Like the hotel, she had only three bedrooms, or to be exact, two bedrooms and a boxroom which she had converted into a bedroom for William. "I know it's a bit cramped," she acknowledged, "but it'll only be until you can get a place of your own." And she smiled brightly as if to suggest, either together, or singly.

Mummy did not look very happy about that, but Joanna was content; the room she was to share with Matilda had twin beds.

Settling in to living in England, and being English, was in the first instance a matter of shopping. This alarmed Miriam because of the expense, but it was very necessary. They had arrived at the end of September, and while the days were on the whole fairly warm, there were sudden dips in temperature, a portent of what lay ahead. And they had only tropical clothing. They needed warm underwear and at least one coat each, and they also needed to buy a school uniform – blazer and grey long trousers – for William, who duly passed his entrance exam, but not for a place in the Fifth at his new school. "Fourth Form!" he announced in disgust. "I can't be a fourth former."

"It's to do with your age," Aunt Ethel explained, not wishing to suggest what she knew for a fact, that educational standards in the colonies were at least one form lower than those in England. "You can't really be a fifth former at fourteen." William refused to be mollified, and went into a mope.

Joanna fared very little better on her introduction to secretarial college. "Mmmm," remarked Mrs Hill, the teacher who had just given her some shorthand to take. "Mmm. We've a lot to do, my dear."

Matilda, predictably, refused all offers of help, and went out on her own, looking for work. "What you need to do," Aunt Ethel suggested, "is sign on at the Labour Exchange. They'll know if there are any vacancies for tap dancers."

She was, as usual, disparaging, confident that Matilda would find out soon enough that her chosen profession was simply not on, and would then have to come down to earth. But Matilda, who went out every day with her golden hair swinging in time to the rest of her, and wearing her shortest skirts, remained equally confident, and they had not been in England a fortnight when she announced that she had found a job. "That's splendid, darling," Miriam said. "As a tap dancer?"

"No." Matilda grinned at Aunt Ethel. "Those aren't thick on the ground. I'm to be a receptionist."

"At an hotel?" Ethel was intrigued; surely one needed some training to work in an hotel.

"At a club," Matilda said.

Now everyone was intrigued. "What kind of club?" Ethel asked.

"Well, actually, it's a dance club," Matilda explained. "They wouldn't give me a job as a dancer, but they said I could work as a receptionist."

"A dance club?" Aunt Ethel was doubtful.

"A very popular place," Matilda assured her. "I work from eight until four."

"Those seem very reasonable hours," Miriam commented.

"You'll have to get up a bit earlier than usual," Joanna said, slyly.

"At night," Matilda said.

There was a sudden silence. Aunt Ethel was first to recover. "You mean you go to work at eight in the evening, and don't come in till four the next morning?"

Matilda nodded. "That's when the club is open."

Ethel looked at Miriam. "I don't think—" Miriam began.

"Now, Mums," Matilda said, "please don't be difficult. The pay is very good. Because of the unsocial hours, you see."

"Yes, but . . . a young girl, coming home alone at four in the morning—"

17

"Oh, I'll always get a lift with one of the other girls," Miriam said, and suddenly flushed, as if she might have said something she shouldn't.

"I still don't think it's right," Miriam said. "Do you, Ethel?"

"Definitely not," Ethel agreed,

"I've taken the job," Matilda said. "The pay is very good." She knew this was important, because Mummy was starting to worry about all the money she had had to spend on their clothes. Thus she had a trump she was quite prepared to play. "If you don't approve, I – I'll move out. I can afford to."

Everyone stared at her in consternation. Even Joanna, who had always known that Matilda had a very strong will, was taken by surprise. "Well!" Aunt Ethel commented.

"Well," Miriam said. "If you're sure . . ."

Ethel glared at her, and Matilda smiled.

"Poor old Mums was really upset," Joanna said in bed that night.

"I know. I did hate worrying her. But she really can't go on running my life. As for Aunt Ethel . . ." Matilda giggled. "I thought she was going to blow a gasket."

Joanna had a practical mind. "I don't see how you're going to keep awake until four in the morning. Is it every night?"

"Except Sundays. I'll sleep during the day, silly." She switched the light on again. "Anyway . . . can you keep a secret?"

Joanna was suddenly excited. "Yes."

"I'm not really going to be a receptionist. I'm going to dance."

"Tap dance?" Joanna was incredulous.

"No. As I said, there doesn't seem to be much of that over here. No, just dance. I'm in a chorus, with a lot of other girls."

"Just like that?"

"I had to audition. Oh, they said I wasn't very good, but I could learn. I think they liked my legs. And, well . . . anyway, I got the job."

"A chorus girl!" Joanna wasn't quite sure whether or not she was being over-critical. Presumably all dancers started in the chorus line.

"I wear a fabulous costume. Would you like to see it? See the show?"

Joanna sat up. "Oh, could I?"

"Let me get settled in first. Then one evening you could say you're going to the pictures, and come along to the club. I'll get you in."

"That would be super." Joanna lay down again.

"But remember," Matilda said, "you mustn't say a word to a soul."

"Because you're to be a chorus girl? What's wrong with that?"

"Mums just wouldn't understand," Matilda said. "Neither would Aunt Ethel. You promised, now." She switched off her light.

Joanna had no intention of breaking her word; she would never let Matilda down. But she was highly excited, and jealous, as she sat at her desk mis-hitting typewriter keys, as Mrs Hill had blindfolded her. "You're supposed to be reading from your dictation, not looking at the keyboard," she insisted. "And using all your fingers."

Matilda had the knack of living an exciting life, while she . . . presumably she was just too timid. Matilda had started going to grown-up parties in Georgetown before Father's death, and on one occasion had taken Joanna along. Joanna had been shocked. The eldest guest had been about twenty, and they had come in all complexions; there had been a good deal of alcohol, mainly rum, the wine of the country, and a good deal of necking, too. Joanna had done her share of necking with boys from Queen's College, Georgetown, at various parties, but she had always checked roaming hands; Mother had instilled in both of them that the preservation of one's body until one's wedding night was an absolute must if one was a lady, and she was not only talking about virginity.

But the necking at Matilda's party was of a variety she had never encountered before, with hands going everywhere, on both sexes, even sliding under skirts. Joanna had had an urgent desire to be home in bed, alone, but had had to stick it out until Matilda had been ready to leave. By then Matilda, with several drinks inside her, had been flushed and excited, while Joanna felt as if she had been at the bottom of a rugby scrum. And when they had reached the safety of their bedroom, she discovered that Matilda no longer had a bra. "Oooh," she had giggled. "That Sandy wanted it. Oh, so badly." Joanna had been left wondering whether the bra had really been 'it'.

Matilda's new lifestyle was very upsetting for the rest of the family. She had to have her evening meal at seven, where Aunt Ethel normally served at eight. Then she was gone all night. For the first few nights Miriam tried sitting up to see her in, but she was invariably fast asleep in an uncomfortable chair when her daughter did return. Following which Matilda had a quick breakfast and retired to bed, just about the time Joanna was getting up. She normally surfaced again for lunch before going back to bed for the rest of the day. She was certainly exhausted, and this was an additional concern for her mother. But she said, "I'll grow into it."

Joanna found it upsetting the way Matilda's hair smelt of cigarette smoke, and the absence of their little chats. But she remained intrigued. "Don't forget you were going to let me come to the club one evening," she reminded her.

"Ah," Matilda said. "Yes. Are you sure you want to?"

"Shouldn't I be?"

"You must promise never to tell Mums about it."

"I have already promised that, and kept it," Joanna pointed out.

"Actually going there will be different," Matilda said.

But she was obviously equally anxious to show her sister what she was doing, and a week later she was awake when Joanna got in from another unsatisfactory day at the secretarial college. "Tonight," she said.

"What about tonight?"

"I've arranged for you to come to the club. Now listen very carefully."

Joanna was so excited she wasn't sure she had listened to everything Matilda told her. But it really was a perfectly simple matter. "Some of the girls from the college are going to the pictures this evening," she told her mother. "They asked me to go along."

"How nice," Miriam said. "I'm so glad you're starting to make friends," and she gave a speculative look at William, seated in the corner doing his homework. There was no evidence of his making any friends, as yet. As if she had, either, Joanna thought. She had little in common with any of the other girls at the college, whose interest in life centred around Skiffle and Lonnie Donnegan, and whose dream was to go shopping in Carnaby Street. But what Mummy didn't know couldn't hurt her, and she put on a smart frock and her new coat and had an early supper with Matilda.

"I'll walk you to the cinema," Matilda volunteered. Once round the corner they caught a bus. Joanna had never known Matilda to be so nervous. "You'll remember your promise," she said, when they got down at Piccadilly Circus.

"Of course I do," Joanna said. "You're making me think this is some kind of crooks' gathering."

"It's a nightclub," Matilda explained, leading her down a side street. "Where people go to have a drink and dance after dinner. It doesn't really hot up until nearly midnight."

"Oh." Joanna was disappointed. "I have to be home by about eleven. That's when the cinemas come out."

"That'll do," Matilda said. "The first show is at nine."

"How many shows do you have to do a night?" Joanna asked.

"Just the two. One at nine, and the other at midnight. That's the big one."

"Then what keeps you here until four?"

"Well . . . it's nice to stay and chat with the customers, don't you think?" She winked. "Makes them come back again."

They had reached a very plain door set in a windowless stone wall. Matilda pressed the bell, and a moment later a panel slid back. The face blinked at Matilda, then the door was unbolted and opened. "Can't be too careful," Matilda explained to her sister.

The man wore a sweater and a flat cap and looked like a boxing second. He looked Joanna up and down. "This the kid sister?"

"Yes," Matilda said, suddenly breathless. "So watch it."

He grinned, and smacked Joanna's bottom. Joanna decided not to make an issue of it, but nearly ran down the corridor behind her sister. "Who is he?" she whispered.

"Just the bouncer." Matilda was descending a flight of steps into a brightly lit lobby, in strong contrast to the passage above them. "Home from home."

The lighting, if bright, was mostly concealed. The room was quite large, but low-ceilinged, and although at the moment empty save for a couple of barmen polishing glasses, still stank of cigarette smoke from the previous night. The bar ran the full length of one side, while in the centre there was a dance floor. The tables and chair surrounded the open space. Matilda walked across the floor, Joanna at her heels. "Boss in yet?"

One of the barmen nodded, and they both ceased work to look at Joanna. She felt that she was on the menu for dinner. "My sister," Matilda said.

"We can see that," the other barman said.

Matilda parted a curtain on the far side of the room and led Joanna into another corridor, off which there opened several doors. The first on the right led into an office. "Here she is," Matilda said.

Joanna was mystified. Matilda had said something about smuggling her in, but she was being announced like a visiting celebrity. But she liked the look of the man behind the desk, who was surprisingly young, with sleek black hair and a handsome face. He wore no jacket, but his shirt and tie were both silk, and his cufflinks gold. He got up, and came round the desk. "Sixteen?"

"Nearly seventeen," Matilda said. But she was again breathless.

The man walked round behind Joanna, but when she made to turn to face him, Matilda shook her head. "This is my boss," she explained. "Anthony."

"And you're Joanna," Anthony said, returning to Joanna's front. "Tilly has told me a lot about you."

Joanna gazed at her sister in amazement, and Matilda winked. "I told Jo she could see the show," she said. "First." She and Anthony were talking some language of their own, Joanna understood.

"Sure," Anthony said. "Keep her sober. Sixteen." He chucked Joanna under the chin. "Nice meeting you, kid."

Matilda escorted Joanna outside, and down the corridor to the second door on the right. "Does he own all this?" Joanna said. "He's so young."

"I shouldn't think he owns it. He runs it," Matilda said. "He's great fun. You'll like him."

Am I going to know him? Joanna wondered, and checked as Matilda opened the door, which gave access to a large, very brightly lit room, filled with a row of dressing tables and full-length mirrors. There were three other girls here already, and to Joanna's consternation two of them were naked, while the third wore only a pair of panties – and one of them was carefully lipsticking another's nipples. "Sammy, and Corinne, and Lou," Matilda said carelessly. "This is my kid sister, Joanna."

All three girls stopped what they were doing to cluster round. Once again Joanna had the feeling she was a particularly succulent dish for supper. Had Matilda not been standing beside her she would have turned and run. "Nice going," Lou said.

"She's come to watch the show," Matilda said, with considerable emphasis. "Over here, Jo." She led the way to a dressing table in the corner. "I'm the new girl," she explained, "so I get this one." Joanna watched in increasing consternation as her sister stripped until she was naked. "What do you think?"

She held up an enormous feathered headdress, sparkling with sequins. "Eye-catching," Joanna said.

Peering at herself in the mirror, Matilda carefully placed the headdress over her hair, pulling it down firmly, then using pins to keep it in place. "Is the rest of it as dramatic?" Joanna asked.

Matilda turned round and gave a little shimmy. "Don't you think so?"

Joanna's jaw dropped in consternation. "You have got to be joking."

"It's what the men come here to see," Matilda pointed out.

Joanna turned to look at the other girls; there were seven of them now, each naked except for her headdress. "Now you can help me make up," Matilda said, and handed Joanna a lipstick tube. "Navel as well."

"You're going to dance naked?" Joanna asked, unable to believe what she was saying.

"That's what I'm paid to do. I lied when I said I was a receptionist. Anthony took one look at me, and said, 'You're for the line'."

"And you went for it? Have you any idea what Mums will do if she finds out?" She didn't dare consider Aunt Ethel's reaction.

"She isn't going to find out, unless you tell her," Matilda said.

"Yes, but—" Joanna felt she should say something about the morality of it, but Matilda was her big sister, to whom she had looked up all her life.

"Twenty pounds a night," Matilda said. "And that's only starters, Anthony says."

The door opened. "Five minutes," a man shouted. With the door open, Joanna could hear a rumble of sound coming from up the stairs.

The girls filed out, chatting to each other as if they were getting on a bus. "You can watch from behind the curtain," Matilda said.

Joanna had a strong urge to run all the way home. But she was supposed to be at the pictures. In any event, she knew she had to see this. Twenty pounds a night! One hundred and twenty pounds a week. Why, that was six thousand pounds a year! But to waltz around naked in front of a lot of slobbering men . . .

She hurried along the corridor. All she could immediately see were legs, as the girls climbed the stairs. She followed them, panting. "That's far enough," the man said, grasping her arm. "You're over-dressed."

She glared at him, and he grinned; he was quite pleasant-looking, but he hadn't shaved for at least twenty-four hours, and had had garlic for lunch. "I'm Ted. You're Tilly's sister, ain't you?"

"Yes," Joanna said, peering through the slight opening in the curtain at a three-piece band playing soft music that was mainly drums, and at the eager faces beyond, as the eight girls stamped around the dance floor, shaking their breasts and bottoms.

"Not much of a crowd, yet," Ted said. "It doesn't really fill up until after ten. But these are the hard-core guys. They come to watch the girls, and maybe have a drink. The ones who come later are here to have a drink, and maybe watch the girls. Some difference. Some of them even bring their women."

Joanna licked her lips and stepped back; she'd seen enough. But she was curious. "Doesn't it . . . well . . . I mean . . ." she could feel the heat in her cheeks.

Ted grinned. "Doesn't it turn me on, having all these bums and tits around all night? You get used to it. Bunch of cows, really."

"You are speaking of my sister," Joanna said, coldly.

"Well, she's a cut above the rest, sure. But not as much as you. You really going to join?"

"To—" Joanna opened her mouth to tell him he was mad, and was checked by a drumroll.

"Queen Bee," Ted said. "Lily."

Joanna peered through the curtain. The woman who had just come on – she was definitely not a girl – was tall and voluptuous, and moved with aggressive thrusts. It couldn't be called dancing. None of it could. But it was certainly posturing. The audience clapped excitedly. "I didn't see her downstairs," Joanna said.

25

"Lily is the Queen Bee, like I said. She's got her own dressing room. You could be up there, one day."

"Not my style," Joanna said, and turned to find her way out. She'd rather walk the streets for an hour, until it was time for her to go hone, than watch any more.

But Anthony was standing beside her. "Nothing to it," he said. "Matilda tells me you want to join."

Chapter Two

On The Make

"Matilda . . . ?" Joanna was incredulous. "I'm sure she didn't mean it."

"Why else did she bring you here tonight?"

"Well . . ." Joanna glanced at Ted, who was grinning.

"Don't tell me you're afraid to take your clothes off?" Anthony asked. "Next thing you'll be telling me you're a virgin."

"I am a virgin," Joanna protested. "And so is Matilda," she added.

"I think the correct word is 'was'," Anthony said.

"You mean – you bastard!"

"Keep your voice down. Look, I haven't laid a finger on your sister. In this business, you don't mess about with the girls, or you find you're doing nothing else. But our customers like to date the chorus after the show, and that's big money. Matilda isn't one to pass up big money." He had just described her sister as a prostitute. Joanna felt she should slap his face. But she had an uneasy feeling that if she did that he might break his own rule and hit her back. More importantly, she couldn't get it out of her head that he might be telling the truth. "So how about it?" he asked. "Come down to the office and let me have a look at you. Not that I think there's going to be any doubt about it."

"I'm sure you mean that as a compliment," Joanna said, as coldly as she could, "but quite frankly, I wouldn't be found dead working in this dump, with or without clothes." She stalked along the corridor, paused at the door to look back at them, half expecting them to be coming after her. But they were both just grinning. She pushed the door open, stepped into the nightclub lobby, where the actual receptionist was just relieving two men of their coats and hats – very expensive coats and hats. Joanna hesitated, and they both turned to look at her. One of them was Howard Edge.

"Well, hello," he said. "Joanna Grain! Don't tell me I've missed you. I'll complain to the management."

Joanna's knees felt so weak she nearly fell down. But he was a dirty old man. Save that now she was looking at him again she realised that he really wasn't that old. "I don't work here," Joanna said, surprised she could speak at all.

"But you must work somewhere," Edge said. "Just name it."

"I work in an office," Joanna said, stretching a point. But she was going to work in an office when she qualified as a secretary.

"Then you should change jobs." He fumbled in his inside breast pocket, produced a piece of cardboard. "Telephone my secretary tomorrow morning, and we'll find you a place."

Joanna goggled at him, and he chucked her under the chin. "Don't forget. Just coming," he said to his companion, who was looking impatient. Parked in the street outside the club was the Rolls.

"You really are a noodle," Matilda remarked, falling into bed and stretching. "God, I'm exhausted. I set everything up for you . . . do you have any idea how many girls apply for a job at the club every week? Anthony only takes the best. And you turn him down flat. You need your head examined."

"I'm sorry," Joanna said; she hadn't actually been asleep; the night had been – she supposed exciting would have to be the word. The most exciting night of her life. But the overwhelming thought was that Howard Edge had spent an evening looking at Matilda, naked. In fact, as he had appeared perfectly familiar wih his surroundings, he was probably a regular. Matilda obviously didn't know that, as the customers sat in semi-darkness – and she wasn't going to tell her. "I am not parading naked in front of a lot of dirty old men."

"You'd rather be a secretary and be felt up by one dirty old man, is that it? Do you know what you'll earn as secretary? I doubt it'll be twenty pounds a week. Anthony pays twenty pounds a *night*!"

"You told me," Joanna rolled over and closed her eyes.

"As it happens," Matilda said, "and luckily for you, you really turned Anthony on. He's prepared to give you another chance."

Joanna pretended she was asleep. But she kept seeing Howard Edge's face. He had not looked lecherous or depraved or even particularly amorous, although he had definitely had a lot to drink. But as regards her, he had simply been admiring. Of course he wanted to get his hands on her . . . she wondered what *he* would pay to accomplish that? And he was a husband and father!

When she got up, as Matilda was fast asleep, she was able to study the card at her leisure. Caribee Shipping Line. Howard Edge, Chairman & Managing Director. Who wanted her to work for him. With what else in mind? In any event, it was all only a pipe dream: she wasn't even yet qualified as a secretary.

Yet the knowledge that she was pretty enough to have turned-on, as Matilda would put it, two such different men as Anthony and Howard Edge could not help but be exciting. Inspiring. She found herself glancing at herself in shop windows as she went to the college next morning, admiring herself. Was narcissism such a terrible crime? The important thing was that it seemed such a waste to possess so much, for only a few years, really, and not put it to its best effect. Which was . . . certainly not showing her all to a bunch of perverts.

Equally it was not something to be conceded to any Tom, Dick or Harry. As it happened his name was Dick. He was also studying shorthand and typing, and was definitely interested. He was quite an attractive boy, although he had acne. But he seemed so *young*. "How about a drink?" he asked one evening in early December when they left the college together. "There's a cute little pub just round the corner."

"I'm sorry. I'm not eighteen."

"Aren't you? Who's to know? You *look* eighteen."

"Do I really?" She was complimented; she had had her seventeenth birthday only the previous week.

"Come on, I'll vouch for you."

She had never been in a pub before, was astounded at the crowd of people, all drinking and talking at the tops of their voices. They had to fight their way through the throng to reach the bar, while Dick bought the drinks. "What is it?" she whispered, eyeing the glass of brown liquid; he was drinking beer from a tankard.

"Port and lemon," he whispered back. "It's what women drink."

"Do they?" Mummy and Aunt Ethel usually drank gin. But she rather liked the taste, and was happy to accept another. Then they found themselves in the lounge bar, where a group of young men were strumming washboards and blowing through combs.

"Skiffle," Dick explained. "It's the in thing."

Time passed so quickly it was half-past seven and Joanna was on her third port and lemon before she looked at her watch. "Crumbs! I must get home."

"Hang about," Dick suggested. "We can get a bite at the fish and chip bar."

"No, I really must go."

"Well . . . it's been fun. How about the pictures?"

"Lovely," she agreed.

Joanna had the sense to stop at a late night chemist on the way home and buy some peppermints to disguise her breath but that did not save her from a wigging for being late for supper. But the family interest was concentrated on William, who had a black eye and a cut lip. "Had a fight at school," he explained, proudly. "Chap called me a colonial."

"You are a colonial," Joanna pointed out. "Have you been to the hospital?"

"Don't you start. Aunt Ethel wanted to take me in, but really, for a black eye?"

"What did your master say?"

William grinned. "That's tomorrow. Happened after school."

Joanna was rather proud of her kid brother too, and even more so when he told her the following day that he had been whacked. "Six of the best," he said. "So did Tommo."

"But he started it," Joanna protested.

"The beak said I shouldn't have responded so violently. We're the best of friends now. Tommo and me, I mean."

Joanna had to rush, to meet Dick at the pictures. It was something with James Mason, but she didn't have an opportunity to see too much of it, for Dick had got them tickets in the very back row, and the feature had only just started when he had one arm round her, one hand on her breasts, and was kissing her cheek. "Come on," he whispered, feeling her stiffness.

"Dick! We're in public!" she protested, making the mistake of turning her head, so that he could kiss her mouth.

"Everyone's doing it," he said, when they got their breath back. Which was perfectly true, and not only in the back row.

Actually, what he was doing was rather nice; no one had ever fondled her breasts before, and he was very gentle. She even let him slide his hand beneath her skirt, although she kept her thighs firmly clamped together; with her eyes shut she could imagine it was Howard Edge. "You could try touching me," he whispered.

But she couldn't bring herself to do that, although he became more insistent over their following dates, while making it plain that he wanted to go the distance. That Joanna would not have. She thoroughly enjoyed the pub and the skiffle groups and the necking in the back row, but when she gave herself completely she wanted it to be with someone memorable, possibly even with marriage in mind. "You are becoming the most utter prig," Matilda remarked, when she attempted to discuss the situation with her sister, who had spent most of New Year's Eve fighting Dick off.

"Just because you've . . . well . . ." Joanna flushed. She had never

31

revealed to Matilda what Anthony had told her on that night at the club.

Matilda knew to what she was referring. "Do you know," she said, "I have four hundred pounds in my bank account? How much have you?"

"I don't have a bank account," Joanna confessed. "As you well know."

"Of course, because you have nothing to put in it. I am going to buy a car next month."

"Whatever for?"

"Everyone who is anyone has a car," Matilda pointed out, crushingly.

Joanna thought of the Rolls, and remembered that she had made no progress towards getting a driving licence. "What sort of a car are you going to buy?"

"A Mini. They're all the rage. Don't worry, I'll take you out in it. Sometimes."

Matilda's obvious success was bewildering. Joanna had never been quite sure of the difference between amoral and immoral, but it did seem that her big sister was both. While she was stuck with the prospects of an extremely low-paid and futureless job – and boys like Dick. And dreams.

Then came the day she awoke to find the other bed empty and unslept in. She sat up in alarm, driving her fingers into her hair. If Mummy and Aunt Ethel were to find out what Matilda really did for a living, or even if they found out she had spent the entire night out . . . She hadn't finished dressing when the phone rang. Aunt Ethel answered it, her voice rising. When she hung up, to face both Miriam and Joanna, waiting on the stairs half-dressed, with William hovering behind them, she wore an expression of mixed triumph and tragedy. "That was Matilda," she announced

"Matilda?" Miriam was incredulous, and instinctively looked at Joanna.

"I . . . I was about to tell you," Joanna confessed. "Matilda didn't come in last night."

"Didn't come in?" Miriam's voice rose to match her sister's.

"She didn't come in because she is in prison," Ethel announced.

"Prison?" The three Grains spoke together. Now all their voices were high.

"Well," Ethel said, "under arrest, anyway. She needs bail money. Twenty-five pounds, would you believe it."

"But why has she been arrested?" Miriam asked, clearly disbelieving the whole thing.

"It appears the club at which she works was raided in the small hours of last night, and everyone there has been arrested. Even the receptionist." Joanna gave a sigh of relief. "That means it was a very shady club," Ethel continued. "I always thought there must be something odd about it, the way they took Matilda on so quickly, and gave her such a good salary."

Miriam sat on the stairs. "My God," she said. "My daughter, arrested? Didn't she tell them her father had been a policeman?"

"I shouldn't think that would have made the slightest difference," Ethel commented. "It might have made things worse."

Joanna sat beside her mother. "We have to get her out. Have you got twenty-five pounds?"

"Well . . ." Miriam looked at her sister.

"I suppose I'll have to lend it to you. But it's a loan. Matilda must pay it back."

"She will," Miriam promised. "Now, I suppose—"

"I'll do it," Joanna volunteered. She didn't want Mummy getting mixed up with Anthony and his people. Or even finding out about them.

"Are you sure? You'll be late for the college."

Bugger the college, Joanna thought. "They'll understand," she said.

William came with her as far as his school. "What am I to say?" he asked, very embarrassed.

"Say nothing. She's not likely to be in the papers," Joanna pointed out.

The police station was more crowded than she had expected, and there were several reporters there. She had to fight her way to the desk. "Matilda Grain," she panted.

The sergeant checked his list. "You're inside," he remarked, puzzled.

"I'm her sister," Joanna explained. "I've brought her bail money."

"Oh, right. Let's be having it, then."

Joanna hesitated. She had never had any dealings with the English police, before. "And she'll be let out?"

"Surely."

Joanna handed over the money, and someone at her shoulder said, "Well, hallelujah." She turned, and gazed at Howard Edge. He was unshaven, and his tie was slipped down to allow the top two buttons on his shirt to be opened. He was also surrounded by people, two of them obviously minders and a third his companion at the nightclub, but the rest from the media, snapping away. As she was in the direct line of fire it suddenly occurred to Joanna that she was also being photographed. Hastily she turned back to the desk.

"Hey," he said. "I'm not actually a criminal. Just in the wrong place at the wrong time."

"I don't want to be in the papers," she muttered.

"Don't blame you. You're here for Tilly, right?"

"Let's be going, Howie," said the friend, wrapping a topcoat round Edge's shoulders.

"Hold on," Howard said. "We'll wait for Miss Grain." He looked past her at the door to the cells, through which Matilda was at that moment emerging, accompanied by a woman policeman. Matilda had obviously been arrested while working, for she wore only a man's coat which barely came down to her thighs, leaving her legs exposed. "My God!" she gasped as she saw Howard. "Mr Edge? You were at the show?"

"Let's get out of here," Howard said. "My car is waiting."

Matilda looked at Joanna. "He'll take us away from here," Joanna said. Her heart was pounding so hard she was sure everyone could hear it.

They allowed themselves to be bustled outside, still surrounded by shouted questions and snapping cameras. Although it was April it was very cold, and Matilda shuddered as the wind got at her. "You drive, Billy," Howard told his friend. "I'll get in the back." He held the door for the sisters. Matilda got in first, and Joanna was in the middle. The two minders got into the front beside Billy. "And put the heating up," Howard commanded.

"You own this?" Matilda asked.

"My company does," Howard explained, and grinned. "But I own the company."

"You are a little devil," Matilda told her sister. "Criticising me . . ."

"It's not what you think," Joanna protested.

"Joanna is absolutely right," Howard said. "We met again at your club one evening, oh, some time ago, before Christmas. She was just leaving, and resisted my every advance. Do you know, I was prepared to fire Billy for taking so long to turn up and get me out of that hellhole. Now I think I'll give him a rise. If he hadn't been so tardy, we would never have met again."

"Yes," Joanna agreed, and looked out of the window. "Where are we going? Home is the other way."

"Is it? You didn't say. I thought you might like a good break-fast."

"I'd love a good breakfast," Matilda said. "But . . . like this?"

"It's a very private place," Howard assured her.

"College! I have to get to college," Joanna protested.

"College? I thought you said you were a secretary?"

"I . . ." she bit her lip. "I'm studying to be a secretary."

"Well, we'll phone in sick." The car turned through an arched gateway into an inner courtyard, pulled up outside a very ordinary-looking door. "My London *pied-à-terre*," Howard explained. "Chaps."

The two heavies got out and formed a sort of guard-of-honour, between whom Matilda was able to dash into the doorway, which had been opened by Billy. Howard escorted Joanna behind her. The heavies remained outside, while the two men showed the girls up a narrow flight of stairs into quite the most sumptuously furnished flat Joanna had ever seen. It was small, lounge, bedroom, and kitchen, but the furniture all came from places like Fortnum and Mason's, and through the opened doorway she could see a magnificent tester bed, with red and gold drapes. This was a *pied-à-terre*?

Billy was in the kitchenette, breaking eggs. Matilda prowled around the flat, examining the various ornaments, pausing before the pictures; Joanna supposed they were prints, because one or two were very familiar. Howard was checking his ansaphone, and listening to a woman's voice, with a quizzical expression. "My wife," he explained, when the machine stopped.

"Your—" Joanna swallowed. "Listen, Mr Edge, I really must get to college."

"I said we'd call in sick. Do you have the number?"

"No, I don't. I—"

"Do you think I could have a bath?" Matilda asked.

"Surely. Help yourself. But don't be too long. I need one myself."

She disappeared into the bathroom, closed the door. "If your wife finds us here . . ." Joanna said.

"My wife is at home. Which happens to be in Berkshire."

"Does she know you spent the night in a police cell?"

"I didn't spend the night in a police cell. It was six hours between the raid and Billy appearing. And that was long enough. No, Alicia doesn't know that. I'm going to have to work out a story. But it won't be difficult. Sit down and have something to eat."

Billy was laying the table. "I've had breakfast," Joanna protested.

"Then have a cup of coffee. We need to talk." He sat down himself, by the phone, dialled. "Darling! Yes, I know. Sorry I didn't let you know, but Billy and I had a few too many and I thought it best to sleep here at his place rather than drive home and risk a d/d charge. Of course I'm all right. No, I don't think I'll go in this morning; I need some sleep. Maybe this afternoon. Kiss kiss." He hung up.

Joanna sipped her coffee. "Do all men lie to their wives?"

"At some time or other." He sat opposite her. "We have to do something about your beautiful sister," he said. "Billy, go and size up Miss Grain, and then go out and buy her some clothes which fit." Billy obeyed with alacrity. There was a faint shriek from the bathroom, then silence.

"He's good at sizing up women," Howard said. "Amazing. I thought Matilda was the prettiest girl in the show, but I knew you'd be prettier." He had to be referring to her body, as he knew what her face looked like. "I've been going there regularly, but you never turned up again. And Matilda wouldn't give me your address."

"You've spoken to Matilda?"

"Of course." And what else, Joanna wondered, feeling utterly jealous of her sister. "But you refused to work there, so Tony told me. Why? It's good money, while it lasts."

"Dancing naked?"

He studied her for several seconds. "I'm glad you feel that way," he said at last. "But what are we going to do with Matilda? Now she's going to have to start all over again. The club will be closed down. They always are, after a raid."

"Oh lord." Absently she ate some toast.

"Now let's talk about you. How much longer have you got at secretarial college?"

"God knows. I'm not very brilliant."

"I regard that as the understatement of the year." He looked up as Billy emerged from the bathroom, looking somewhat hot and bothered but also very pleased with himself. "Got everything?"

"Oh, yes," Billy said.

"Off you go, then. You'll catch them just opening. Don't be too

37

long. But I want a complete outfit." Billy nodded, and ran down the stairs.

"Are you really going to buy Matilda a complete set of clothes?"

"I can't very well send her home in a short jacket, now can I? She'd catch cold. And she'd be arrested all over again, and on the same charge – indecent exposure. Where is home, by the way?"

Joanna gave him the address without thinking.

"Your mum's place? I know about your dad. Captain Heggie told me. I'm very sorry."

"Thank you." But Joanna couldn't resist a slight giggle; she was feeling fairly hysterical. "He was a police inspector."

"In British Guiana. I remember. Do you remember that night, in the storm?"

"You said you owned the company."

"Well, I have a majority shareholding, and I am both chairman and MD. But I'd rather talk about you."

The bathroom door opened, and Matilda appeared, wrapped in a man's dressing gown. "That man—"

"My man. He's gone out to get you some clothes."

"Oh." She sat down on the settee, knees pressed together. She had washed her hair, and it lay as a golden mat on her shoulders.

"Jo has been telling me something about you. May I be very rude and say that yours doesn't sound the sort of family background for a go-go dancer?"

"Well . . ." Matilda licked her lips. "We're not very well off since Daddy died."

"And Anthony paid well. I can imagine. You do realise that's gone? He'll lose his licence. He may even be charged with operating a brothel." Matilda clutched the dressing gown more tightly. "I'm not criticising," Howard told her. "I'm explaining. Will you find another dancing job?"

"Well . . . do I have an alternative?"

They gazed at each other, and Joanna realised that she was watching a very subtle negotiation. Matilda was hoping to become

mistress to a very wealthy man, who was also young and handsome.
"Do you have any skills?" Howard asked. "I mean, out of bed?"

Joanna gasped. She had never heard it put quite so bluntly.

"Only dancing."

"Ballet?"

"Tap."

He stroked his chin. "I might be able to find you a job. Would you
like me to do that?"

"I'd be ever so grateful." Matilda's eyes were liquid. Joanna just
could not believe what she was seeing. And hearing. Her adored big
sister, offering to sleep with a man in return for some help . . . but
hadn't Matilda already been sleeping all over London?

"Then we'll see what we can do. Now I'm for a shave and a bath.
Billy'll be back soon with some clothes for you." He grinned at
Joanna. "Look up the number, call your college and tell them you
have whatever it is women have. We still haven't had our chat."

The door closed behind him. "Talk about falling on our feet," Matilda
remarked. "Jesus!" She hurried to the table and began wolfing food.

"Tilly, listen," Joanna said urgently. "Howard may be very handsome and dashing and rich, but he's on the make. He lies to his
wife, he—"

"All men lie to their wives," Matilda said.

"And you'd go to bed with him, just like that." Joanna snapped her
fingers.

"I should think that would be rather fun," Matilda said. "But it's
not me he wants to get between the sheets, goose. It's you."

"Me?"

"No accounting for tastes. Or maybe he likes virgins."

"I think we'd better get out of here." Joanna got up, put on
her coat.

"Don't be silly. Firstly, we can't get out of here until I have
something to wear. And secondly, if we pass this up we need
our collective heads examined. And don't start that crap about

39

morality. He's going to find me a job," Matilda said. "I need a job. But if you walk out on him he probably won't help me. Men are like that, darling. Believe me. You've just told me that he's a cad. So—" Matilda looked up as the outside door opened, and Billy came in, accompanied by his two henchmen; each carried a stack of boxes.

"Quick, eh?" he enquired. "I was there when the doors opened."

Matilda was on her feet, peering at the labels. "Harrods? They're all from Harrods!"

"It's the nearest," Billy said, somewhat apologetically.

Matilda was on her knees, allowing the dressing gown to fall apart as it chose, tearing paper apart, cutting ribbons with scissors Billy had helpfully produced, pulling open the boxes beneath. "Oh!" she cried. "Oh!" as she took out the black lace underwear, the beige twinset, the green skirt. "Oh, my."

"Those must have cost a fortune," Joanna gasped.

"Not a cheap store, Harrods," Billy agreed.

"I think you should try them on," Howard suggested, from the doorway. Like Matilda, he was wrapped in a dressing gown.

"Oh, yes," Matilda said. "Help me, Jo!"

Joanna scooped up the various garments and hurried behind her sister into the bedroom, closing the door as she did so. "You can't accept these," she said.

"Why not? How am I supposed to get home?" Matilda asked, smoothing the black lace panties around her midriff and bottom, and turning in front of the mirror.

"I'll go home and get some of your things," Joanna said.

"You have got to be nuts." Matilda was adjusting the bra straps.

"Tilly, that man is a complete stranger."

Matilda giggled as she pulled the jumper over her head. "Of course he isn't. We've sailed on his ship, had dinner with him every night for a week. Anyway, he's quite a regular at the show. He knows what I look like."

"You don't mean he's one of those—"

"I do not mean that," Matilda snapped, pulling on the skirt. "But he's looked often enough, hasn't he?"

"And you don't think that if you accept all these gifts he'll want to do more than look?"

Matilda had put on the cardigan, and was again turning in front of the mirror. "That would be rather nice. But as I said, I think it's you he wants to get his hands on. I'm not complaining. I think you're on to a winner. How does that look?" She had used one of Howard's brushes on her somewhat tangled hair.

"You look like a million dollars," Howard said, having opened the door, unheard. Joanna turned, flushing scarlet. "Now," Howard said. "Give me your phone number."

"Don't you dare," Joanna said.

"She's very young," Matilda explained, sitting at the desk to write out the required information.

Howard folded the piece of paper in two. "Give me a day or two, and I should be able to call you about a job. Meanwhile, I'm going to a party on Sunday. I'd be flattered if you two young ladies would accompany me." He smiled at Matilda. "Billy's going as well."

"We'd love to," Matilda said.

"Will your wife be there?" Joanna asked.

"Ah, no. On Sunday Alicia is taking the children to see her mother."

Joanna sat down on the chair beside the bed. "Then I really don't think we can accept."

"She'll be there," Matilda assured him. "Even if wearing hand-cuffs."

"Dress casual," Howard said. "But bring swimsuits."

"Have you any idea what Mummy is going to say?" Joanna asked, huddling in a corner of the back seat of the Rolls. She was trying not to think about Aunt Ethel at all.

"We won't tell her." Matilda sat upright, smiling through the window at those who would gawk.

41

"I'm talking about the clothes."

"Ah, well . . . let's worry about that later."

Which was all of ten minutes away, after the car had stopped outside Aunt Ethel's house. Both the ladies had apparently been watching from behind half-drawn curtain – as was everyone else in the street – and they waited for the front door to close before emerging. "Where have you *been*?" Miriam cried when they were safely indoors. "I called the police station, and they said you'd left hours ago."

"Well," Matilda said. "We needed to have breakfast, and a chat."

The two older women had finally taken in her clothes. "Where did you get those?" Miriam demanded.

"Someone gave them to me," Matilda said.

"You . . . that's over a hundred pounds worth!"

"At the very least," Matilda agreed. "I think they're super. Do you mind if I go upstairs and lie down? I've had a very harrowing night."

The two older women stared at her with their mouths open.

"Why aren't you in school?" Miraim inquired of Joanna.

"I felt I should stay with Tilly," Joanna explained.

Once again Miriam and her sister were speechless.

The situation was irretrievable, although perhaps no one recognised it at that moment. It took time to sink in. The fact that the two girls had come home in a Rolls was overlooked in all the other trauma, but it surfaced again on Sunday when the Rolls reappeared. "Whose car is that?" Miriam demanded.

"Just a friend's," Matilda said carelessly. She had spent some of her hard-earned money on a new sporty outfit, and even bought a new jumper for Joanna as well, and new bathing costumes for each of them; black one-pieces which made them look extraordinarily sexy. Joanna had wanted to protest, but had been carried along with the idea. It was certainly exciting; her life seemed to have entered a new dimension, even if she knew in her heart it was going to be disastrous from a family point of view. As did Matilda. "I really don't think I can go on living there anymore," she said as they drove away. They were alone save for the chauffeur. "I feel as if I'm being stifled. Don't you feel that, Jo?"

Actually, Joanna did, but she wasn't going to admit it. Her family was all she had in the world, and she didn't feel up to cutting off those links. Besides, she couldn't legally. But then, neither could Matilda. Or could she? Tilly was nineteen. "I bet Howard could find us a flat somewhere," Matilda said, half to herself. "Where we could do our own thing."

"And who'd pay for it?"

"Well . . ." Matilda winked. "If you played your cards right . . ."

"You are just impossible," Joanna snapped. "I have told you before—"

"Sssh," Matilda said, for the Rolls was stopping at a pub to pick up Howard and Billy, and two more young women. They had all already had a good deal to drink, and were in a very happy mood.

"Oooh, pretty," one of the girls said, and kissed Matilda. "He said you were pretty."

The other girl was seated next to Joanna, regarding her somewhat disparagingly. "Which cradle did they get you from, darling?"

"If they annoy you, say so," Howard said, "and I'll tan their asses. Or better yet, you can tan their asses."

"Chance would be a fine thing," the first girl said.

"Annie and Lou," Howard introduced. "Joanna and Matilda. Two very special friends of mine."

He and Billy occupied the jump seats opposite, and Joanna could feel his eyes boring into her all the way out to the friend's house, which was well out of London, and set in a walled park. The house was large, and there were at least fifty people there – not counting the waitresses – cavorting in and out of the swimming pool. Joanna had never actually seen a bikini before, in the flesh as it were, and was at once embarrassed and astounded. "I must get one of those," Matilda muttered, as they changed, together with

Annie and Lou, both of whom wanted to kiss and cuddle and hug as they did so.

"I thought we were here to entertain the men," Joanna muttered, wondering if she was about to be raped.

"Men!" Annie said, disparagingly. "All they're good for is paying the bills."

Joanna freed herself, adjusted her strap, and hurried outside, to be greeted by a chorus of wolf-whistles. She took refuge by diving into the deep end of the pool, forgetting that she had not intended to wet her hair. She went a good way under water – brought up in Guiana's rivers, she swam like a fish – and surfaced at the shallow edge. "That was quite something," said an admiring male. "Champagne?"

At eleven in the morning? But she took the glass anyway.

The other girls had joined them by now, and there was a good deal of horseplay going on. Joanna moved back into deeper water, where she felt safer, carrying her glass in one hand. There she was joined by the man who had given her the drink. "I'm Andy Gosling."

"Joanna Grain."

"You don't really look as if you belong in this crowd."

Like her, he had one arm on the coronation, where they had both put their glasses, now being topped up by an attentive waitress, all black-stockinged leg. Now he allowed his own legs to drift against Joanna's. "Don't I?" she asked; he was being dismissive of her own sister. But really, Matilda, at that moment being fondled by two of the men to the accompaniment of squeals of laughter, deserved to be dismissed. "Too elegant," Andy said. "I gather you're Howie's discovery." Joanna raised her eyebrows, and drank some more champagne. "Quite a lad, our Howie," Andy said. "But you want to be careful. He's a love 'em and leave 'em lad. On the other hand, I'm a great snapper-up of unconsidered or cast-off trifles. Do remember that."

"I am not a trifle, Mr Gosling," she pointed out, finished her champagne, and took another dive under the water. When she surfaced, at the deep end, she found herself facing another young man. But this was like no one she had ever seen before. He was dazzlingly handsome, his good looks and superb body enhanced by his dark complexion.

"The sun," he said, "has risen." Joanna goggled at him, and wondered if she should submerge again. But he too was offering her champagne. "Dare I say that you are the most beautiful woman at this party? Perhaps in London."

Joanna had got her breath back, following a sip. "You can say it."

"And do nothing more. Because your name is Joanna Grain, and you are Howie's ladylove."

"Has he told everyone? But you're wrong. I am not his ladylove. I am not anyone's ladylove."

"Then there is hope for me yet. Dearest, beautiful lady, allow me to take you away from here. We will mount a magic carpet together, and travel forever towards the moon."

Once again she was breathless. She was quite relieved to discover Howie standing behind her charmer. "She's bespoke, Hasim," Howie said.

"I feared that," the man called Hasim said. "May I at least help you from the pool, Miss Grain?"

He took her hand and lifted her from the water with the greatest of ease. "I hope, no, I know, that we shall meet again, Joanna Grain," he said. "Perhaps when Howie is occupied." And to her consternation he kissed her hand.

"Who on earth was that?" she whispered, as she got her breathing back under control.

"His name is Prince Hasim ben Raisul abd Abdullah."

"Did you say 'prince'?"

"He is the son and heir of the Emir of Qadir. That's in the Gulf. His family is one of the richest in the world. That allows him to be an international playboy, who gobbles up sweet young things like you."

"You're jealous!"

"Of course. Both of his money and his looks. But he's a good friend." Wearing trunks, he was splendidly built himself. And he had told everyone she was his! She really should be annoyed about that. "You swim to the manner born," he said.

"I'm a West Indian."

"I thought you came from the mainland?"

"I do. But British Guiana is always considered part of the British West Indies. I should have thought you'd know that, trading with them."

He grinned. "I did. Are you planning on going back?"

"Not immediately."

"Because if you do, you must certainly travel by Caribee Lines."

"How many ships do you have?"

"Four eight-thousand tonners. So you see that I am not in Hasim's class. But I'm hoping you'll be faithful." Chatter and laughter flowed around then, and he secured two more glasses of champagne from a passing tray.

"If I have much more of this stuff I'm going to pass out," she told him. "What time is lunch?"

"Another half hour, maybe. But I think you should get dressed. You're looking chilled." He wrapped her in a large towel. No one took any notice; Joanna had an idea that they had been told to ignore them. He led her into the house, and to her alarm, came with her into the girls' changing room, closing the door behind them.

"Do you mind?" she asked.

"Have a hot shower," he recommended, sitting down and crossing his knees.

"While you watch?"

"You can draw the curtain." She hesitated, but he obviously had no intention of leaving. She stepped into the shower stall, draped the towel over the rail, took off her swimsuit, and turned her face up to the deliciously warm jet. There was shampoo, and she washed her hair, rinsed, then wrapped herself in the towel.

46

"That must feel better. Do you know, every time I look at you I am more and more sure I am falling in love with you."

"I don't suppose you'd have a hairdryer?" she asked, because she had to say something noncommittal.

"No. But if you look in that cupboard you'll find another towel." She did, and wrapped her hair in it. "How're things at home?" he asked. "Was there any problem with Matilda's night out?"

"I think she means to move out. If you can find her a job to pay the rent."

"Suppose I said I'd take care of the rent?"

"For Tilly?"

"For both of you."

"I can't leave home. Mummy wouldn't go for that. I'm only seventeen, you know. Anyway, your wife—"

"Please don't bring Alicia into this. She's my wife. Period. But I have fallen in love with you."

"You're crazy. You've never touched me. Or—" she bit her lip, thinking of that kiss.

"I know. Love is a crazy thing." He got up, and came towards her. "I want you more than I have ever wanted anything in my life." He stood against her. "And I want you to want me. Do you think you could do that?"

Joanna stared at him. It would be so easy to do. "It's not possible," she whispered.

"Everything is possible." He kissed her on the mouth. Again.

Chapter Three

Surrender

It seemed the most natural thing in the world for Joanna to allow her lips to be parted, for Howard to delve as deeply as he wished. Nor did she make any attempt to resist him as he gently freed the towel and let it fall to the floor around her ankles. Yet her brain was whirring, telling her that she had to stop this while reminding herself that she was entirely in this man's power at this moment. That she wanted to be in his power. His hands stroked her thighs and came up to her breasts. "Where have you been all of my life?" he whispered into her ear.

He stepped back to look at her. His arousal was easy to see in his bathing trunks, but he had as yet made no move to take them off. Joanna concentrated on getting her breathing under control. "We have three ways of playing this," he said. "I will buy Matilda a flat. Tomorrow. Your choices are, one, to run away from home. Unless either you or your sister tell her, your mother will not know where the flat is." He studied her expression. "But that's not your scene. Your second choice is to let me come and have a talk with your mother. I will make it worth her while to allow me to take responsibility for you."

Amazingly, he had still not yet made any move to touch her again. But she had to protest. "You mean you think you can buy me, like some slave? Mummy would probably call the police."

"There is nothing criminal in asking for a woman's company. All she has to do is say no."

"You said there was a third alternative." She was having trouble with her breathing again.

48

"That we play it secretly. You continue as you are now, but we arrange to meet at Matilda's flat whenever possible."

This is incredible, she thought, that I should be standing here, naked, with a man who has barely touched me, talking about . . . him touching her a whole lot more, and having the right to do so. She licked her lips. "There is a fourth alternative," she said. "If you truly love me as much as you say."

They gazed at each other. "I did not say I loved you," Howard said. "I said I wanted you, very, very badly. I will pay a lot of money, grant a lot of privileges, for the right to have you. But I cannot break up my marriage, and perhaps lose my children, for the sake of a fuck." He grinned. "We might not take to each other."

"So your idea would be that we give it a trial spin."

"Is that such a heinous concept?"

"In a man's world, I suppose it is quite natural. But what happens to me if, as you say, we do not take to each other?"

"I would make it worth your while."

"You would make me a whore."

He was beginning to get angry. Joanna supposed he had never before encountered such opposition, when he chose to put his money on the line. "So you tell me how you want to play it," he said.

"I would like to be taken home, now," she said.

"You mean you have accepted my hospitality, displayed your all, and think you can just walk out when you're ready?"

"It's a free country. If you attempt to stop me, Mr Edge, I will see you in court." She turned her back on him, dressed herself. She expected him to grab her, touch her . . . she wasn't at all sure she wouldn't carry out her threat. But instead she heard the door close, gently. She turned, totally confounded. He was gone.

She finished dressing, opened the door again, and found his chauffeur waiting there. "You wanted to be taken home," he said.

Joanna was again utterly surprised. "Yes, please. But I should tell my sister."

"Matilda seems to be occupied," he said.

Joanna went on to the pool surround. There were still several people in the water, but Matilda was not one of them. And the most delicious smells were coming from the dining-room. "Is she eating?"

"Lunch has not yet been served. *Do* you wish to go home?"

Joanna chewed her lip. But she did wish to leave, and she had no desire to come face to face with Howard or any of his friends again. While Matilda could certainly take care of herself; she was probably earning hundreds of pounds right that minute. "Yes, I do want to go home," she said.

Having announced that she would be out for lunch, there was not a lot at home; Mummy and Aunt Ethel and William had also gone out. But Joanna was just happy to be alone, had some bread and jam, and went to bed, to stare at the ceiling. I should be in bed now, she thought. With a man on top of me. Or would it be underneath her? She had no idea. And she did so want to find out. But not as someone's mistress, to be discarded the moment he got bored with her.

The real catastrophe was that she had almost certainly cost Matilda the flat she dreamed of. She decided against telling her; what the eye can't see the heart doesn't grieve over. Matilda naturally treated her behaviour as a joke. "Too hot for you?" she enquired when she finally came home, about six.

"I suppose it was. Too . . . jet-setty."

"That's the way to live. But I thought you and Howie had something going?"

"We don't," Joanna said, definitely.

Matilda did not pursue the matter, and Joanna returned to her world of typing and stenography, and Dick, who was angling for the same result as Howard Edge, but was far less sophisticated and confident. Have I burned my bridges? she wondered. Is my world going to be entirely that of Dicks rather than Howards?

She started reading the newspapers, looking for little bits of information. But Aunt Ethel took the *Daily Mail*, which didn't go in for ship movements or business news other than the sensational; the sensation that summer was the Americans putting a man into space; that did not seem likely to affect her future. So Joanna started spending a few hours a week at the local library, where she had access to *The Times*. Caribee Shipping was really a very small company, with rather small ships, but every so often she would come across a mention. Trading with the West Indies! With British Guiana! She wondered if she would ever have the money to return to her birthplace? Travelling once again by Caribee Shipping. Suppose Howard was travelling? Would he know she was? As Chairman of the line he would obviously have access to all passenger lists. If he was still interested.

But would she ever wish to go back, really? British Guiana seemed to be slipping into virtual civil war as the ethnic clashes between blacks and East Indians became ever more violent.

"I hope you won't mind, Mums," Matilda said at breakfast, one chilly morning in the new year. "But I'm moving out."

There was total silence for a minute, then William dropped his spoon. "Moving out?" Aunt Ethel was first to recover.

"I've found a flat," Matilda explained, ears pink.

"But . . . you're only nineteen," Miriam protested.

"I'm an adult. And I shall be twenty this year."

"How can you afford a flat?" Aunt Ethel enquired.

"My new job pays very well," Matilda told her.

As before, no one knew what her new job was, not even Joanna. But Joanna suspected the worst, because, again as before, she kept some very odd hours. She could hardly wait to get her sister alone. "You louse."

"I'd have thought you'd be pleased. Now you can have this room all to yourself."

"You could've told me you were flat-hunting."

"Actually, I wasn't. I did, but as Aunt Ethel says, they really are

51

very pricy. Most girls my age share. I'd just about made up my mind to do that when Howard came along."

"Howard?"

"And the beauty of it is, if you want to meet him there, you can, with no questions asked."

"Howard?" Joanna said again.

"Your boyfriend, remember?"

"He's not . . ." Joanna frowned. "Has he ever made a pass at you?"

"Well, he actually makes passes at almost everyone in a skirt. But I told you, it's you he's really after. Don't tell me he hasn't had you?"

"I have not laid eyes on Howard Edge since that party last summer."

"And what happened there? I saw him follow you into the changing room."

"Nothing happened. I turned him down."

Matilda gazed at her for some seconds. "You have got to be nuts. He's loaded. Didn't you know that?"

"He's also married, with two children. Who he has no intention of abandoning."

"What did you expect? He's one of *them*, and we're two of *us*. We may have been aristocrats in BG, merely because our father was a police officer and we have white skins, but over here we're sweet Fanny Adams. Don't you realise that? But . . . if you didn't give him a fuck, why's he bought me this flat? And he has bought it for me; I've the papers."

"You'll have to ask him," Joanna said. The bastard! He was still on the hunt. And buying a flat for Matilda would be like her putting a shilling in the poorbox at church.

"You are going to come and look at it?" Matilda asked. Joanna couldn't resist that, whatever the risk. They took the bus into the heart of Westminster; the flat was in Maddox Street. "Isn't it super?" Matilda stood in the centre of the lounge, hands on hips.

"Bit garish," Joanna suggested, feeling enveloped by the deep pink wallpaper.

"Oh, I mean to change all that. And in here." She opened the bedroom door. Here the decor was in deep red.

"Just who had this place before you?" Joanna enquired.

"God knows. I'd say he was a bachelor with an inflamed libido. But it's mine. All mine."

"Presented to you by Howard. With not a single string attached?"

"Well, he found me this job as well. Dancing."

"With nothing on?"

"Well, yes. But I'm the main attraction. And it's a cut above Tony's because it's a private club. To which Howard belongs. He's deep. The string is obviously you."

"What do you think he would say, or do, if I up and married someone, right now?"

Matilda, inspecting the plumbing in the bathroom, turned in consternation. "You're not doing that?"

"Who knows," Joanna said. "I might."

It was her turn to gasp in consternation as the front door opened.

"I have keys," Howard explained.

"And you knew we'd be here?"

"Well, it's Saturday, so when I called at your house and was told you were both out, I reckoned you weren't at school."

"You called at the house?" Joanna went to the window to look down at the street, and . . . but it wasn't the Rolls. It was something sleek, and stream-lined, and obviously very fast.

"It's a Jaguar. Called an E-type," Howard explained. "The very latest thing,"

"You've sold the Rolls?"

"Good lord, no. The Rolls is the company car. This is my runabout. Would you like a run about in it?"

She wondered what Mummy and Aunt Ethel would make of her being driven home in that!

"It's super." Matilda hurried in from the bathroom.

"Bit garish, I'm afraid."

"That's just what we were thinking. I'll redecorate." Now she looked out of the window as well. "Oooh! Is that yours?"

"A Christmas present I gave to myself."

Joanna was peering at him, frowning. He had changed. He had lost weight, and allowed his hair to grow too long, and he hadn't shaved that morning, and . . . "You're drunk," she accused.

"I am not," he protested. "I may have a hangover. In fact, I do have a hangover. You wouldn't happen to have anything, would you, Tilly?"

"I haven't actually moved in yet," Matilda said.

"Ah. Right." He felt in his pocket and produced a wad of notes. "Be a doll and go down to the off-licence and buy two bottles of champagne. Is that fridge on?" He knelt before it, turned various switches. "Try to get one of them cold, will you."

Matilda looked at Joanna, uncertainly. "Oh, I'm coming with you," Joanna said.

"No." Howard pulled himself to his feet. "You and I need to have a chat."

"Alone?"

"That's the idea."

"I don't think it's a good idea."

"Listen," he said. "I am not going to touch you. Unless you ask me to. You have my word. Before a witness."

"I'll get the champagne," Matilda said, and ran from the flat.

"Sit," Howard invited. Joanna sat on the settee; her knees were in any event feeling weak. She expected him to sit next to her, but he chose a straight chair on the far side of the room. "Alicia has left me."

"What did you say?"

"She's packed up, taken the children, and gone home to mother."

Now Joanna was feeling weak from the waist down. "But why?"

He shrugged. "We had a fight. We often do. She's hot-headed.

And it seems one of the people at that party last year told a friend of hers how I'd been seen sneaking into the ladies' changing room. Goddamed cheek, spying like that. So this friend told Alicia. She didn't say anything about it at the time, but she was clearly simmering. And then the little bitch started having me followed."

"But we haven't seen each other since then."

"She found out I'd bought this flat, in the name of Matilda Grain. She only knows that the mistress I'm supposed to have acquired is named Grain."

"Shit, shit shit!" Joanna muttered.

"Anyway, once again she just simmered, until we quarrelled the night before last. Then she came out and said, why don't you get off with your little West Indian whore. I lost my wool, told her you were a far more moral person than she could ever be – well, she was my mistress for a year before we married."

"So she went off in a huff. She'll be back."

"I'm not sure I want her back."

Joanna stared at him. "You mean you're going to divorce her? What about the children?"

"We'll have to sort something out. But if she's spying on me, and generally poisoning the air, I'm not sure the best thing for them *is* for us to be together. As for divorce, well, in time. She's left me. I have a case for desertion. It's in the hands of my solicitor."

"But if you take up with me—"

"She can sue me for adultery. That's the idea. Desertion is a long term prospect. Adultery is immediate. You have any objection to being named?"

"Well, of course I do. Especially as it wouldn't be true."

"That could be adjusted."

"Oh, no," she said. "Oh, no, no, no. That would be conspiracy."

"I am asking you to become my wife," he said.

Her turn to stare. "Are you?" she asked at last.

"That's what I said."

"And I'll accept, once you're free."

He made a gesture of irritation. "You realise that means I'll have to commit adultery, somewhat publicly, with someone else?"

"I'm sure you'll find someone, Howie."

"You are really the most absurd girl I have ever met. I love you. I want to marry you. All I am asking—"

"Is that I stick my neck out, and say, chop it off."

"You are saying that you don't trust me, that I belong to the fuck 'em and flee 'em brigade. After, well . . ." he made another gesture. "I've played fair with Tilly."

"You have the wealth to play fair with whoever you choose, Howard, so long as you choose to do so. I should hate to think that you will now throw Tilly out. But I possess only one asset. Would you, a businessman, expect me to throw that on the floor and say, take it or leave it?"

He held her hands. "I thought we were talking about love. I love you, Jo."

"That's not what you said at the party."

"Well, you didn't expect *me* to put all my cards on the table first time around. The fact is, I have loved you from the minute I first saw you. Do you know, I have never heard you say that you love me."

He was drawing her forward, and she allowed him to kiss her. "I could love you, Howard," she said. "Very easily, and with all my heart. But there's a big difference in how we stand. You have to raise me to equality, if we're going to love each other. I won't be purchased off the peg."

She released him as the door opened. "Champagne!" Matilda announced.

"I was just leaving," Joanna said.

What have I done? she asked herself when she got home. That man, a millionaire, handsome, eager, has asked you to marry him. And you have turned him down flat! He had claimed to love you. The first man ever to do that. And you have turned him down flat. Who are you keeping yourself for, Dick?

She had, in fact, been supposed to meet Dick at the local palais de danse that night, but she didn't go. Thankfully, Matilda had not returned by then either. "I wish I knew what was going on," William complained, coming into her room after tea. "Mummy and Aunt Ethel keep muttering at each other, and then clamming up whenever I appear."

"I don't think they're happy about Tilly moving out," Joanna suggested.

"Golly, I wish I could move out," William said. "I will, you know, just as soon as I can afford a place of my own."

"Me too," Joanna agreed.

But of course Mummy and Aunt Ethel had more on their minds than just Matilda moving out. "Someone came here for you this morning," Aunt Ethel said at dinner. Matilda still hadn't come home. "A Mr Edge. In one of those new fast cars. A Jaguar. We didn't know you knew anyone who drove a Jaguar."

"He's a friend of Tilly's." Joanna had already determined the story in her mind.

"But he asked after you, dear," Miriam said.

"Yes, well . . . he probably thought I knew where Tilly might be," Joanna said, desperately.

"And just who is this man?" Aunt Ethel inquired.

"He's that shipping magnate," Joanna said, enjoying their consternation. "You remember, Mums? We met him on board the *Caribee Queen*, two years ago. Mr Edge. He owns the line."

"Such a nice man," Miriam said. "But . . . whatever can he want to see Matilda for?"

"I'm sure I have no idea," Joanna said,

When she awoke next morning, Matilda was in the other bed, also awake. "You really are a noodle," Matilda said. "You don't deserve him."

"Well, I'm obviously not going to get him," Joanna said. "His ideas and mine are poles apart. I'm sorry if I cost you the apartment."

"The apartment has nothing to do with you," Matilda said. "I'm moving the rest of my things today. You going to give me a hand?"

"If you can promise me Howard won't turn up again."

They took a taxi with Matilda's various boxes. Mummy and Aunt Ethel sniffed and disapproved as much as was possible but William, equally excited, accompanied them. "Wow," he said. "This is swell. And all your own! However did you afford it?"

Matilda and Joanna gazed at each other. "I've put something by," Matilda said. "Not as much as your sister, of course."

Joanna opened the fridge, and spotted immediately that the two champagne bottles were absent. "I see he's a careful man with his money," she remarked.

"Who?" William asked.

"Willie, I'd be ever so grateful if you'd take the garbage down," Matilda said. "There are bins in the front forecourt."

"Oh. Right." William dragged the paper sack out of the holder, and a champagne bottle fell out, struck the carpet with a dull clunk, and rolled across the room.

"Ooops," William said. "Sorry."

"You are a clumsy oaf," Matilda remarked, reaching forward. But Joanna reached the bottle first, picked it up, and opened the sack to thrust it in. The other one nestled, waiting for its partner. William disappeared through the door.

"I'm very happy for you," Joanna said.

"Don't be even more of a noodle than you already are," Matilda said. "The bottles were there, so we drank them. He means to marry you, Jo. I have never known a man with such single-mindedness."

"He'll get over it," Joanna said, taking clothes out of the suitcase and spreading them on the bed preparatory to finding hangers. "He'll get over ideas about the divorce. Do you have any idea what it would cost him? Adultery?!"

"He has that all sorted out," Matilda said. "Companies within companies within companies that his wife can't touch. She can bankrupt him, but she can't bankrupt *him*, if you follow me."

"I always knew he was an utter thug."

"Your future husband."

"No way."

Matilda held her shoulders and shook her. "Listen to me, idiot. He loves you. He's rich. He's going to make you rich."

"With companies inside companies inside companies?"

"It's up to us to sort that out. Before you say yes. But it's up to you to say yes, when we have it right."

"Us?"

Matilda kissed her. "We're partners, right?"

Joanna felt that she was caught up in a gigantic whirlpool, carrying her . . . where? For another fortnight she heard nothing from either Matilda or Howard, was left entirely to herself. Yet she found herself putting off Dick time and again, to his obvious annoyance. So much so that she at last accepted a Saturday night dance date. Dick was wildly passionate, rubbing himself against her on the dance floor, and when a rock number came on, grabbing her all over the place, ostensibly to throw her about, but leaving her feeling as if she had been in a wrestling match. "Whew!" she said when the music finally stopped. "I think I've had enough for one night, Dicky. Let's go home."

As usual, they caught a bus on the corner, sitting on the upper deck, which at this time of night held only one other couple, who were very obviously courting. They paid no attention to the pair behind them, and no sooner had they sat down than Dick had his arm round Joanna's shoulders, while his other hand was caressing her breast. "Dicky," she protested. "We're in public!"

"Who cares? There's nobody looking at us." He kissed her, with the same urgency he had shown on the dance floor, and she realised with some alarm that he had come to a decision about them. Didn't she have a say in that?

But she submitted to his kisses, because she didn't want a scene on the bus. Then suddenly he stood up, pulled the cord, and led her to the stairs. "This isn't our stop," she protested again.

"It's three away. Let's walk a bit."

"Oh . . ." but the conductor was grinning at them, and she allowed Dick to help her off the bus on to the pavement.

"Super night," he remarked.

Joanna looked up at the nearly full moon, and wondered if it was having some effect on his libido. They held hands as they strolled along the pavement. "I think we're at least a mile away from home," she grumbled.

"So what have you got against taking a walk? Good for you. Listen. I've been thinking about us. It'd be great if we could set up, someplace. Together."

"You have to be nuts. What would we live on?"

"I'm graduating next month. I have a job all lined up."

"As a male secretary? What are they paying you?"

"Not a lot. But you'll be out in the autumn. With our joint incomes we could afford a flat. I'd marry you, if you wanted that." What a throwaway line, she thought.

"Does that turn you on?" he asked, squeezing her fingers.

"I'll have to think about it."

"I'll take that as yes. Hey, a friend of mine lives over there."

Joanna looked across the street. Although it was nearly eleven, there were lights on in the house, behind the drawn curtains. "Oh?" she asked, without interest.

"He's still up. Let's drop in for a nightcap."

"I don't really think we should."

"Listen, you have to be home by midnight, right? That gives us more than an hour. Let's live a little."

"Calling on a friend, who's probably in bed?" But she allowed herself to be led across the street, waited while Dick pressed the bell.

"Who's that?" asked a voice from the other side of the panel.

"Dick. And lady."

"Well, hi." The door swung in to reveal a young man in his shirt
sleeves; the shirt was half out of his pants. Behind him the corridor
was conventional enough, but there was a peculiar smell in the air.

"I always keep my word," Dick said. Joanna glanced at him,
frowning, wondering what he meant.

"Then doubly welcome. I'm Ron."

"Joanna." Joanna stepped into the hall, and to her consternation
was seized and both hugged and kissed by her host. She looked at
Dick, but he merely winked.

"Come on in," Ron said, and opened a door on the right of the hall.
Here the lights were low, and there were about eight people present,
Joanna estimated from a quick glance. They were all smoking, and
the strange scent was much stronger in here; in fact, the air was heavy
with it. The sexes were equally divided; the four girls had kicked off
their shoes, and were sitting or lying on the floor, being fondled by
the men, while passing their cigarettes from hand to hand.

She didn't like the scenario at all. "I really think we should be
going," she said. "We only dropped in for a nightcap . . ."

"But as you're here, you have to have a drag," Ron said.

None of the other people in the room had taken the least notice of
their entrance. "I'm sorry," Joanna said. "I don't smoke."

"This ain't tobacco," Ron explained. "It can't do you no harm."

Joanna found herself sitting in a chair, and the cigarette, as she had
supposed it was, was taken into Ron's mouth for a long suck, before
he gave it to Dick. It's unhygienic, she thought. But as it came to her
from Dick's mouth it didn't seem very important. She only wanted to
humour them and then be away. The rasp of the marijuana took her
breath away, but she had sucked twice before she realised she had
done so. Then the roll was taken away to be passed around, while
Ron busied himself making another one, carefully pouring the grains
in the paper before rolling it over. "You okay?" Dick asked.

"It was ghastly. God, I'm thirsty."

He got up and went to the bar, poured a glass of some liquid. She
took it with suspicion, but to her relief it was water. Nothing had ever

tasted so good. She began to take in her surroundings, the people scattered about the furniture and on the floor. She watched one of the girls allowing her knickers to be pulled down about her ankles before kicking them right off, while the man lying beside her sent his hands beneath her skirt. She watched a girl unzipping a man's pants and putting her hands inside. She kept thinking to herself, this is some kind of orgy, I must get out of here. But Dick was sitting beside her, caressing her breasts as he so liked to do, pushing up her jumper to get his hands beneath, sliding over the brassiere and trying to get round behind to release the catch, while she pressed her back as hard as she could against the settee. She hadn't allowed Howard to do this to her, so why was she allowing Dick? Then the weed was back. "No," she said. "I really don't want another."

"Yes, you do," Ron said. "You'll like this one better."

Amazingly, she did, and now he was sitting on her other side, kissing her mouth before joining Dick's explorations under her sweater. She was surprised Dick didn't object to that. Then Ron was really deep kissing her, and she gasped, while Dick's hands were on her knickers. "No," she said, but she had no idea how loud she was saying it, or if she was saying it at all. She seemed to have lost the will to resist them, found that she was rather enjoying what was happening to her, as the nylon was pulled down her thighs. It caught on her buttocks, and she raised herself to allow it to be pulled right off. Then they were both sliding their hands up and down her thighs, and between her legs, and she experienced a quite heavenly feeling of physical pleasure overlaid with a mixture of guilt and relaxed acceptance.

"Another drag," Ron whispered. "You really are a doll, Jo-girl."

Joanna began to shudder as impulses raced away from her groin. She didn't know whether she was being raped or they were using their fingers, but she didn't want them to stop. Then there came a thunderous rap on the door. "Shit!" Ron snapped.

One of the girls screamed. "Lights," said someone else, and the room was plunged into darkness.

Again came the rap. "Back," someone said.

"They'll be there too," another argued.

Joanna felt herself being dragged to her feet and hurried to the door. She couldn't believe this was happening, and the room was going round and round in any event. But at the door there was a large policeman. "Gotcha!" he said.

Dick had to keep his arm round Joanna's waist as they stood before the desk, or she would have fallen. "Name?" the sergeant said, without raising his head.

Joanna was taking deep breaths, as she had been all the way from Ron's house, trying to clear both her lungs and her brain. "Joan Smith," Dick said.

"Try again, son," the sergeant said. "She has a lot of sisters. All named Joan. All here tonight."

"My name is Joanna Grain," Joanna muttered.

The sergeant wrote it down. "Age?"

"Eighteen."

The sergeant raised his head to peer at her for the first time. Then he shook his head, somewhat sadly. "The charge is possession and use of cannabis. Don't say anything," he advised, as she would have spoken. "Now, you can have bail of twenty-five pounds. Do you have twenty-five pounds?" Joanna shook her head. The sergeant looked at Dick.

"Search me," Dick said. "Look, sarge, we weren't in possession of anything. We went to a party, and—"

"I'd save it, if I were you," the sergeant recommended. "You can make a phone call. Each of you. Twenty-five pounds each." He gestured to the phone.

Dick looked at Joanna. "My old man will beat the tar out of me," he said. "If he finds out."

"My sister will get us out," Joanna said. After all, she thought, I got her out once.

Matilda was in bed. "Do you know the time?"

"Listen," Joanna said.

"Oh, you little fool," Matilda remarked, having listened.

"Save it," Joanna said. "Get us out of here."

"Us?"

"Me and my boyfriend."

"Shit!" Matilda commented.

"I won't lock you up," the sergeant said. "Just sit down over there until your sister comes for you." He wasn't so gracious to the rest of the party, who had already been charged; it appeared that some of them were known to the police. But Dick was allowed to sit beside her.

"How did you get to *know* these people?" Joanna whispered.

"I get around." He seemed proud of being involved with them.

Joanna hunched herself into a ball, and suddenly realised that she was not wearing knickers. She hunched herself into a still smaller ball. If Mummy and Aunt Ethel found out . . . but they were certain to find out. "Over there," the sergeant said.

Joanna looked up, at Howard Edge.

Joanna stood up, then sat down again; her knees felt weak. "You're paid for as well," Howard told Dick. "Come along, the pair of you." They trailed behind him into the night; Billy opened the back door of the Rolls. "Where can we drop you?" Howard asked Dick.

He refused to be overawed by the car. "We're together."

"You," Howard said.

Billy started the engine and they drove away from the station. "Now listen," Dick said. "Where Jo goes, I go. Who are you, anyway?"

"I'm a friend of the family," Howard said. "And if you don't want to be put out on the pavement, I'd give Billy an address."

Dick looked at Joanna. "Please," she said.

"And leave you alone with this guy?"

"Like he said, he's a friend of the family."

Dick scowled, but gave his address. When they got there, he said, "I'll call you."

"Not tomorrow," Joanna said. "You could at least thank Mr Edge for putting up your bail."

"Thank you, Mr Edge," Dick said, and got out. Howard caught the door before it could be banged, closed it, and Billy drove off.

"Grass," Howard remarked. "What on earth made you do that?"

Joanna shrugged, preparing to defend herself. "We felt like some fun."

"Fun," Howard remarked, even more disparagingly. "These yours?" From his pocket he took her knickers.

Joanna pressed her knees together. "How did you get those?"

"The sergeant gave them to me when I paid your bail. He thought they might be yours. He'd spotted you weren't wearing any."

"Shit," she muttered. "Do you mind looking the other way?"

"Is that really necessary? After all . . ."

"You have seen me in the nude. That's not quite the same thing."

"You'll have to explain that." But he looked out of the window while she dressed herself.

"We seem to have been driving forever," she said, looking out of the window herself, and not recognising anything. "This isn't where I live."

"I think you need taking care of," he said. "And I can't do that if you go home to mother, who doesn't seem all that interested. So I'm taking you to my home. I'd have a nap, if I were you; it's a long drive."

"And suppose I demand to be set down, right now?"

"You can charge me with kidnapping."

She glared at him, but she was still too confused by the events of the evening to sustain a defence. "How did you know about me?"

"Tilly called."

"At your home in the country?"

"No, no. I was spending the night in town."

"And she knew how to get hold of you?"

"Well, of course she did."

"I really would like to go home."

"And I have said I think that would be a bad idea. Tell me about that young punk you were with."

"He is not a punk."

"He took you to that party."

"Well, yes. He's at the secretarial college with me. We date, sometimes."

"He take off your knickers?"

"I . . ." she bit her lip. "That is absolutely no business of yours."

"Listen. I'm going to marry you."

"With, or without, my consent?"

"You gave your consent, remember? On certain conditions. I'm prepared to fulfill them."

"With or without your present wife's consent."

"The divorce is going through. I'm afraid it'll take a little while. But until then—"

"I'm to be your mistress, right?"

"You will be my ward. I will not touch you until our wedding night . . . if that's how you want it."

She stared at him, unable to see his eyes properly in the gloom. "You're a romantic."

"Aren't you? Tell me if that chap has had you."

"If he had, would you put me out on the street?"

"No. I don't think I could ever do that. Jo, I want you. I want you on any terms you have to offer. But I also want to take care of you. That crowd you're running around with is no good. I'm not even sure you're still a virgin."

"Well, I am," she muttered.

"And the panties?"

"I know." She sighed. "I think I was going to be raped, without even knowing it. Then the police arrived."

"Hooray for the fuzz. But you understand why I want to look after you. Once you get hooked on cannabis—"

"What harm does it do?"

"Actually, not a lot. It induces unreality, but then so does alcohol, and cannabis at least isn't ruining your liver. The big risk is that once you get hooked on it, and the more you smoke the less effect it has, you start to want new sensations, new unrealities, and so you move on to the hard stuff."

"What's that?"

"Morphine. Cocaine. And ultimately, heroin. These are killers. Especially heroin. I don't want that to happen to you, Joanna. And the only way I can stop it is to have you in my care, always."

"And what about my mum? My studies?"

"We'll say, stuff your studies. As for your mum, I think we will have to get in touch with her, tomorrow, and explain the situation, and expect her to understand."

"She won't. She could take you to court."

"I don't think she will," he said.

Against her will, Joanna did sleep in the car. She was exhausted, and the cannabis fumes were still whirling around her head. Her brain was both active and feeling soporific, at the same time. If only she hadn't let Dick talk her into going to that party. But if she hadn't gone to the party, she wouldn't be here now, sitting next to Howard, feeling so warm and protected.

She blinked at the huge gates through which they were passing, and the curving drive beyond, bordered with oaks. And then, a blaze of light. She sat up, looked at her watch; it was four in the morning. Billy must be very tired. And Howard? He sat beside her and seemed not to have moved throughout the drive. But he turned his head when she stirred. "Home," he said. Joanna looked out of the window again. The house was at least three stories high, and there were lights on every floor. "They are expecting us," Howard said.

Joanna's heart and stomach seemed to roll over at the same moment. They! They consisted of a dozen or so servants, all eager to greet their master, and his new mistress. Because that was what she was, whatever he had promised. "I think the young lady wants only bed, Mrs Partridge," Howard was saying. "I'm afraid there is no luggage."

Mrs Partridge, a thin, somewhat severe-looking woman, did not allow her expression to register any emotion. Presumably. Joanna thought, she was used to this sort of thing. "Which room, Mr Howard?"

"Ah . . . the blue."

"Of course. Come along, my dear."

Joanna looked at Howard, who winked, and nodded. "I'll be up shortly."

Joanna followed Mrs Partridge into what could only be called a baronial hall, from, high chandeliered ceiling to potted palms and suits of armour. The grand staircase occupied the centre, and Mrs Partridge led her up this to a deep gallery, off which there opened several reception rooms. "There is a lift," she said over her shoulder.

"I can walk," Joanna said.

Mrs Partridge inclined her head, and led her along the gallery to a secondary staircase, which was as luxurious as any Joanna had previously known, and they went up to the next floor, where a corridor wide enough to be called another hall led between various doors. Mrs Partridge opened the third on her right, and showed Joanna into a bedroom which was definitely decorated in blue, from the bedspread and pillows to the walls and ceiling, and even the pictures. The housekeeper walked across the room, and opened an inner door, to reveal a bathroom that matched everything else, for both luxury and colour. "There's a shower, if you prefer." Mrs Partridge tapped the fitting. "I'm sure you will be comfortable. May I get you anything?"

Joanna licked her lips. "A toothbrush?"

Mrs Patridge opened a cupboard in the bathroom and showed her several brushes, still sealed in cellophane, and several unopened tubes of toothpaste as well.

"Thank you," Joanna said.

"Please ring if you require anything," Mrs Partridge said.

Did the woman never sleep? Joanna went to the window to look out at the dawn, which was just coming up. Everywhere there were trees, although she thought she caught a glimpse of water. Howard owned all this? And more. She turned as the door opened behind her. He was followed by a butler, carrying a tray with an ice bucket in which there was a bottle of champagne, and two flutes. The butler placed the tray on the table and withdrew without a word. "Or are you too tired?" Howard asked.

"When I go down, it's going to be for months," Joanna said.

"Then a drink won't do you any harm." He poured, and gave her a glass, touched it with his own. "Here's to happy days. Lots and lots of them." He drank, and she did also. Then he said, "You never did answer me. I'm talking about the short term."

Joanna drank some more, and sighed. "I couldn't possibly sleep in here alone," she said.

Chapter Four

The Mistress

Joanna supposed that as seductions went, hers was a disappointment. This was partly because she had been seduced long before they got to bed, had known it was going to happen for so long, had merely been flapping her wings against it like a bird caught in a closed window. Even more was it because her brain was still in a spin, from the marijuana, then the arrest and then the champagne, so that she was hardly aware of what was happening to her. When she awoke, it all seemed an almost surrealistic dream. She had enjoyed his stroking, had even tentatively stroked him back, wondering if he'd mind. There had been less pain than she had expected, but some discomfort remained.

But now she belonged. She was sufficiently old-fashioned, and sufficiently well brought-up, to accept that having given Howard her virginity, she was his. To have sex with anyone else would make her a whore, or at best a loose woman. Was that what she really thought of Matilda?

Matilda! She sat up in bed, for the first time truly realising where she was. She was alone, in this magnificent bed, in this magnificent bedroom, wearing . . . absolutely nothing! And the door was opening! She slid back beneath the covers, pulling them to her throat. It was Mrs Partridge, carrying a tray. "Breakfast, my dear," she said cheerily. "I hope you're hungry."

Joanna could only stare at her, speechless with embarrassment. Mrs Partridge placed the tray on the bedside table, lifted the covers off the various plates. "I told Cook poached eggs for today. Cold milk for your cereal, but hot milk for your coffee." She paused, anxiously. "You do drink coffee in the morning?"

Joanna licked her lips. It all smelt awfully good. And she wasn't going to tell this woman that at Aunt Ethel's they had always begun the day with tea. "Yes," she said faintly.

"Well, you just eat to your heart's content. You know where your bathroom is. There's no need to come down."

Was that a suggestion, or a command. "Is—?"

"Mr Howard has gone to town. But he'll be back for lunch."

There was so much that needed doing. "Did he—?"

"He said you were to have anything you wished, and that he would be back for lunch. That's not very far off, now," she added, and closed the door behind her.

Joanna sat up again. She was starving. She started with orange juice and cereal, followed by toast with the eggs and then more with marmalade and finished with two cups of coffee, feeling utterly replete. She had never had a breakfast like that in her life.

She drew a bath and wallowed for half an hour, then got dressed. Her clothes weren't as clean as she would have wished, but they were all she had. If only she knew what was happening in the outside world. Mums probably had the entire police force looking for her; save that the police would know where she had gone, or at least, who she had gone off with. To be a man's mistress!

She stared at the telephone on the bedside table. The temptation to use it was enormous. At least to call Tilly. But she couldn't call anyone, until she knew what was going to happen next. She went to the window overlooking the drive, and saw the Rolls-Royce coming towards her.

She turned with her back to the window, watched the door opening again. Howard carried a tray on which there was another ice bucket with another bottle of champagne, and two glasses. "I've already been seduced," she said, trying to be sophisticated.

"I always drink champagne before lunch," he explained, put down the tray, and came towards her. "Do you know you are quite the most beautiful creature on God's earth?"

"I think you're prejudiced." She was folded into his arms for a hug and a kiss.

"I'm sorry I had to dash off, but there were things to be done."

"I know. Where did you begin?"

"With your mum. She's waiting to see you. Are you up to it?"

He drove the Rolls himself. Joanna sat beside him, her knees pressed tightly together the whole way. It had to be done, of course, if only to collect her clothes. Although no doubt Howard would have bought her a complete new wardrobe, if she'd wanted it. But it had to be done. Trouble was, it was Sunday, and everyone in the close was home. Men were washing and polishing their cars, children were playing in the street; on Sundays, the close looked like a slum. An inquisitive slum.

All movement stopped as the Rolls slowly pulled up outside Aunt Ethel's house, except at the windows, where curtains stirred windlessly. But the door was opened for them, by Matilda! "I telephoned her to suggest that she might be useful," Howard murmured, walking beside her up the path.

"You look just super," Matilda whispered, hugging her, as if she had expected her to be a beaten-up wreck, Joanna thought.

Mums was waiting in the lounge, wearing the expression Joanna remembered from the day Daddy had been brought home dead. Aunt Ethel was nowhere to be seen. Neither was William, although Joanna knew he was home; his coat and cap were hanging in the front hall.

"Mrs Grain!" Howard kissed Mums' hands. "We've spoken on the phone."

Miriam goggled at him as if he were the devil. Then she looked at Joanna. "Are you all right?"

"I'm fine," Joanna said.

Miriam peered at her more closely.

"Perhaps we should all sit down," Matilda said, brightly.

"Yes, please," Miriam said, and chose the settee. The slight impasse was overcome when Howard sat beside her, causing her to withdraw to the far corner. Matilda and Joanna sat in chairs opposite. "Matilda said you had something to say to me," Miriam suggested, at large.

Howard cleared his throat. "I am here to ask for your daughter's hand in marriage. Joanna," he added hastily.

Miriam stared at Joanna. "Where did you spend last night?"

Joanna knew she was flushing. "At . . . at Howard's house."

"She was upset," Matilda said. "Well, after being arrested, and all that—"

"Had you taken drugs?" Miriam asked.

"I . . . I didn't know what it was," Joanna protested. "But, like Tilly says, I was upset. Then Howard came along and bailed me out—"

"Just like that," Miriam said, perhaps to herself.

"I telephoned Howard and asked him to help," Matilda explained.

"My solicitor will take care of the charge, Mrs Grain," Howard said.

"Just like that," Miriam repeated.

"Joanna, with your permission, of course, is going to be my wife," Howard pointed out.

"Just like that," Miriam said a third time. "How long have you known my daughter, Mr Edge?"

"Ah . . ." Howard looked at Joanna.

"Nearly two years now, Mums," Joanna said. "We met on the ship, remember?"

It was Miriam's turn to say, "Ah. And when will the marriage be, Mr Edge?"

"Well . . . as soon as my divorce comes through."

"I see. Thus your proposal of marriage is dependent upon . . . circumstances."

"Not really. My wife, my present wife, and I, have irrevocably split."

"Does your wife know you plan to marry again?"

"Well . . . no, not at this moment. I didn't want to tell her until Joanna had agreed, and yourself, of course."

"But you assume she will accept the situation?"

"Well . . . perhaps she may be unhappy with it."

"You mean *she* may not regard the split as irrevocable."

"I really don't know. It *is* irrevocable."

"But if she does not accept it, your divorce may be a long way off. And what exactly will the grounds be? Desertion is a matter of years."

"Well . . ." Howard looked embarrassed. "I think I can persuade her to go for adultery."

"With my daughter named as co-respondent?"

"Do you object to that?" Howard looked at Joanna, who knew her flush was deepening. "You wouldn't have to appear in court," Howard said. "Only your name would be used, and evidence would be provided . . . I know it's embarrassing, but that is the quickest way. And as for the name, well, as we are going to be married anyway, that wouldn't matter. Would it?"

"Perhaps not to Joanna, Mr Edge," Miriam said. "But the whole world would know that my daughter had committed adultery."

"Oh, Mums," Matilda said. "This is 1962!"

"In which everything goes. I could apply to have my daughter made a ward of court, Mr Edge. She is only eighteen."

"You have that right, Mrs Grain," Howard said. "In that case, we would have to wait for three years to get married. But we would get married, as soon as it became possible. And in the meantime—"

"It would estrange Joanna and myself," Miriam said thoughtfully. Her shoulders rose and fell, helplessly. "I do not approve. I think you have both behaved disgracefully, and intend to behave even more disgracefully. But as there seems to be nothing I can do about it, save have Joanna locked up . . ." Another shrug.

"Oh, Mums!" Joanna knelt beside her. "It's all going to work out, you'll see. Say you'll come to the wedding?"

"Ask me again, nearer the time," Miriam said.

There was really very little time to feel distressed by the estrangement from Mums. No doubt this was as Howard had intended it should be. First of all there was the establishing of Joanna in Caribee House. This was entirely painless. Mrs Partridge had undoubtedly entertained Howard's lady friends before, but she was able to take in her stride the fact that this lady friend was to be permanent, and to be her mistress. She recognised immediately that Joanna was entirely out of her depths, and took over as a sort of surrogate mother, aided of course by Matilda, who was wildly excited about the whole thing. But Mrs Partridge even managed to accept the constant comings and going of Matilda.

Had Howard and Matilda slept together, Joanna wondered? And did it matter if they had? It was she he was going to marry. But even with Matilda's hovering presence, and with Mrs Partridge always about to explain and convince, Joanna found herself somewhat lonely. The other servants were remote, and apparently regarded her with some suspicion. Was she really a permanency? But she wasn't sure of that herself. She was sure of only one thing, that she didn't want to leave the security of Caribee House and face the world, until she was Mrs Edge. And that promised to be a little way off. She viewed the world through Howard's television set.

She telephoned home several times in the first few days, but Mums was always busy. It was William she was really after. She and William had in many ways been closer than she and Matilda. She wanted William to visit, and perhaps spend a weekend. And he seemed quite keen. But he never came. Mums and Aunt Ethel had got at him.

Meanwhile, the divorce. A private detective came and inspected the wardrobe in the master bedroom with great care and even greater embarrassment. But there were her clothes hanging in the closet next to Howard's. This was apparently terribly important. "What happens now?" Joanna asked him.

"I make a report, miss. I mean, madam. I mean . . . it'll all be all right, you'll see." Just what she had said to Mums.

The great moment of every day was when Howard came in from the office; he had entirely given up using the London flat, and drove out every day, sometimes not getting home until eight. Joanna quite understood that the wheels of commerce had to keep turning, whatever his domestic problems, but with him home all the fears that overlaid her during the day disappeared. The principal fear of course was that he was deceiving her. She adored him, everything about him, but she was not a fool. He had had dozens of women in his time. He even, so Matilda suggested, went to clubs such as Anthony's to pick out the more attractive chorus girls and take them either to his flat or, if Alicia was away, to his house. Matilda even hinted that, had he not encountered Joanna that first evening, he might have chosen *her* instead, as a permanent companion. Except that there was a quality of immorality that lurked around Matilda like a miasma. Howard might well have considered her for a one-night stand – Joanna could not escape the feeling that he had in fact done so – but he would never have considered her as a mistress, much less as a wife.

But he had chosen her sister. Did that speak volumes for his perspicacity, or for her transparent innocence, or simply, as she was coming to accept, that she was so much better-looking than Matilda? Or, even more simply, that he had been looking for a reason to get rid of Alicia, and had found in this colonial hick the answer to his problems?

But as usual he seemed able to understand her every thought, and certainly her every fear. She had only been resident at Caribee House three weeks when he opened his briefcase on the bedroom table. "I have some things for you to sign," he said,

"Me? Sign? Sign what?" She was instantly suspicious.

"Certificates of ownership. These are shares."

She peered at the sheets of stiff paper. "Shares in what?"

"Caribee Holdings. My company. There are a thousand of them but you can sign for them in block."

"And what happens then?"

He kissed her, and poured champagne. "You own them, goose."

"A thousand shares in your company?" Cautiously she flicked the sheets. "Are they worth anything?"

"I sincerely hope so. We are currently quoted at six pounds, ten shillings on the Stock Exchange. So that pile is worth six and a half thousand pounds. At the moment."

Six thousand pounds? Just like that? "I don't understand."

"It's a gift, from me to you. A preliminary gift. It means you own part of the company. I have to tell you that at the moment it is a very small part. Caribee Holdings has one million shares, so you have a one thousandth stake in the company."

"A million shares . . ." Joanna had always been good at mental arithmetic. "You mean the company is worth six and a half million pounds?"

"At the moment."

"And you own it?"

"I control it. I have sixty-nine per cent of the shares, once you've signed."

That still meant he was worth . . . nearly five million pounds!

"Who owns the others?"

"Twenty-five per cent are owned by my three co-directors. Five per cent of those are owned by Alicia. And one per cent is about to be owned by you. However, I am going to see that increases. We are planning a rights issue in the next year or so, and you'll have the chance of increasing your stake."

Alicia had five thousand shares. That meant she had over thirty thousand pounds. Joanna was beginning to understand. "Who owns the house?"

"The company owns the house, as it owns my car, and all the ships."

"And you control the company," Joanna said thoughtfully. "But if Alicia now votes against you—"

"Her five per cent can have no impact whatsoever."

"But . . . can't she claim some of your shares in the divorce settlement?"

"No, because my shares are actually held in a trust company. It's managed by Billy. You remember Billy? The idea was thought up by my father, to avoid death duties. The shares are actually mine. I receive the income from them, and I can use them to control the company, but I cannot sell them or disburse them in any way without the agreement of the trustees. The trustees agreed to let Alicia have her five per cent. But she knows if she demanded any more they would refuse." He grinned. "They are all close friends of mine. Billy is in fact my closest friend."

"And you persuaded your trustees to give me this thousand."

Another grin. "Billy is very fond of you."

"Well . . ." She flicked the shares again. "You mentioned that they produce income?"

"Oh, indeed. I expect our next dividend to be one shilling and eleven pence per share. I'm afraid we are a little close-fisted, but the upkeep of the ships is high."

"One shilling, eleven pence, and I have a thousand of those . . . I'll have to work it out."

"It'll be just over ninety-five pounds."

"Oh, great. That's not two pounds a week. I could earn ten times that dancing at Anthony's club."

"It's not a salary, darling. It's all pin money. And incidentally, we pay dividends half-yearly, so it's really a hundred and ninety."

That sounded a little better. "And you have sixty-nine thousand, so . . ."

"Just over twelve. Thousand. From the shares. I am also paid a salary as managing director."

"So you're rolling in it?"

"Let's say I can afford you," he said, and opened a bottle of champagne.

Her initial feeling that he was treating her rather meanly was soon removed. He gave her an allowance of five hundred a year, on top of her dividends, and she began to feel a wealthy woman. And there was so much more. "There really is no necessity for you to lock yourself away out here, you know," he told her. "I have opened accounts in your name at Harrods and Fortnums, and at the following restaurants." He gave her a list; they were all the very best. "I have also opened an account for you at this firm of chauffeur-driven hire cars. All you have to do is telephone them, be picked up, go where you like, buy what you like, eat where you like, and be driven back here."

Instinctively she looked out of the window. "There's nothing to be afraid of, really," he said. "No one knows who you are. Listen, go out and buy yourself a mink."

She telephoned Matilda first. "Meet me at Fortnum and Mason's," she said.

"You're kidding."

"Eleven o'clock."

The car dropped her at the doors, which were opened for her. Feeling somewhat like a queen, she entered, looked right and left; she had not been here before. Needless to say there was no sign of Matilda. "Madam?" asked the young man in the morning coat.

"I'm looking for a fur coat."

"Ah . . ." He was taking her in. She was wearing her best day dress, but it had clearly not come from any couturier. Nor were her shoes absolutely right. "What sort of fur did you have in mind, madam?"

"I thought of mink."

"Oh, quite. I'll have someone take you up. Miss Loam?" The woman hurried forward. "Furs," the floorwalker explained. "And perhaps, well . . ."

"Absolutely," Miss Loam said.

"My sister was supposed to meet me here," Joanna explained. "Matilda Grain. I'm Joanna. Joanna Grain."

The name obviously did not immediately register. "I will tell your sister where you are to be found, Miss Grain," the floorwalker said.

Joanna was whisked upstairs. "Furs really need to be very carefully matched up," Miss Loam remarked.

"I know. I do need some clothes."

"Ah." Miss Loam brightened. "But we'll start with the coat." Languid young women surrounded her, but she was obsessed with the feel of the fur. "Pastel shades suit you best," Miss Loam suggested.

Joanna surveyed herself in the full length mirror, and looked past her shoulder at a horrified Matilda. "Whatever are you doing?"

"Choosing a coat."

"A perfect fit," Miss Loam suggested.

"I think so too," Joanna said. "I'll take it."

"Of course, madam. The price is a thousand pounds." Miss Loam waited, expectantly.

"I have an account," Joanna told her.

Miss Loam's eyebrows went up and down like yo-yos. "Then I'll just enter it up. Shall I take the coat, madam? To wrap?"

"Not necessary," Joanna said. "I'll wear it out."

Miss Loam hesitated, then said, "Of course, madam." She hurried for the exit, pausing for a quick word with the woman standing by the door.

"She's afraid you'll do a runner," Matilda whispered, stroking the fur. "But Jo . . . can you afford it?"

"I think so. Would you like one too?"

"Would I?" Matilda's eyes began to match Miss Loam's.

"Excuse me, miss," Joanna said to the waiting attendant. "May we have another of these? I think it should be a size larger." The assistant summoned another woman to keep an eye on them while she went for the other coat, but by the time she returned, Miss Loam had also returned, a different Miss Loam this, all breathless obedience to Joanna's every wish.

"We spoke of a new dress, perhaps . . . But it would be best to begin with lingerie, don't you think, Miss Grain?"

"Oh, yes," Joanna agreed. "Coming, Tilly?"

But Matilda was trying on her coat.

"Are you going to beat me?" Joanna asked spreading the sales slips before Howard.

"I might. But only because I think it might be rather fun. However . . . this is quite a whack for one day."

"You said to get a fur. Don't you like it?" She paraded in front of him, wearing the mink and nothing else.

"I think it's superb. But I didn't say anything about getting Tilly one as well."

"She was so jealous, Howie."

"I can imagine."

She knelt beside him. "Say you forgive me."

He stroked her hair, ran his hand over her shoulders and then down to cup her breasts. He was reassuring himself, she knew, that she really did belong to him, and that therefore she really was worth it. "I forgive you. But . . . no more days like today until your birthday."

Joanna giggled. "That's next month."

But she knew she'd gone right over the top, and did not repeat the spree. On the other hand, it was fun to be driven into the West End, to meet Matilda for lunch at a smart restaurant. She did this at least three times a week. She would have loved to entertain William in such style, but it simply wasn't possible through Mums' unrelenting hostility. She wondered how he was getting on. But then, she wondered how Dick was getting on. She heard nothing more about the cannabis charge; as he had promised, Howard got his solicitor to sort it out.

She heard nothing more about the divorce, either. Howard never spoke of it, and she saw no mention of it in the newspapers she had taken to reading from cover to cover. The important thing was that Howard seemed perfectly happy, and it was her business to keep him so. She enjoyed that. She was discovering that she was perfectly happy herself, did not want anything to change, until the day in the New Year she and Matilda were lunching together in the West End, and she looked up to find Alicia standing beside the table.

Joanna was so surprised she knocked over her glass of wine. "Well," Alicia said, loudly, "if it isn't the tart."

Joanna found herself sliding across the seat to come to rest against the wall, while Matilda goggled at Alicia in equal consternation. The maitre d' hurried up. Clearly he knew Alicia. "Oh, Mrs Edge," he said. "Is there something wrong?"

"I don't like the quality of customer you have in here, Jacopo," Alicia announced loudly, and heads began to turn. "Tarts belong on the street."

"But madam—" the maitre d' said.

Joanna stood up. She had had a couple of glasses of wine and was in no mood to be insulted. "You'll apologise for that remark," she said.

"Ha!" Alicia commented, and turned to her luncheon companion, another very well-dressed woman. "This is the little whore I was telling you about, the one Howard picked off the street to sleep with." She was still speaking very loudly.

"Madam, please," the maitre d' begged.

"You unutterable bastard," Joanna said.

"Don't you dare insult me!" Alicia shouted.

"I don't see how I can," Joanna pointed out. "You're beneath insult."

"Why, you—" Alicia swung her hand, but had it caught by Matilda, at last coming to life, and to the defence of her baby sister. "You—" Alicia turned to hit Matilda in turn, while the other woman looked as if she was going to take part.

The maitre d' seemed about to faint, and stepped back into the ranks of the half-dozen waiters who had suddenly accumulated. "Oh, no, you don't," Joanna said, and picked up the carafe of water from the table, upending it over Alicia's head. Alicia shrieked. By now everyone in the room was staring at them. "That's how we deal with loud cats at home," Joanna said.

Alicia stared at her through a watery haze, then turned and ran from the restaurant. "Oh, lord," Matilda said.

"You haven't heard the last of this," Alicia's companion said, and ran after her friend. Matilda sat down with a thump.

"Madam," the maitre d' said. "Ladies . . ."

"I'm sorry about the mess," Joanna said. "Would you like us to leave?" The maitre d' looked at her; they had ordered a very expensive meal. Then he looked behind the disappearing Alicia, sizing up the future. "I believe I have an account with you," Joanna said, sitting down. "It's in the name of Howard Edge, and my name is Joanna Grain."

"Oh. Ah. Mr Edge. Miss Grain! Yes, of course. Clean up this mess," the maitre d' commanded a waiter. "Dessert! Would you like dessert, madam?"

"Whatever is Howard going to say?" Matilda asked when they had placed their orders.

Howard knew all about it before he got home: Alicia had telephoned him at the office. "I suppose we're just lucky there were no reporters hanging about," he said. "But it's sure to make the gossip columns."

"Are you very angry?" Joanna asked. "I mean, she started it."

"Of course she did," Howard agreed. "It may all turn out for the best. She's finally got the message that you and I are a permanent item, and is prepared to take the divorce. For another two thousand shares. She wanted more, but we talked her down."

"Oh! Isn't that serious?"

"Not really. I told you, we're planning a rights issue in the next year or so. This is really to raise sufficient capital to upgrade our fleet, which is getting a little old. What it does mean, however, is that all individual holdings will be, if you like, watered down."

Joanna considered this. "Mine as well?"

"Not if you follow my advice. As an existing shareholder you will receive two for one anyway. But I suggest you also buy into the issue."

"I haven't any money."

"I'll lend you the money."

But her brain was racing away at another tangent. "If a whole lot of new shares are being sold, won't that lower the value of the existing shares?"

"Momentarily, perhaps. If we have a good reaction it should push the value up, in the long run, and we'll all be wealthier."

"But won't an issue of shares dilute your control of the company?"

"Not really. I also receive two for one. My stake will actually increase. But in any event, as long as I have fifty-one percent, I'm in charge."

"It all sounds terribly, well . . . nerve-wracking."

He grinned. "I've been doing it for years."

Joanna suddenly realised she had no idea how old he was – and she was going to marry him.

Howard was forty-one. This came as a considerable shock: Mums was only forty-five. "Age," he declared, "is a man-made mathematical formula. I'm as fit as many a man of thirty."

She also discovered that the first thing he did every morning on leaving the house was drive to a gym in London and exercise for an hour. "Do you think it's safe?" she asked Matilda. "At his age?"

"He always seems all right to me." Matilda giggled.

"Have you ever slept with him?"

"Well . . . a long time ago," Matilda said. "Does that make you mad?"

"Of course not. I always knew it, anyway. What . . . well, what is he like in bed?"

"Don't you know?" Matilda was astonished.

"Of course I know, as regards me. But you've had a lot more experience than me."

"Well, he always gets it up," Matilds said.

"You mean, some men don't?" It was Joanna's turn to be astonished.

"You'd be surprised," Matilda said. "But then . . ." she sighed. "I've always been in the weirdo side of the business. A, guys who are really past it but still want to try, and B, guys who are so high on booze or drugs they don't know which side is up." She giggled. "Or C, guys who do know which side is up, and don't want to know, if you follow me."

"I don't."

"Well, count yourself lucky. Although . . . Howard is very orthodox," she said seriously. "He doesn't even do fellation."

"Eh?"

"Where you suck him."

"Where I . . ." Now Joanna was horrified. "That's illegal. Isn't it?"

"Not between consenting adults."

"And you've done that?"

"When I'm doing what I'm doing, I'm a consenting adult. But he sucks you, right?"

"Well . . ." Joanna flushed. He did have a tendency to bury his head in her pubes, embarassing her as much as it had excited her. "That's not illegal, is it?" she asked anxiously.

"Not so far as I know, as long as you're a consenting adult." Another giggle. "Or a consenting wife. Listen, quit worrying. You're going to be Mrs Howard Edge, wife of the Chairman and Managing Director of Caribee Shipping. You're going to have the world at your feet. And in your handbag. You are never going to have to fear or want again."

Joanna shivered, and hugged herself. "Until Howard finds someone he likes better, and splits with me as he did with Alicia."

"If he ever does that, Jo, then you're a twit. For God's sake, you're eighteen, he's forty-one. You're young enough to be his daughter. All you have to do is keep him happy until he's too old to take on anyone else."

85

"Don't you think that's a trifle cynical? I happen to love him."

"You were the one worrying about him leaving you."

"It's a fact of life. He is a very attractive, very wealthy man. He's eligible, even if he is married."

"Now who's being cynical?" Matilda laughed. "You just follow my instructions, in everything. But mainly sex. You say he sucks you."

"I never."

"You didn't deny it. You have to do it back. Men like that. I'll bet you've never even touched his prick," Matilda said.

"Well . . . not really."

"Men like that," Matilda repeated. "Just go with him. And then you need a couple of pregnancies. Just a couple. He'll want children by you, but he won't want you out of action for too long."

"You mean it's all planned," Joanna said. "Whatever happened to spontaneity?"

"That's the biggest secret of all," Matilda told her. "Making him believe, now and always, that it is all spontaneous." She kissed her sister. "Enjoy it. Be happy. And make him happy too."

Chapter Five

The Tragedy

After the fracas at the restaurant, which made the gossip columns, the first time Joanna had ever seen her name in print, Alicia did decide to go for adultery, with the result that the whole business was settled within a year. Howard arranged the wedding for the very day the divorce became final.

It had been an incredibly busy year, too busy indeed for Joanna to feel any embarrassment about being painted a scarlet woman by the press. Actually, she was so young, and so patently innocent, she received more sympathy than criticism, and to her great pleasure even Miriam got swept up in the preparations, and moved into the house for the last month, ostensibly to oversee things like the gown, but in reality, Joanna knew, out of sheer curiosity. She was afraid that Howard might object, but he remained urbanely content, or so it seemed, and welcomed his prospective mother-in-law with open arms.

The reconciliation meant that William could visit as well. Joanna was delighted to be back in the company of her brother. William was now sixteen, big and strong, and seemed to be getting on much better at school. "What are you going to do?" Joanna asked him, one Sunday morning in late summer as they strolled in the garden.

"Go to university, I suppose," he said.

"Can Mums afford it?"

"Well, I'll have a grant, of course. I don't suppose there'll be much on top of that . . ." he paused.

"Would you like me to have a word with Howard?"

"Do you think he'd be interested?"

"Of course. You're going to be his brother-in-law."

"Let's see how it goes," William suggested.

Obviously he didn't want a hand-out. Joanna was pleased about that. She could of course give him some of her allowance, but Howard would be sure to know about it; she would prefer to tell him what she was doing. She was relieved that there did not seem any great urgency. William still had to pass the necessary examinations. She got the impression that he wasn't doing as well, scholastically, as he might; he seemed to be more interested in sport. But again, she supposed, early days.

He also seemed to have lost his earlier interest in girls. "That's odd," opined Matilda, who naturally saw a lot more of him. "Queer?" She gave one of her giggles. "Do you think he is?"

"Of course he isn't."

"Well, he only ever has boys about him, and some of them are definitely push-me pull-you," Matilda said, disparagingly.

"You simply have to face the fact that not everyone in the world relates their entire lives to sex, unlike you," Joanna pointed out, even more disparagingly.

She was having the time of her life, because now that the wraps were off, as it were, Howard wanted to show her off. He took her dancing, to concerts and the opera, and he held several cocktail parties at the house, where she was very definitely the hostess, wearing a succession of extremely expensive dresses. These occasions were at once exhilarating and disturbing. She could not help but respond to the open adulation of the men – Prince Hasim was always present, and as gallant as ever – or the envy of the women, to the champagne and the canapés and the feeling of being in control. But she was disturbed by the fact that Matilda was never included, and that they were never invited back to other people's houses. "It's a difficult time, for my friends," Howard explained. "Because they were all friends of Alicia's as well. Probably still are." He grinned, and kissed her. "I am the guilty party, you see. But it'll all settle down, once the divorce is final and we're married."

"If you're guilty, then I must be even more guilty," she said.

"You are guilty of nothing," he told her.

So far he had wanted only what Matilda would no doubt have described as the most orthodox of sexual responses from her. He liked to kiss her naked body from mouth to toe, and he liked to stroke her, but he demanded nothing back from her, and she didn't think she should take the initiative in that direction. He entered her in a perfectly straightforward manner, with her lying on her back. There too she thought she should wait for him to make the first move. He did not like wearing a condom, nor did he wish her to wear or use any protection herself, but she did not get pregnant. She wondered if this concerned him, but it did not appear to.

The fact was, they had a very odd relationship, she supposed. Although she was his fiancée, she was also his mistress. Although she had her charge accounts and all the money she could spend, the bills were paid, and no doubt scrutinised, by him; this knowledge had an inhibiting effect on her buying, and although she could, it appeared, go where she liked and meet who she liked, she rapidly realised that she was being overseen all the time, as everyone seemed to be in his pay, and thus that she really had no freedom at all. Not that she wanted to be any more free than she was; it was just the *feeling* of being caged. Her only friend was Matilda, and Matilda, she realised, was to be kept at arms' length from Howard's friends: she had a reputation, and besides, was a common-or-garden dancer. Matilda never indicated any resentment at her exclusion from her sister's social life, which was a great relief – but she had to be aware of it. Joanna entertained her to lunch at least once a week. They gossiped, and giggled and often got quietly tight, but did not again get down to any intimacies, while, inside her, she was aware of a growing build-up of resentment, that she should be so helpless, even to promote her own sister, who, so far as she knew, was still having to parade naked in front of a gaggle of lecherous old men and more, having to sleep with them afterwards.

The wedding date was set for the second week in December, a week after Joanna's twentieth birthday. On her birthday, the two sisters had lunch together as usual at a smart West End restaurant. "Where are you going for your honeymoon?"

"Do you know, I have actually no idea. Howard hasn't told me. I'm wondering if we're even going to get married."

"Eh?"

"Well, this Kennedy thing—"

"That's done, darling. We can't mourn him forever."

"Well, I can tell you that Howie has been very concerned, these past few weeks."

"And so you haven't asked him about the honeymoon." Matilda frowned. "You *are* going on a honeymoon?"

"Well . . . I imagine so. Unless he's too busy."

Matilda continued to frown as she played with her wine glass. "Do you and he ever talk? Or do you just make love?"

Joanna flushed. "Of course we talk."

"But only about his choice of subjects."

"Well . . . we can't talk shop, because I don't know anything about the business . . ."

"Have you ever been to his office? To Caribee Buildings at all?"

"Well, of course I haven't. As I said—"

"You don't know anything about the business. And Howard aims to keep it that way."

"I have no objection to that."

"Hm," Matilda commented. "I still think you should honeymoon, somewhere really exotic. And I think you should know where it is you're going."

Matilda was in many ways a troublemaker, Joanna reflected. But the nest had been stirred. Joanna felt more than ever thoroughly out of sorts as she dropped her sister after lunch. "Home, madam?" asked Wyndham the chauffeur.

"Oh, yes, home," Joanna said.

He engaged gear and the car moved to the corner, and waited for the traffic flowing by on the major road. Joanna regarded the passers-by without much interest; she had had a liberal helping of wine with her lunch and doubted she would stay awake until they reached Berkshire . . . and then found herself blinking at the face that was peering at her through the tinted rear window. "My God!" she remarked.

"Madam?" asked the chauffeur.

"Hold it a moment," Joanna said, and rolled down the window.

"Joanna?" It was Dick, looking untidy in an ill-fitting suit, with a battered-looking briefcase dangling from his left hand.

"Dick!" What a pleasure it was to see him again.

"But—" he looked left and right at the Rolls.

"I'm holding up traffic, madam," said the chauffeur.

"Oh . . . listen, get in," she said, and opened the door, and Dick half fell into the spacious car. Joanna banged the door shut. "Now you can drive," she told Wyndham.

"Yes, madam. Where would you like to go?"

"Just some place quiet," Joanna told him. He made no comment, filtered into the traffic.

Dick was scrambling on to the seat beside her. "I have to get back to the office."

Joanna giggled. "Tell them you had an accident."

It was so good to see him again, someone of her own social background, social structure . . . although Mums would probably say he was inferior. Aunt Ethel certainly would.

He was remembering their last meeting. "This is just like the car you drove off in after that drug bust . . . heck, two years ago."

"All but," she agreed.

"And since then . . ." he grinned. "The class was struck dumb when that old bag announced you wouldn't be coming back. You should've seen her face."

"And yours?"

"Oh, heck, Jo . . . you know, I damn near wept? Oh, what the hell . . . I did weep. I was so fond of you." Tentatively he touched her hand, and she squeezed his fingers. Damn that second bottle of wine, she thought. If I am not careful, I am going to do something very, very stupid.

But how she wanted to do something very, very stupid. With Dick. They had come so close to it, on so many occasions. "So," he said. "Now, I suppose . . . you're married or something." She pulled off her left glove, and realised, for the first time, that Howard had never even given her an engagement ring! "Well, hell," Dick said. "But this car must be costing a bomb."

"I am going to get married," Joanna said carefully.

"Oh. To that fellow?"

"Yes."

"But . . . he's, well . . ."

"Old enough to be my father," she agreed. "I suppose you could say that I have sold myself, hook, line, and sinker."

Wasn't that the absolute truth?

"Shit!" he muttered, and flushed.

They were out of the West End now, and the streets were quiet. "Can you find some place to park for a few minutes, Wyndham?" she asked. "Somewhere green. There has to be a park some place."

"Yes, madam." His ears were glowing.

"So, what are you doing now?" she asked.

"Well, I've left college, of course, and I have a job—"

"And you're married, and have kids."

"Chance would be a fine thing, on my salary. Listen, I have to be getting back, Jo. If I lose my job—"

"I'll make it up to you," she promised, with a wild idea that she might get Howard to give him a place at the shipping company.

"Right now, I want to . . . pretend. Pretend that it's two years ago. That there's nothing else."

"We're two years older," he said soberly. "We—"

"I know." They were suddenly in a green area, with trees and thick undergrowth. But she didn't need undergrowth. She had the car. "This is ideal, Wyndham."

The car pulled in to the side of a quiet lane.

"I don't suppose you'd care to go for a walk?" Joanna asked.

"It's a nice day for a walk, madam." Wyndham opened the door and got out. "How long a walk should I take?"

"Oh . . . half an hour," Joanna suggested. He touched his cap and walked away from the car.

"Gosh," Dick said. "To have that kind of power . . ."

"It's called money." She held his face between her hands and kissed him on the lips.

"Were you planning on a honeymoon?" she asked Howard that night at dinner.

"Of course."

"Oh! Am I allowed to ask where?"

He grinned. "It's a secret. My wedding present to you."

There really was no answer to that.

Nor was it his only present to her. On the morning of their wedding he gave her an enormous ruby solitaire. "Gosh," she said, as she flipped up the lid on the little blue box. "Oh, gosh."

"I never did give you an engagement ring," he reminded her. "So, better late than never."

She continued to goggle at the huge red stone. She had no idea what it might be worth, but it had to be a lot. Then a thought struck her. "You shouldn't be here at all."

"Eh?"

"It's bad luck for the bride and groom to see each other on the wedding day, until they're married."

"I never knew you were superstitious."

"Well . . ." she flushed. "I'm not."

"You just believe in old wives' tales. But I've always made my own luck."

As always, it was impossible to argue with him, and in any event the rest of the day was entirely taken up with the preparations. The house became filled with hordes of caterers and waitresses, with the dressmakers attending to last minute details, while Miriam fussed. Matilda arrived at ten. However much she might have been pushed aside during the past few months, Joanna had been determined her sister was to be her maid of honour, and Howard had not objected. Her first step into society, Joanna thought, giving her a hug and a kiss. "I'm so glad you're here," she said.

"Have you found out where you're going yet?" Matilda asked. "Oh, you ninny."

William turned up soon after, wearing a new suit – only the second suit he had ever owned – and looking terrified. Then the parson came. "It would have been so very nice to be able to marry you in the church," he said, squeezing Joanna's hand, "but there it is. Rules are rules. But I can bless you," he added brightly.

By then it was time for Joanna to get dressed, fussed over by Miriam and Matilda, and utterly surprised halfway through by the sudden appearance of Aunt Ethel. "What are you doing here?" Matilda asked.

"I was invited," Ethel said.

"Well, of course, but we didn't expect you to come."

Ethel merely snorted. "Can you really, in all conscience, wear white?" she inquired of the bride.

"You may not believe this, Aunt Ethel," Joanna said. "But Howard is the only man with whom I have ever been to bed."

Aunt Ethel clearly didn't think that was any argument.

The house was packed, partly with people Joanna had already

entertained at cocktail parties or met at dances, but also with people she had never met before, but who she gathered were staff from Caribee Lines. "Be nice to Young, Joanna," Howard said, all smiles. "Without him we would be in deep shit."

He passed on, and Joanna smiled, nervously, at the somewhat cadaverous looking man. "I thought I'd met Howard's solicitor."

"I'm not a solicitor, Mrs Edge. I'm chief accountant at Caribee Lines."

"Ah." It occurred to her that he might also be perusing all of her accounts. In which case he knew almost as much about her as Howard. "Then we have no secrets from each other," she said with a bright smile.

"None at all," he agreed, gravely.

Then there was Prince Hasim, resplendent in a morning suit, raising his topper and kissing her hand. "How I wish I were in Howie's place at this moment."

"Oh, come now, Your Highess," Joanna said. "Don't you have a full quiver of wives and concubines back home in Qadir? Or even here in London?"

"Concubines, yes. Wives, no, would you believe it? My English education, I suppose. I keep waiting for the right one. And when I find her . . . she belongs to another."

"You say the sweetest things," Joanna told him, and hurried away before he could say anything else. Not only did she not wish to think of any man save Howard on her wedding day, but the Prince gave her goose pimples . . . in the most erotic possible fashion.

The ceremony droned about her head. Howard had wanted music, even if they couldn't be married in a church, and this was provided by a hi-fidelity phonograph, mostly stirring stuff. The wedding luncheon took upwards of four hours, with gallons of champagne and endless speeches. Howard's was the most brilliant, that of his best man – the host of the bathing party that seemed so long ago –

the most boring. Then Matilda was ushering Joanna away to change her gown for a frock, and Mums was weeping, and Aunt Ethel was looking more po-faced than ever, before she was being hurried down an aisle of people, all reaching to touch her or kiss her. She hardly drew breath until she was seated in the back of the Rolls, and they were driving out of the estate.

"Do you know," Howard said, "there is only one person in the world who knows where we are going? No, two."

"Who are they?" Her head was still spinning from all the champagne.

"Peter Young. And . . ." he kissed her. "That's another surprise."

It was only four in the afternoon, but the day seemed to have been going on forever. She felt she should be full of scintillating conversation, or at least amorous intentions, but instead she fell fast asleep, only to awake a couple of hours later as they pulled into heavy traffic. She sat up with a start. "Gosh! I'm sorry, Howard."

He smiled at her. "I dozed off too."

"Where are we?" She looked right and left at the unfamiliar houses.

"Southampton."

"You don't mean . . ." She watched the docks approach. And alongside the Caribee dock, a ship . . . "That's the *Caribee Queen*!"

"Bound for the Caribbean and all places exotic."

"Oh, Howard!" She hugged him. "Where, exactly?"

"You know the itinerary. Out to Georgetown with dry goods, stopping at Bridgetown, load with rice and sugar, then back home, stopping at again at Bridgetown. Twenty-four days the round trip. Christmas at sea. It'll be terrific."

"Oh, Howard!" She hugged him again.

"You've no doubts about returning to British Guiana?" he asked in her ear.

"I don't think so. Anyway, I won't be Inspector Grain's daughter; I'll be Howard Edge's wife."

"Absolutely," he agreed.

He had of course told Captain Heggie that he would be travelling with his bride, but had issued the strictest instructions that there were to be no celebrations or undue attention. So he and Joanna took their places with the other passengers to board, although the purser could not help but be deferential as he showed them to the forward cabin himself.

The door closed, and Howard took her in his arms. "Just you and me, for twenty-four days."

"And a crew of thirty and ten other passengers," she smiled.

"Not one of whom is going to interfere with us in the least," he promised.

He was quite right. They unpacked their gear, as they were actually making the round trip and would not be leaving the cabin for those twenty-four days, and went on deck in the gathering darkness to watch the ship leave. Here they were just two of the group of passengers, mostly West Indian businessmen and their wives returning home after a summer in England. The purser did sidle up to Howard and mutter that the Captain would be happy to have him and Mrs Edge on the bridge if he wished, but Howard sent him off with a quick shake of the head. "Mrs Edge," Joanna whispered. "I like the sound of that."

At dinner as well, served at one long table in the saloon, they melded in with the rest of the passengers. As was traditional, the Captain did not join them on the first night out, but the first officer did. However, he too had been well briefed and paid Howard no obvious attention, although the special attention was there, had anyone cared to look too closely. But the talk was all about the Profumo Affair and changing conditions in the West Indies following the collapse of the federation, and both Howard and Joanna had to do nothing more than listen politely. And then at last the privacy and comfort of their own cabin. "Do you remember our first meeting?" Howard asked.

"I shall never forget it."

"Did you know that I wanted to bring you to this cabin, then?"

"I didn't," she confessed. "Matilda thought you did, and I told her she was an idiot. And," she added, "a married man. Actually, that's a lie. I didn't know you were a married man until we docked."

"And what did you think then?"

"That you were a lousy, despicable, but very typical man."

He kissed her, then eyed the nightdress she was carefully taking out of the drawer. "You're not meaning to wear that?"

"I bought it specially for tonight."

"I've never seen you in a nightdress before."

"Well . . . I don't normally wear one. I'll put it back."

"No," he said. "Put it on." Tongue between her teeth, Joanna settled the lace and satin on her shoulders, smoothed it down her hips. Howard had also undressed, but he didn't have any pyjamas. "You do realise," he said, "that these internal bulkheads aren't all that thick. No noise, or the neighbours will come rushing in."

"Do I usually make a noise?" she asked.

"There's always a first time," he said, and stepped up to her, digging his fingers into the bodice of the nightgown, and pulling down with all his strength.

It was in fact all Joanna could do to suppress a scream; he had never been violent before. She found herself backed against the wall while he proceeded to tear the beautiful garment into shreds, finally bursting the shoulder straps to let it gather in folds of tattered material about her ankles. Then he kissed her. "I've always wanted to do that," he said.

She didn't know whether it was the fact they were actually married, or the feeling of romantic isolation from normal convention inescapable from being on a ship at sea, but she had never known him in such a mood. His love-making took on a new and more vigorous aspect too, and having gone through his kissing and stroking routine, which always aroused her, as he knew, he rolled her on her face and lifted her thighs to enter her from behind. Another new experience, but one which quite transcended all the others, as he seemed to fill so much more of her, make her so much more aware of herself.

Suddenly she knew that she was indeed going to climax, and it was by far the best she had ever had. While just to lie there feeling him still in her and his weight on her back crushing her into the bunk, while the ship rolled gently as she made her way down the Channel, slowly because of the fog, and always behind her blaring horn, gave her the greatest feeling of security she had ever known.

The rest of the voyage was paradise, even if, by breakfast the following morning, it appeared that everyone on the ship, including the passengers, knew both who they were and that they were honeymooning. But as that also meant that everyone on board understood that they were in the presence of the Owner, when they clearly wished to be alone, as when lying in deck-chairs on the boat deck, they were left alone. Every night was a dinner party, in which at least one of the officers always joined. It was a happy ship with a happy crew, which made the passengers happy as well. "We've been carrying some of these people, to and fro, for ages," Howard told her, and she could well believe that.

The weather remained fine, as it was after the hurricane season and before the winter storms, the sea was unfailingly blue, as was the sky, and the *Caribee Queen* chugged steadily on her way before a broad white wake, passing through the Azores, and then making for Barbados. This was special, not only because of the attractiveness of the island itself, but because it was where Howard had joined the ship three years before, and thus where he had first met her. As they spent a day in Carlisle Bay, discharging cargo, he took her ashore, hired a car, and drove her up to the north of the island, where the sea caves were, and then down the west coast, past rockstrewn Bathsheba, past Sam Lord's Castle – "There's talk of turning it into an hotel,"

Howard said – and then on to the cliff above the Crane, where they could look at the huge rollers breaking on the Cobblers Reef, before racing in to churn up the beach.

From Barbados it was only a night's further sailing for British Guiana.

"Tell me something about the firm?" Joanna asked, as she lay in his arms.

"Planning a takeover?"

"I'm interested. Your life is my life, now."

He considered for a few minutes, then said, "It's not all beer and skittles. Like right now. We had huge hopes about federation, but since that has collapsed, and all the West Indian colonies are becoming independent states, trade has taken a downturn. Then we have two ships that need replacing . . . there are a few problems ahead."

"Oh," she said. It wasn't what she had expected, or hoped, to hear. "But it'll all be okay once you float your new stock issue, or whatever. Won't it?"

"Hopefully. If it's a success."

"But then you'll have a lot more shares. What do you do with them all? I mean, when it's dividend time?"

He grinned, and kissed her. "I don't actually own any shares in Caribee Shipping."

"Eh?" She rose on her elbow in alarm.

"It's a legal matter. Remember, I told you, the shares are all held by a trust company in Jersey. That's where Billy comes in: he manages the trust. That's to avoid death duties, you see, when I go. In the meantime, I get the income from them, and I control them for voting purposes within the Company."

"Just as the Company owns the house and the car . . . does it own me as well?"

Howard kissed her. "I own you, sweetheart. Do you object to that?"

She snuggled against him. "It's a comforting feeling."

"Excited?" Howard asked, as they picked up the pilot on the edge of the mid-flats, some ten miles off the coast.

"Oh, yes," she said.

"We spend three days here, so I've arranged a trip into the interior. Ever been to Kaieteur?"

"No, I haven't. You mean we're going up there? Can we afford it?"

"We're not broke yet."

They spent a morning in Georgetown, and she showed him the Eve Leary barracks, where she had lived with her parents before her father's murder. Then they drove up to Atkinson Field, the air base built by the Americans during World War Two, and there boarded the Grumman amphibian which would fly them into the interior. They held hands as they looked down on the endless reaches of forest, pierced only from time to time by the great rivers. "Most of that is still unexplored," Joanna told him, happy to be playing the mentor at last.

"It's not somewhere to come down," Howard agreed. They landed on the broad Potaro River, upstream of Kaieteur itself, and were led by their guide through a forest path to emerge on a flat rock that overhung the fall. "You don't suffer from vertigo, I hope?" Howard shouted, for now the noise of the cascading water was utterly deafening.

"Not till now," she assured him, and then held her breath as they emerged from the trees on to the rock and gazed at the most awe-inspiring sight in the world.

"When you think," Howard shouted, "of the way they carry on about Niagara and Victoria . . . they're cascades compared with this."

Joanna tried to take in the immensity of the scene, as the three hundred foot wide river, emerging from the trees about a mile to their right with a slow and almost purposeful intensity, rolling up to the lip only feet away from where they stood, and then plunging over, for . . . "How deep *is* it?" she shouted above the roar.

"The gorge is getting on for 1,000 feet," the pilot told them. "The sheer drop is 741; that is, two and a half times the drop of Victoria. The total drop is another hundred."

"A river the size of the Thames, dropping 800 plus feet," Howard said.

"It's been doing that for thousands of years," the pilot said. "Can you imagine the size of the cavern it must have dug out behind that water?"

Joanna couldn't. "Has nobody ever been there?"

"Not possible. There's no way anyone can get through that liquid wall. Unlike Niagara, it never freezes over here."

"Gosh," she said. "There could be all the riches of the world behind there."

"There sure is one vast cavern. One day, I guess, it'll have eaten back so far the river bed will collapse into it."

"But then there'd still be the fall," Howard pointed out.

"That's true. Anyway, it isn't likely to happen in our lifetimes. Not even yours, Mrs Edge."

They remained at the lip for an hour; the roaring water, plunging so far, had a mesmerising effect. But the biggest adventure was yet to come: taking off. They rejoined the Grumman, upstream, and taxied back several hundred yards. Then the engine was thrust up to maximum power, and the little aircraft raced over the surface of the river, water flying to either side. While ahead of them was the end of the world, where the river abruptly ended, and beyond, thousands of feet away, they could see nothing but the forest, huge and green and looming. "Here we go!" shouted the pilot.

Joanna closed her eyes, then forced them open again. This was something that had to be seen and remembered forever. She looked down through the window as they arrived at the lip. She saw the water cascading downwards, the immense rise of spray at the bottom, eight hundred feet away. She caught her breath as the plane dropped, level with the river behind them, before soaring upwards.

"Whew!" Howard said. "You should make your customers have a medical before this trip, just to be sure none of them has a heart attack." The pilot grinned. Presumably he did this so often he never even noticed.

"Where to, now?" Joanna asked. "Back to Atkinson?"

"We have two days left," Howard said. "I thought we'd have a look at the interior."

From Kaieteur the Grumman flew north-east for about a hundred miles before landing on another river, the Mazaruni, and before a settlement, Tumareng. "Ever been up here before?" Howard asked, as they taxied in to the bank.

"Not here. I've been up to the savannah, you know, the high prairie they call the Rupununi." He nodded, studying his map. "But as a young inspector, Dad was based up here for a few years," Joanna said. Howard squeezed her hand.

There was quite a crowd waiting for them on the bank, several black policemen, a couple of white men, and a large number of American Indians, descendants of the Arawaks who had used to own the country. Joanna had encountered them on her visits to the Rupununi; they were short, squat people, not terribly attractive, physically, but full of good humour and enormously strong.

"Mr Edge?" One of the white men shook hands with Howard. "John Dayton. I'm the DC. And . . ." he frowned at Joanna.

"Hello, Mr Dayton," Joanna said.

"Good lord," Howard said. "You mean you two know each other?"

"Gordon Grain's daughter," Dayton said. "My dear girl!" He embraced her. "How's your mother?"

"Very well, thank you."

"And . . ." he groped, mentally.

"Matilda and William," Joanna said. "I'm Joanna," she added, as he obviously didn't recall her name either.

Howard continued to look quizzical. "I've been to their house for dinner," Dayton said. "Oh, some years ago. You would have been . . . ?"

"Twelve, Mr Dayton," Joanna said.

"You've changed a bit. Well, this calls for a celebration. Oh, by the way, this is Inspector Calham. He's the local chief bobby." Calham, a young man wearing khaki uniform with shorts and stockings, shook hands.

Then they were hurried away to the Commissioner's bungalow for celebrations. Apparently neither Calham nor Dayton was married, and they thoroughly enjoyed the company of an attractive young bride; the meal was eaten on the bungalow verandah, behind mosquito screens, beyond which the Amerindians gathered to stare at them. "So, what would you like to do and see while you're here?" Dayton asked as they drank thick, sweet, black coffee.

"You tell us," Howard suggested. "Some gold workings, of course—"

"That's rather like watching a tree grow," Calham grinned. "Ever done any white water?"

"I'm not with you."

"He means rapid shooting," Dayton explained. "There's a river close by, a tributary of the Mazaruni, that has some spectacular falls."

"Now that sounds like fun," Howard said, turning to Joanna. "You game?"

"Isn't it dangerous?" she asked.

"Not if the boatmen know what they're doing," Dayton said.

"We'll give it a whirl," Howard said.

"Then we'll make an early start in the morning."

"I hope you don't think I'm chicken," Joanna said, when she and Howard were alone in their bedroom in the guest bungalow, isolated

104

from the world by their mosquito nets, although the sounds of the village and the jungle beyond overlaid the evening, softened always by the constant swish of the river. The Grumman had returned to town, but would come back for them the day after tomorrow; the *Caribee Queen* sailed that night.

"Of course I don't," Howard said. "You have every right to be concerned. But these chaps know what they're doing."

"It's just that I'm not sure I should be bounced about too much." He had been looking at his maps, as usual. Now he slowly turned his head. "I missed last month. I put that down to all the excitement over the wedding. But I was due again four days ago," she explained. "I didn't say anything then, because, you know, with all this travel, it seemed quite reasonable to be late."

"Holy Hallelujah!" He hugged and kissed her.

"Only four days," she reminded him.

"Okay. But if there is a little fellow in there, we certainly don't want to bounce him about. You'll have to take a rain check on this one."

She squeezed his hand, then frowned. "But you're still going?"

"Darling, I'm not pregnant. It'll be the experience of a lifetime."

They slept in each other's arms, although Joanna was awake most of the night. She was not disturbed by the unfamiliar jungle sounds which drifted through her window, or by the sudden very heavy shower of rain just before dawn. It was merely a feeling of euphoria that swept over her from time to time. She had never been so happy in her life. She had been a little afraid that Howard might not really wish to start another family, but he had seemed over the moon.

And she would not have been human if she had not reckoned it would be one in the eye for Alicia.

They were up at dawn to breakfast with Dayton, before driving off along a rather bumpy track to look at some of the gold workings. As Dayton had warned, this was not terribly exciting, but Joanna was presented with a nugget, about half the size of her little fingernail.

"Pure, twenty-four carat metal," Dayton told her. "A quarter of an ounce weight."

"Which would be worth, how much?" Joanna asked.

"Oh, seventy-five dollars, maybe."

"I'm going to keep it, forever," she vowed.

Then there was an alligator farm, where they were shown hundreds of newly hatched babes. "Oh, aren't they just superb," Joanna cried, as one of the inch-long replicas was placed on her palm. Although born and bred in Guiana, she had never actally seen an alligator outside of a zoo; they were not normally to be encountered on the streets of Georgetown. Now the infantile reptile opened its jaws to yawn at her. "Can I have one, Howie? As a pet?"

"Of course you can," Howard said. "Just let's ask if it's practical."

"Well, sir, madam," said the black manager, "you can have one if you like. But you want to remember, these creatures grow. And then some."

"How big?" Howard asked.

"Well, sir, come a couple of years, if you was keeping him in your bathtub, you'd find his tail hanging over one end and his head over the other. His jaws would then be about three feet long."

"My God!" Joanna commented.

"I think maybe we should think about that one," Howard suggested. "Whatever would Mrs Partridge say?"

They drove over to the river, about half the size of the Mazaruni. "Listen," Dayton said.

It was by now a familiar sound, the road of water rushing downhill very fast.

A double-ended wooden boat was waiting for them, with a crew of eight paddlers. The boat was called a bateau, fittingly enough, but the word, in Guiana, denoted the specific double-ended construction rather than merely boat. They had by now been joined by Calham, and he and Howard got into the boat. "I'll take care of the little lady," Dayton said.

"See you in ten minutes," Howard said, taking his seat amidships, while the paddlers dug their blades in and the bateau moved away from the bank. Joanna felt she should say something, but nothing came to mind beyond the admonishment to take care, and that seemed rather puerile.

She got into the jeep beside Dayton and they followed the path down the gently sloping hillside. This was extremely bumpy, and she began to wonder if it would not have been more restful in the boat. Then Dayton braked and pulled off the track on to the bank. "There," he said.

Joanna gazed at the rocks, the tumbling white water. "How far is it?"

"It stretches about a quarter of a mile, but they'll be going so fast it'll seem more like a few seconds," he said.

They got back into the jeep and drove another hundred yards, then Dayton stopped again. Now they were virtually in the middle of the rapids, which went racing and bubbling past only a few feet away. "This is the easy part," Dayton joked, noticing her anxiety. "When they get to the end, the men have to haul the boat back upstream, overland."

Joanna was looking upriver, and at that moment the bateau appeared. It was already travelling quite fast, the eight paddlers' arms and blades moving in perfect unison. "They're a highly trained team," Dayton explained. "When they get to the rocks, it's a matter of adjusting their strokes to make the boat move with the current and avoid hitting anything."

"But they've done it before?" Joanna asked.

"Often," he assured her.

"How deep is it?"

"Only a few feet. If they do get tumbled, it's a matter of walking ashore."

She found that very reassuring, as the boat now came hurtling down towards them. Howard was grinning with excitement as they struck the white water. A rock reared in front of them and Joanna suppressed a scream, but a deft touch by one of the rear paddlers sent the boat slewing round. Before it could be picked up broadside by the rushing water, another deft stroke on the other side straightened it up again. Their technique was fantastic. Another two twists and they were level with the jeep. Howard waved. The bateau surged on.

"They'll be there before us," Dayton said, and turned back to the jeep. Joanna remained watching the boat as it did another twist. But the man on the left side did not respond quickly enough this time, and the bateau was picked up, broadside on, by the stream. There was a wild flurry of paddles, but she reached the next level before she could be straightened, and went over, still broadside on. "Shit!" Dayton commented, hurrying back to Joanna's side.

Joanna remained standing absolutely still, unable to move or speak. The bateau was upside down, racing on, out of control, striking a rock to splinter herself, and then again. Behind her were bobbing heads. "Rope," Dayton snapped, and ran back to the jeep to collect the coil of rope in the back. This he dropped on the ground, before hurling the end as far into the water as he could. But the heads were already scattering, shouting. "They'll be swept down," Dayton said, gathering up the rope. "Come on."

Feeling she was in a dream, Joanna got in beside him, holding on as he went bumping down the path, for another hundred yards. When he braked again, they looked at relatively calm water, although only a few feet further upriver it still tossed and stormed beneath clouds of spray. Already staggering towards the bank were several of the paddlers. "What about fish?" Joanna asked. "Piranha?"

"There are no piranha about here," Dayton assured her. "If any did get swept down the rapids they'd be suffering from shock. There's Calham." The policeman emerged, looking like a drowned rat. All eight paddlers were now sitting on the bank, gasping for breath. "Just Mr Edge," Dayton said, staring upstream. "Should be here by now."

Everyone was now looking, while Joanna's heart seemed to have stopped beating. The water was only five feet deep, Dayton had said. Well, all the other men had been able to stand. But . . . "Where is Mr Edge?" Dayton asked, his voice suddenly taking on an edge itself.

"He was thrown out with the rest of us," Calham said. "My God, you don't think—"

Dayton ran back up the track, two of the crew with him. "There!" shouted one of them.

"Oh, thank God!" Joanna gasped.

But there was no elation in Dayton's voice. "Fetch the rope," he shouted.

Calham led the others upstrean, carrying the rope. Joanna went with them, stopped to look at Howard, who seemed to be wedged between two of the rocks. He was neither moving nor holding on. Slowly she sank to her knees.

Part Two

The Heiress

'Why, I hold fate
Clasp'd in my fist, and could command the course
Of time's eternal motion'

John Ford

Chapter Six

The Widow

Dayton and Calham put the body in the back of the jeep for the drive back to Tumareng, Joanna sitting beside it. They had covered it with a blanket, for which she was grateful. Howard's mouth was open where he had gasped for the air that had not been available, and there were also bruises on his face where he had struck the rock. Joanna's brain was numbed. She had not been allowed to see her father's body. But she could only think, first father, now husband. And I am bearing his child. She had no doubt of that now.

Because of where they were, only a degree or two north of the equator, there were horrible connotations to death. There was a radio at Tumareng, and Dayton got on it right away, but it would still be four hours before the Grumman could be taken off its present assignment and got up to them, and now it was almost noon. Joanna watched as the big fridge at the DC's bungalow was emptied of its contents, and Howard's body placed inside, while the generator, normally run for only a couple of hours every evening – the fridge was mainly battery operated – clacked into life. She saw Dayton and Calham exchange glances, and could read their thoughts: this is going to cost a fortune.

But they had their duty to do. Joanna was invited to lie down on the Commissioner's bed, and when she declined, was seated in an armchair in the lounge and offered brandy. "I'd rather have coffee," she said. "Can't I have coffee?"

Coffee was brought. She sipped it, both hands wrapped round the red-hot cup, staring in front of her, only slowly becoming aware that people were standing around her, black men as well as white, and Indians too. "Please," she said. "I am all right."

Some of them left, shooed away by Dayton. Calham, having changed his wet clothes, sat beside her. "We were all thrown out," he said. "I didn't see Mr Edge after that. I don't know what to say. The drill is . . . well, every man gets ashore as best he can."

"Have you been capsized in a rapid before?" she asked.

"Yes. Yes, I have."

"And were lives lost?" He shook his head. "Then it was just an accident," she said.

They gave her another cup of coffee, and this she realised *had* been laced with brandy. She didn't really want to drink it, because she had so much to think about. But it did relax her, kept the unthinkable thoughts at a decent distance. She was a wife of just two weeks, and now she was a widow. And a mother. She was surprised, and somewhat ashamed, at how little grief she felt. But she had never loved Howard. She had been overwhelmed by him, from the moment of their first meeting. He had been a dream man, who had suddenly, amazingly, become reality. She had been swept off her feet, only managing a few faint flutters, like a butterfly caught in a jalousie. She had known all along that their marriage could never last. Howard had been a sexual rover, and soon enough he would have roved again, as she had been warned, in different ways, by both Alicia and Matilda. Both had recommended she make hay while the sun shone. Had she made hay? She had a thousand shares in his company, currently producing an income of just under two hundred pounds a year. But all her charge accounts would presumably end with his death. That man Young would see to that the moment the news reached him. She had not taken to Peter Young at all.

Well, she thought, I still have my mink. And the ring Howard gave me. That must be worth a fortune! She wondered if she had enough money to get home? But they would have to pay her passage; she would be travelling with her dead husband. Their boss. Who was their boss no longer. She realised that her fingers had curled into fists, and that her nails were eating into her flesh.

John Dayton, who would not leave her alone for an instant, gave her another cup of coffee, and offered her lunch, but made no comment when she declined. He ate himself; as the dining-table was on the far side of the lounge, he could still watch her. "The plane will soon be here," he promised her.

It took six hours for the plane to get to them, because the pilot had had some rounding up to do. With him were a doctor, an undertaker, and a man who introduced himself as Norman Peters. "I'm Caribee Shipping's agent in Georgetown," he explained. "My dear Mrs Edge, I don't know what to say. If there is anything you wish, you have but to tell me."

"I want to go home," Joanna told him. "With Howard."

"Of course."

The undertaker had a cold bag, into which Howard's body was loaded, rather as if he were a side of beef, Joanna thought. This was placed in the luggage compartment of the Grumman, with their suitcases. Then they flew back to the coast. No one spoke much, the exact tale of what had happened having been given to them at Tumareng. Inspector Calham would of course look after the local police formalities. At Atkinson Field there were reporters, but Peters ushered Joanna through the throng and into a car for the drive down to Georgetown. "I've booked you a hotel room—"

"I'd rather sleep on the *Caribee Queen*," she said.

Her last experience of being Mrs Howard Edge, she thought.

"Of course. Whatever you wish," Peters gushed. He obviously hadn't as yet been in touch with Peter Young.

Sailing was delayed for two days, to permit the autopsy and inquest. Joanna was required to appear in court, surrounded by sympathetic British expatriot officials, all of whom had known her father and remembered her as a little girl, who, with their wives and children – some of whom she remembered – wanted to hug her and kiss her and tell her how sorry they were at the terrible tragedy. She wanted only to be away from them, but had to sit and listen to how Howard's death had been caused by drowning while temporarily unconscious, he having apparently hit his head on a rock when thrown out of the bateau. No blame could be attached to anyone.

Then at last the *Caribee Queen* sailed, Howard now in the ship's refrigeration room. Joanna deliberately did not look at any newspapers or listen to any radio broadcasts, and the crew were clearly under orders not to disturb her in any way, so she had no idea how widespread was the news of Howard's death. She did observe that the *Caribee Queen* sailed with two empty cabins. This was because she was picking up two passengers in Bridgetown: Peter Young and Billy Montgomery.

Joanna was sitting on the boat deck beneath a broad-brimmed hat, looking across Carlisle Bay at the Careenage and the attractions of Bridgetown, when the launch came alongside. She did not look over the rail to see who was boarding, and thus was utterly taken aback when the two men, looking very hot and bothered, emerged at the top of the ladder. "My dear Joanna," Billy said, kissing both her hands.

"Mrs Edge," Young said. "My deepest sympathies." They were both wearing white tropical suits with black armbands, and white panama hats.

"I don't understand," Joanna said.

"We flew out yesterday, as soon as we heard the news," Billy explained, dragging a deck-chair alongside hers to sit down. Young did the same on the other side.

"I see," she said. "Business."

"That's about it," Young said. "The company."

"Yes," she said. "All I want is to go home. I won't trouble you any more."

Young and Billy exchanged glances. "We do understand your

feelings right this minute, Joanna," Billy said. "But . . . well . . .
business must go on. It transcends death."

Joanna frowned. "What has that got to do with me?" Another
exchange of glances between the two men.

"Did Mr Edge never discuss business with you?" Young asked.

"Sometimes. I have a thousand shares in the company. Do I have
to give those up?"

Young took off his hat to scratch his head.

"Joanna," Billy said, "did Howard never discuss his will with
you?"

"No, he didn't. We weren't into things like wills. He didn't
expect to die."

"Of course he did not. But . . . there it is. We have a copy of his
will with us. Do you want to look at it?"

"No."

"Well, with your permission, I'll tell you what matters. Howard
left his entire holding in Caribee Shipping to you."

Joanna raised her head, slowly.

"That is," Young said carefully, "sixty-nine per cent of the shares."

For a moment Joanna could not grasp what he was saying.
"That is to say," Billy explained, "you now own the company.
Which means that you continue to own the house, and the apartment, and the car, and . . . well, everything. It's all in trust, of
course. But you own the trust. Naturally, there are some provisions
for his children by Alicia, but these do not affect your overall
position."

"In effect," Young said, "he also willed you his authority as
Chairman and MD. Now, of course, it is quite impossible for a
girl of twenty to be chairman of a large company, much less MD,
however . . ."

The calm sea suddenly appeared to be very rough, and the deck was
going up and down. Howard *had* loved her, after all. He had left her
everything. Every single, little thing. The entire world. Would you
like to sail forever? he had asked her when they had first met. Now

117

he had enabled her to do that, or anything else she chose. "Joanna?" Billy asked, having seen her eyes glaze.

"Who else knows about this?" she asked.

"Why, no one, at the moment," Young said. "We thought it correct that you should be informed first. As soon as I get back to England I shall of course acquaint all the other shareholders with the situation . . ."

Alicia, Joanna thought. My God, she'll curdle in her cornflakes! "As I was saying," Young went on, "while no one would expect you to take on the duties of Chairman and MD, the gift, shall I say, the choice, is within your keeping. The appointment."

He paused, and there was another exchange of glances. Because each of them is hoping for such an appointment, Joanna realised. "Is there any legal impediment whereby I should not be Chairman and Managing Director myself?" she asked, very softly.

"Well . . . no. But the difficulties—"

"Tell me about them."

"Well . . . apart from the day-to-day running of the company, an immense task, believe me, there is the effect the news would have on the shares. They would tumble."

"Would that matter, so long as we did not have to sell any? If the company continued to make the same profits as before, it would not affect the dividends, would it?"

Young and Billy gazed at each other; such a simplistic approach was unknown to them. "It's not quite as simple as that," Young said, wiping his neck with his handkerchief. "The value of the company affects the amount of money we can borrow. You are probably not aware of it, but there is an overdraft. Two million pounds. Also, Howard was planning a flotation next year. We need a considerable capital influx, you see."

"Why?" She continued to pretend ignorance.

"We need to liquidate our borrowings. In addition, of our four ships, two are coming up for replacement. In fact, they have really reached the end of their working life, and can only be disposed of for scrap. So we need that financing from the city. Now, this tragedy will certainly create a problem. I haven't told Miller & Sparks myself as yet, but they will certainly know of it by now. I imagine the wires are red hot right this minute. So—"

"Who are Miller & Sparks?"

"The brokers who were going to handle the issue."

"And you think they will refuse to do that, now?"

"No, no," Young said hastily. "But . . . well . . . they'll want to know that a responsible person is in charge of the company."

"Are you saying that I am irresponsible, Mr Young?"

Young mopped away, and looked imploringly at Billy. Who came to his rescue. "Of course Peter doesn't mean that, Joanna. But you must look at it from the point of view of these hard-nosed city analysts. You, we, Caribee Shipping, are asking them to invest several million pounds in the company. In return, they will wish assurances that the profits will be maintained at least at their present level, and will hopefully increase as the new, improved ships come on the route. Now, the key to the maintenance of profits is management, control, strength of will at the top . . ." his voice faded away as he looked into Joanna's eyes.

"I quite understand," Joanna said. "What you are saying is that I will have to find a chairman and managing director who can command the confidence of the City of London."

"Well, if you put it that way . . . yes."

"Then you must give me a little while to consider. But we have that time, haven't we? Until we dock?"

The *Caribee Queen* left Barbados that evening, steaming into the Atlantic. In five days time they would be home. And by then . . . Joanna lay awake in her bunk that night, listening to the growl of the engines. She was alone in a four-berth cabin, because this was the cabin the Owner always occupied when he, or she, was at sea. And she was the Owner. It had all been too sudden for her to grasp that afternoon. She had refused to join Young and Billy and the other passengers for dinner, had dined alone in her cabin. She was faced with an immensity she could only consider in total privacy.

What had she and Howard worked out he was worth? Four million pounds! So, she was now worth four million pounds. She tried to envisage what four million pounds, in bank notes, might look like, stacked up in front of her and couldn't. Well, then, she tried to envisage how it could be spent. The most she had ever spent in one day was two thousand, five hundred pounds, on that glorious morning she had bought both Matilda and herself fur coats, herself some new outfits, and then treated them both to a bang-up lunch. If she spent two thousand, five hundred pounds a day, every day, from here on . . . she got out of bed, switched on the light, and sat down with a pad of the ship's notepaper and a pen. It would take her one thousand, six hundred days to go through the lot. That was less than five years! That didn't seem very long. But that took no account of the income coming in and of course she wasn't going to spend two thousand five hundred pounds a day, not for a single day, much less a thousand odd.

So, approach it from the other angle. She was twenty. Supposing she lived until she was eighty, she could . . . she got busy with her pen. She could spend sixty-six thousand, six hundred pounds every year before the money ran out. That was more than five thousand pounds a month, or more than a thousand pounds a week. That suddenly put everything in perspective. Tilly! What was Tilly going to say? What was Tilly going to *do*? Tilly would need controlling. So would her spending, if she was going to remain a millionairess. But so would the company.

The company! No doubt it was self-perpetuating, even if astro- nomically in debt. But only with the right MD who would be able to gain the confidence of the city. Such a man should not be hard to find. She didn't altogether trust either Young or Billy, not for their honesty, but for their ability. But there had to be someone . . . Why *not* her? She could take over the chairmanship simply by announcing it. The other shareholders – including Alicia, delicious thought –

would have to accept her decision. They might all sell their shares and quit. She wondered if it might be possible to own every share? But the suggestion was that the company would go straight down the drain without the backing of its stockbrokers and its bankers. Her big task would be to convince the City that she knew what she was about!

She got out of bed, put on her robe, opened the cabin door. The saloon was empty, with dimmed lights. She crossed it and opened the door on to the deck. Immediately the breeze plucked at her clothes and hair. But it was a self-created breeze, caused by the speed of the ship; the sea remained calm. And they were still far enough south for it to be warm. She climbed the ladder to the bridge, stood for a moment on the wing, looking through the open door at the quartermaster standing at the helm, and the officer of the watch, who was on the far side, leaning over the high table and writing in the log.

She drew a deep breath and stepped into the house. Both men turned in the same instant, jaws dropping. "Good morning," she said.

"Good heavens, you gave me a start, Mrs Edge," the Second Mate said. "Thought you were a ghost."

Both her nightgown and négligé were white satin, given her by Howard as a wedding present; he hadn't got around to tearing them off her before his death. "Is all well?" she asked.

"Oh, surely, Mrs Edge. No problems." He gestured at the starlit night, the broad path of the moon across the sparkling water. "Perfect night." He tapped the radar. "Nothing within forty miles of us."

"Then do you mind if I talk with you for a while?"

"Why, it'd be a pleasure, Mrs Edge." He waited, perhaps expectantly. Presumably he had never before been in the position of entertaining, on the bridge, a beautiful widow . . . who also happened to be his employer.

"I want you to show me, and tell me, and explain to me," Joanna said, "everything about navigation."

Second Mate Mullin swallowed. "Navigation, Mrs Edge? That's a very big subject."

"I know. But we have five days and nights before we reach Southampton, don't we?"

"Yes, ma'am," Mullin said, with sudden enthusiasm.

At dawn Joanna returned to her cabin, showered, and dressed herself. She had a quick breakfast, then went down to the engine room. She had already had First Mate Crowther, who had replaced Mullin at two for the morning watch, and been equally scandalised at what he was required to do, and had then got every bit as enthusiastic, inform Chief Engineer Wilson that she wished to meet him in his kingdom, and he was waiting for her, eyeing her somewhat suspiciously. "It's not all that clean down here, Mrs Edge."

"That's why I am wearing jeans, Mr Wilson."

She had also tied her hair up in a bandanna, and for the next two hours followed him about as he explained about temperatures, ratios, gauges, pressure and oil consumption, while she tried to put thoughts of latitude and longitude, currents and leeway, sextants and logarithmal tables, Greenwich Mean Time and Ship's Time, out of her mind, and replace them with boiler pressure and designated speed, fuel consumption and induced horsepower. "You going to remember all of this?" Wilson asked when they had finished.

"No," she admitted. "But I am going to come down here again tomorrow, and the day after, and the day after that, and you can show me it all again and again." He scratched his head.

Captain Heggie was waiting for her when she returned to her cabin for a wash after the engine room. "You're being a busy lady, Mrs Edge," he said. "Suborning my officers." But he grinned as he said it.

"I didn't want to disturb your beauty sleep," she said. "But now that you're up, there's a lot you can teach me, too. About cargoes and costs, routes and alternatives."

"You mean to run this line yourself?"

"Just let's say that I am interested in how it works, at every level. But if I did decide to take over, would you object?"

"I think it would be the best idea since sliced bread. Let's go up to my office."

Young and Billy were up by now, breakfasting with the other passengers in the saloon. They looked at Joanna quizzically as she accompanied the captain up to the bridge, but preferred not to make any comment at that moment. Joanna spent the rest of the morning looking at manifests and cost sheets. "I hate to say it," she remarked, "as I was born there, but the trade with BG is the weakest."

"They have the weakest economy. But it should pick up when the territories recover from the failure of federation." Heggie said.

"Is that really going to happen, Captain?"

"Given time."

"Time we don't seem to have. You don't think we should be tempted to look for other routes, other markets? My husband has spoken of dwindling profit margins in the Caribbean."

Heggie scratched his head. "That's not my province, Mrs Edge. But I have to say it would be a hell of a gamble. We have these routes, we have these customers. You'd have to get both local permission and guarantees to go elsewhere."

"Just a thought, Captain."

"We're hearing rumours that you've been all over this ship, from top to bottom," Billy said, as he and Young finally cornered her in her favourite relaxing position on the boat deck.

"Don't you think I should know all there is to know about one of my possessions?" she asked.

There was the usual exchange of glances. Neither man had yet worked out how to take her, seriously or as an irrelevance. But her mind was fast hardening. The decision was composed of several things. She felt that Howard would not have left everything to her had he not intended her to succeed him eventually, although obviously he could not possibly have expected it to happen so soon or so suddenly. Thus she felt guilty for her earlier appraisal that she was just a passing fancy, and was determined to prove herself worthy of his trust. There was the matter of the child she was certain was in her womb, something known only to her. That child was the entire future.

Then there was the very real understanding that if she appointed a chairman and managing director, he would certainly shunt her aside as an ignorant young woman, and seek to run the company his way. While she had so many ideas on how to run the company *her* way. More than any of those, however, was the desire to meet, and beat, a challenge. To show the world, and particularly a few members of it, such as Aunt Ethel and Alicia, and even Matilda, who always treated her as a child, what she could do. She was a hick from the furthest possible sticks. But she wasn't stupid, and she knew what she wanted. Well, she was going to get what she wanted. Get? She would take.

She smiled at the two men. "By the way, I have informed the radio operator, through the captain, that I do not wish any business matters transmitted from the ship for the remainder of the voyage. As you said, Mr Young, the wires are no doubt red-hot in London. Let's keep them that way. After all, we'll be home in four days."

"While thousands are being wiped off the value of the company shares, every one of those days?"

She gave him a sweet smile. "That's my problem, isn't it? Tomorrow is Christmas Day. Lunch with me."

They wandered off, disgruntled, and she checked with Captain Heggie. "What time are we supposed to dock?"

"Six in the morning, Mrs Edge."

"On Monday."

"That's right. Sorry about the hour, but it means we can start unloading within a couple of hours of clearing customs."

"I think it's a splendid time to dock, Captain. Now tell me, do you have an up-to-date *Who's Who* on board?"

"I have last year's. We need to be able to identify our passengers, when we can."

"May I look at it please?"

She went into the radio shack, where the operator hastily stood to attention. "I have some telegrams for you to send. And I would like the replies brought directly to me."

"Of course, Mrs Edge." She wrote out the messages, gave themn to him. Then it was simply a matter of waiting.

Early as it was, Miriam, Matilda and William were on the dockside waiting for her. They were allowed on board by a sympathetic customs officer, now aware that he was dealing with the Owner's family. "Oh, my darling." Miriam held her close. "Howard . . . ?"

"He's on board," Joanna said. "He'll be buried in the family plot."

"You're so calm . . ."

"Well, I've had ten days to come to terms with the situation."

"Jo!" Matilda hugged her and kissed her. "I am so sorry for you." William said nothing, just held her for several minutes.

"You may go ashore whenever you please, Mrs Edge," Captain Heggie said. "We'll see to your gear. And—"

"We'll look after that, Joanna," Billy said. "There'll have to be an embalming, and, well—"

"What are you doing on board?" Matilda asked.

"Billy was Howard's man," Joanna said. "Now he's mine. Well, in a manner of speaking." The family stared at her. "I shall want to see you, whenever you've finished unloading, Captain Heggie"

"Of course, Mrs Edge. Just name the date and time."

"Keep in touch with the office," Joanna said. Once again the family stared at her. She smiled at them. "Shall we go?"

They followed her down the gangplank, to where the Rolls waited. Billy looked as if he would have liked to join them, but Joanna merely smiled at him, and closed the door. "Where to first, Mrs Edge?" asked the chauffeur.

"Harrods."

"Yes, ma'am."

"Harrods?" Miriam and Matilda spoke together.

"I need widow's weeds," Joanna explained. "I didn't take anything black on my honeymoon."

"But . . . Harrods?" Miriam was aghast.

"I think you should know," Joanna said, "that I am now the Chairman and Managing Director of Caribee Shipping. In fact, I own the company, to all intents and purposes."

Now their stares came at her as if she was a stranger. Well, she supposed, she was, now, to them.

"You own the company?" Matilda, predictably, was first to recover; Joanna could just imagine her brain tumbling over itself as she tried to determine what that might mean for her.

"Howard left me all his shares, yes."

"And you're going to run the company yourself?" William was delighted.

"I have that in mind, although there are certain things to be sorted out."

"Wowee!"

"But, you can't—" Miriam began.

"Don't say it, Mums, please. I can do anything I please, if I have enough guts and determination. Shouldn't you be in school, Willie?"

"They gave me the day off to meet you."

"Well, I'm sure you don't want to hang about women trying on clothes. Go to the games department and buy yourself something. Tell them to bill it to me."

William gulped and hurried off, and the three women swept inside, Miriam looking, as always when she entered this store, like a frightened rabbit.

"There's so much we have to talk about," Matilda ventured.

"I know," Joanna said. "We'll have a powwow after the funeral."

"Not till then?"

"I have a lot to do today," Joanna pointed out.

She bought herself three black dresses in varying styles and for varying occasions, and a black turban into which she could fit her hair. The assistant was most apologetic when she presented her card. "I'm not sure—"

"Telephone Caribee Shipping," Joanna told her. "Ask for Mr Young, and ask him if that card is still valid."

"How embarrassing," Miriam whispered.

"Not at all. It's correct business procedure. Everyone knows my credit is backed by Howard's. What they don't yet know is that Howard's credit is now mine."

The assistant came hurrying back. "So many apologies, Mrs Edge. It's just that—"

"Don't give it a thought," Joanna told her. "Now," she said, "I am going to drop you all home. I have some appointments."

"Aren't you going to come in?" Miriam asked. "There's so much—"

"Later," Joanna reminded her.

They dropped Miriam and William first, then drove to Matilda's flat. "I don't know whether to be over the moon or under it," Matilda confessed.

"Just remain absolutely calm," Joanna said.

"Like you. You really are something, little sister."

She was setting up to dominate. But Joanna just smiled. "I'm not little any longer, Tilly."

The car stopped. "About my work," Matilda said.

"Are you on tonight?"

"Yes. I'd like to quit."

"I wouldn't do that yet," Joanna said. "I don't have Howard's contacts yet. It might take me longer to find you a new job."

Matilda glared at her. "You are a bitch."

"I'm feeling my way," Joanna told her.

Chapter Seven

The Bargain

"His Highness will see you now, Mrs Edge." The secretary was English, very prim and proper, in her mid-forties. Hasim obviously did not mix work and play. Joanna was not sure if that was a good thing or not, in her position.

He was on his feet, standing in front of his desk, in a large, light office, huge windows overlooking London. "Joanna!" He came forward to embrace her. "I am so terribly sorry. When I got your wire, I just could not believe it." His eyes, as she had anticipated, roamed up and down the trim black dress she had just bought, settling on the black turban beneath which her hair was entirely concealed.

So here I am, she thought. Joanna Edge, *femme fatale*? Or Joanna Edge, blatant whore. That verdict would depend on how successful she was. "Thank you."

He held her hand and led her to a chair. "And you actually saw it happen? How terrible for you."

"It's all a bit hazy now."

"I can imagine." He sat beside her. "So . . . there is no trouble, is there? If there is anything I can do to help . . ."

"There is no trouble, Hasim. But I do need your help."

"You have but to ask."

"Well, I should tell you that I intend to manage the company myself."

Hasim's mouth made a small O. "Can you do this?"

"There is no legal reason why I should not. I suppose there is, in your country?"

"I'm not sure there is any legal reason there, either. It's just that no woman in my country would ever dream of attempting such a thing."

"But do you have any prejudices against dealing with a woman, in England?"

"Of course I do not. It is necessary all the time, nowadays. But there is also the question of your age . . ."

"I am legally an adult."

"Experience?"

"I shall get that. I'm working on it already. But I understand that almost everyone with whom I come into contact will hold your point of view."

He held her hands. "My dear Joanna, I wish only to help you. I was merely pointing out the obstacles."

"There are others. Caribee Shipping hasn't been doing too well."

He frowned. "Howie always gave the impression that he was on a roll."

"Howie was great at giving impressions. Trouble is, I think he believed them himself. I haven't seen the books yet, but as far as I can gather, the situation is this: profits are falling, partly because of the general situation in the West Indies, and partly because at least two of our fleet aren't up to it any more. They're costing us more to keep them running than they can possibly earn."

"Well, as to the West Indies, I know they are going through a period of uncertainty at the moment, since the collapse of the federation—"

"I don't believe they are going to recover all that quickly, Hasim. Not from what I've heard."

Hasim released her hand to ring a bell. "You must let me take you out to lunch."

She smiled. "I'm not that poor, yet."

"I would still be honoured." He gave his secretary instructions, and the door closed again. "But when you get your new ships—"

"Am I going to get new ships?"

"Howie spoke of a flotation—"

"We have a kind of chicken and egg situation," Joanna said. "There is no hope of us improving our financial situation, even if trade picks up, if we don't get those ships. At the present time, there is no hope of us getting those ships unless trade and profits pick up. What is more, there seems *absolutely* no hope of a flotation with a twenty-year-old managing directress in charge."

"So you would like me to underwrite some of the shares."

"Can you?

"I'm afraid it would only be a very small part of what you need."

"Then that is not the answer, although I am very grateful for the offer. But I think I have a possible solution."

"Tell me."

"When I leave here, Hasim, I must go to see, first of all, my stockbrokers, and secondly, my bankers. As we have agreed, they are both likely to take a very downbeat view of my situation. I need to present them with something that will make them believe that Caribee Shipping is going up, not down. We've agreed ships alone won't do it, while Caribbean trade is down. But if I could tell them that I have secured an entirely new trade route, one with a burgeoning and spreading economy, from which we could not fail to make a growing profit, that might just swing the odds in my favour."

Hasim released her hands, got up and sat down behind his desk. "You would be plunging into areas of which you and your captains know nothing. I mean, physically."

"They can navigate. So the waters around the Persian Gulf can be treacherous. You don't have hurricanes, right?"

Hasim pinched his lip. "There is also the matter that politically, the area is not as stable as the Caribbean."

"You reckon? What about the missile crisis a couple of years ago? And if that's been sorted out, Castro is still running riot."

"That is true, I suppose. One does tend to worry about personal problems to the exclusion of all else."

"Then you'll give me a guarantee, and slots?"

"It would mean treading on some corns," Hasim said, thoughtfully. "As it happens, the company that is presently handling most of our commodity trade – we are obviously not talking about oil here – has been letting us down somewhat over the past year or two. But it would cause quite a stir were we to put them out altogether—"

"I'm quite prepared to compete."

"You cannot compete, my dear Joanna. You can only replace. All shipping contracts in and out of Qadir are government controlled. So, you either have the backing of the government, or you have nothing."

"And you are the government."

He smiled. "I am a part of the government. Perhaps I could persuade my father . . . but it would be difficult."

Joanna drew a deep breath. "I'm not really any good at bargaining, Hasim. I have no experience of it. I know I have only one asset which I feel would be of any value to you."

"My dear Joanna," he protested, "you know how much I adore you. But . . . you are a widow of not yet a week."

"Then perhaps you would be prepared to wait a little while. I will not break any promises I may make to you, if you will not break any promises you may make to me."

His gaze drifted from her head down to her thighs, which were all of her he could see at the moment, and then back up again. "I would be prepared to wait a very long time for you." He gave a quick smile. "I already have done so."

"Then, do we have an understanding?"

"It will have to be a *little* while," Hasim reminded her. "I have my father and my uncles to persuade."

"I can be patient. If you can. But I will need some sort of time scale. For the bankers."

"I would say . . . four months. I will have to go to Qadir."

"Four months," Joanna said, half to herself. In four months time she would be showing.

"Will that be satisfactory?" Now he was anxious.

"Four months will be perfectly satisfactory," she said. "But . . . I also need ready cash. A good deal of ready cash. I must order the new ships right away. Will you back an increase in my overdraft? To be repaid out of the flotation?"

"Of course you may count on me."

"It's a large amount," she said. "I will need an additional four million." She held her breath.

Hasim waved his hand, and she realised she was moving into financial circles of which she had no experience.

"You mean, I can ask my bankers to call on you for an endorsement?" She had to get it absolutely straight.

"Of course. However," he said, "I would like it to be a confidential matter, between you, me and your bankers. At least for the time being"

"I will have to tell my board. And my stockbrokers."

"I understand that. I was thinking of the media." He stood up, came round his desk. Joanna stood also, and tensed herself. But to her surprise, he merely stroked her cheek and the line of her jaw with his forefinger, then stroked the bodice of her dress, knowing exactly where her nipples were, then kissed her gently on the lips. "Shall we lunch?" He had taken possession, in his own way.

Joanna only just made her next appointment; Hasim wanted to have champagne with his meal. "You understand," he said, "much as I would like to, I cannot marry you, Joanna. As the heir to the throne of Qadir, I must marry a Muslim. I don't suppose—"

"I'm afraid not," she said. "I take my religion very seriously."

How easy was it to lie convincingly, where someone was as sincere as Hasim ben Raisul abd Abdullah.

"But you will always be my first choice," he assured her.

"As you will be mine." In for a penny, in for a pound, she reflected.

*   *   *

"Mrs Edge. A terrible tragedy." Jonathan Prim's voice was just that, as well as a trifle cold.

"Thank you."

"Please sit down." Joanna did so, reflecting that neither the office nor the chairs were a patch on Hasim's. But then, Johnathan Prim was only a stockbroker. He was also an exact replica of his name, from long face and body to pince-nez. "Now," he said, placing his elbows on the desk and his fingertips together.

Joanna decided to take the initiative. "I assume Peter Young has been in touch with you?"

"Yes, he has. With some rather unusual, and, I may say, disturbing, intimations."

"You object to my taking over the company, Mr Prim?"

"My dear young lady, as you have a controlling share interest, you may do whatever you choose. But I am afraid you may find yourself a little short of support. I assume you have already spoken to the bank?" Of course he would know she had not.

"No, I haven't, Mr Prim. I have an appointment for tomorrow morning."

"I see. Well, then—"

"When I do see the bank people," Joanna said, "it will be necessary for me to have a firm assurance on the share issue."

"I'm afraid that will have to be left in abeyance for the time being, Mrs Edge. Until things have sorted themselves out."

"You mean, right now, no one will take it up. At least, in sufficient bulk to make it worth while."

"I'm afraid that is exactly the point, Mrs Edge. A flotation like this needs, as perhaps you are unaware, a substantial underwriting. A big insurance company, a big pension fund, these are the people we need to get in on the ground floor, to guarantee to us that they will take up a substantial proportion of the stock to be issued. City businessmen, well, they're a hard-headed lot, and while they may be personally sympathetic to you in your – ah – frightfully sad circumstances, they will still wish to see a viable return, at the end of the day."

"What exactly will they have against me, Mr Prim?"

"Well . . . apart from your age and inexperience, of course—"

"And my sex?" she asked, softly.

"Well, obviously it is unusual to have a woman, a very young woman, stepping straight into the chairman's shoes. But," he hurried on, "there is also the matter of the viability of your ships—"

"Which the share issue is intended to address."

"Oh, quite. But then there is the profit margin, steadily shrinking over the past three years—"

"But my husband, my late husband, was still intending to go ahead with the flotation, with your backing, I understand."

"Well . . ." Prim looked a trifle embarrassed. "Mr Edge had a way with him. He had planned a vast meeting of present and potential investors, at which he had intended to convince them that an upturn was just around the corner."

"Do you think he would have succeeded?"

"Yes, I do. Which is why my firm was prepared to issue the flotation."

"And you do not think I can do that?"

"Well . . . have you ever done anything like this before?"

"One must start somewhere," Joanna said, equably. "But Howard would have had to offer these potential investors some facts to support his case, would he not?"

"He would have pointed to an almost certain upturn in West Indian trade as the territories recover from the idea of federation."

"But he could not guarantee that would happen." Prim took off his pince-nez to stare at her. "My information is that it is not likely to," Joanna said. "At least in the short term."

"Did Mr Edge know this?"

"I think he must have done. But as you will know, Howie was always the supreme optimist. As you just said, he had a way with him."

"But . . . if the West Indian trade remains depressed, that would cause a very serious situation. For Caribee Shipping, certainly."

135

"I agree with you."

"Well, then . . . in the circumstances, Mrs Edge, I am going to have to advise my partners that in no way can we agree to handle a share issue in the name of Caribee Shipping."

"Not even if I told you that the Company is about to undertake a vast expansion, into new trade routes, with guaranteed profits?"

Prim allowed himself a self-satisfied smile. "Dreams are wonderful soporifics for tragedy, Mrs Edge."

"What I am going to tell you, and what you will soon hear from another source," Joanna said, "is entirely confidential. For the next four months. But you were not planning the issue for at least six, were you not? So that will not be a problem. What I wish you to do is prepare the issue and leave the rest to me."

"My dear young lady—"

Joanna refused to be annoyed by his constant use of the word young. "You have heard of the Emirate of Qadir?"

"Well, of course I have."

"It is one of the richest emirates in the Gulf, is it not?"

"Indeed it is."

"And I imagine you are aware that the Emirate's business affairs in the West are handled by Prince Hasim ben Raisul abd Abdullah, the heir?"

"Of course."

"Have you ever met Prince Hasim?"

"Yes, I have. May I ask—"

"I would like you to pick up your telephone, and dial Prince Hasim's personal number. I have it here." She opened her handbag and took out the card. "He will answer the phone himself. When he does, I would like you to ask him if it is being arranged for Caribee Shipping to take over the handling of the major part of Qadir's commodity trade. Providing, of course, that our new ships are on order. In this regard, Prince Hasim is prepared to underwrite a certain percentage of the share issue himself."

Prim continued to stare at her for several seconds, then he reached out his hand and picked up the phone.

The Rolls was waiting for her, and Joanna had Charlie drive her to the London flat. She didn't have keys, but he did. "You going to be all right here by yourself, Mrs Edge?" he asked.

"I'll be fine," Joanna said. "Just don't tell anyone where I am, Charlie."

"You can count on me, Mrs Edge. If there is anything I can do to help . . ."

A big handsome hulk of a man who was relishing his change of employer. And should he not, in view of what she was contemplating? What she had indeed set in motion? Save that she did not intend to go through with it, because of that saving grace in her womb. That would have to be confirmed right away.

"I know you will always be around, Charlie," she said, and closed and double-locked the door behind her, taking a deep breath. From the very start she had thought this flat the most elegant place she had ever seen. And now it was hers!

She kicked off her shoes, threw her mink across a chair, opened the fridge. Naturally there was a bottle of champagne in there. Several. Howie had always been prepared for a celebration. She opened a bottle, poured herself a glass, and sat down beside the phone. She was both curious and apprehensive. She wound the tape back to the beginning, let it play. Friends, condolences. Friends, condolences. Then . . . "I think you and I need to have a little chat, Joanna. Call me." Alicia. Of all the goddamed cheek.

"Joanna, oh my dear, dear Joanna. What can I do?" Andy Gosling! What could he do, indeed.

More condolences. She flicked the tape off, opened Howard's desk, hunted through his diaries and appointment books, found what she wanted, dialled. An Indian? Well, if he was good enough for Howie he had to be good enough for her. Save that the thought . . . but she was a big girl now, and growing bigger every moment.

Besides, now the idea had taken root, as it were, it was becoming more exciting by the second.

"Dr Alva's surgery."

"My name is Edge," Joanna said. "Joanna Edge."

"Oh, Mrs Edge," the receptionist gushed. "We are all so very sorry. What can we do to help?"

"I would like an appointment with Dr Alva, for tomorrow morning."

"Tomorrow morning? Oh . . ." There was the rustle of pages being turned. "Tomorrow is full. We could fit you in a week today . . ."

"Tomorrow," Joanna said.

"Ah . . ." There was an audible gulp on the end of the line. "Would you hold a moment?" Joanna waited. The girl came back on the line. "Dr Alva can fit you in, Mrs Edge. At eleven."

"Thank you," Joanna said. She drank some champagne. There was still so much to be done. Not least about Howie. She dialled Caribee Shipping. "Mr Young, please," she told the switchboard girl.

"I'm afraid Mr Young is in a meeting, If you will leave your name and telephone number—"

"This is Mrs Edge," Joanna said. "I wish to speak with Mr Young, now."

Once again the gulp was audible at the end of the line. "Of course, Mrs Edge, right away."

Am I being a bitch? Joanna wondered. But it was such fun. For so long she had been frightened of her shadow . . . now the shadows were all frightened of her.

"Mrs Edge! Where have you been? I have been trying to get hold of you all day."

She simply had to make him drop that didactic tone. "You mean Mr Prim hasn't called you?"

"No." Young's voice was flooded with curiosity.

"He's probably suffering from shock. If it is of interest to you, I had a meeting with him this afternoon, and Miller & Sparks will be handling our stock issue this coming summer. What I would like you to do, therefore—"

"Pardon me, Mrs Edge. Did you say they will be handling the share issue?"

"Is there something the matter with this line?"

"Do forgive me. But I spoke with them this morning, and they definitely declined."

"Amazing what a difference a few hours can make. Now, I've been rather busy today, but I would like to come in as soon as possible to have a look at the books, and other things. Can you tell me when the funeral is?"

"Ah . . ." She could almost hear his brain whirring. This woman doesn't even know when her husband is being buried? "Wednesday morning, at the village church."

"I see. Well, I have an appointment tomorrow morning, and another tomorrow afternoon. I assume you are going to the funeral?"

"Of course, Mrs Edge."

"Yes. Well, we can have a chat then. And I will be in the office on Thursday morning. But that is three days away, and there are things to be done. I wish you to put out tenders for the building of two new Caribee ships immediately. The designs can be roughly the same as the existing ships, improved where possible, but special attention must be paid to the refrigeration plants and the air conditioning."

Another telephonic gulp. "Are you sure this is wise, Mrs Edge? Whatever firm takes up the contract will require a down payment."

"How soon will the tenders be back? I wish you to emphasise that it is urgent."

"Well . . . within a few weeks, to be sure."

"Make it three weeks maximum, or there is no contract."

"Three weeks! Well, I suppose we could string along our decision for another month or two."

"We will make our decision in twenty-four hours, Peter."

"But . . . the deposit!" Now he was almost wailing.

"I will arrange it. Please get on with it, now."

Joanna hung up, drank some more champagne. There was still so much to be done. She telephoned a florist, ordered an outsize wreath. Presumably all she had to do was make her wishes known to Howie's secretary and all this would be taken care of for her, but she hadn't yet met Howie's secretary . . . and she was enjoying doing things for herself. Never had she been on such a high.

The doorbell rang, and she sat up straight. There were only about half a dozen people in the world who knew she might be in this flat at this moment, and she wasn't sure she wanted to see any of them. She took a deep breath, stood up, straightened her dress, adjusted her turban, which she had quite forgotten to take off, and opened the door.

"I've been looking everywhere for you," Matilda said.

"So, it seems, have a lot of people."

"I only just remembered where you probably were. Where you had to be, in fact, as you never went home. Or out to Caribee House."

"Well, come in." Joanna closed and locked the door again. "Champagne?"

Matilda gazed at the bottle in consternation. "Who's been here with you?"

"How many glasses do you count?"

"You've drunk nearly a whole bottle of champagne all on your own?!"

"I'm prepared to let you help me with the second one." Joanna took it from the fridge, and another flute from the cupboard, poured. "Or do you have to be sober?"

Matilda took the glass, sat down, and crossed her knees. "That's what I wanted to talk to you about."

"Tell me."

"Well . . . Jo . . . you can't really want me to go on parading around naked in front of a lot of old weirdos?"

"I thought you enjoyed it. Or at least, what came afterwards."

"I never did. I just wanted to make some money. Be independent. Didn't you always want that?"

"I suppose I did."

"Only you went about it the right way. Jo, let me quit."

Joanna raised her eyebrows. "Isn't that up to you?"

"I can't quit unless I have another job. Let me work for you."

"Can you type?"

"You know I can't type."

"Have you any experience of PR work?"

"Well, no."

"Then I don't see—"

"Jo, I'm your sister!"

"I know that, Tilly. But I have to be able to employ you as *something*."

"Well . . ." Matilda drank some champagne. "Let me be your bodyguard."

"My *what*?"

"Howie always had a couple of heavies knocking about. Where are they, by the way?"

Joanna shrugged. "Haven't a clue. I haven't seen them since I got back. And frankly, I've been too busy to look."

"But Howie felt he needed them."

"I think they just gave him a sense of power. Although, when you're a well-known and very wealthy man, I suppose there is always the risk of trouble."

"You are now a very wealthy woman," Matilda pointed out. "And I imagine you'll soon be fairly well-known, as well."

Joanna considered; she hadn't really thought about that aspect of things, as yet. "Mmm," she commented. "I suppose I'll have to keep them on."

"They went with Howie everywhere. Even to the loo, when he was out. You going to have them go to the loo with you? A bodyguard should always be there. You can't have men always there, unless you intend to sleep with them. And even if you did, as there's more than one, it would cause trouble. And think of the scandal. Whereas, I'll be with you, always, and no one will be able to say a word."

Joanna realised she was serious. She put down her glass, held Matilda's hands. "Tilly, you can't be a bodyguard."

"Why not?"

"Because you're a woman! What would you do if a heavy came in here now? Apart from screaming for help?"

"I'd lay him out."

Joanna stared at her with her mouth open.

"I'm a brown belt at karate," Matilda explained.

"You? You never told me. How did you do that?"

"I attend classes," Matilda explained. "Well, you see, a girl in my position needs to be able to take care of herself. You have no idea what weirdos sometimes ask me out."

"Have you ever had to use it?"

Matilda giggled. "Only once. Boy, it was fun. I'd go on and get my black belt if you'd pay for the lessons."

Joanna considered her for several seconds. But she had long been aware of the overwhelming loneliness of her position, a loneliness that could only get worse now she was the Chairman of Caribee Shipping. And Matilda was quite right in saying that a male confidante was only practical if he was also a bed partner, because that would be what he'd start thinking of very rapidly. Over the past couple of years she and Tilly had undoubtedly drifted apart, mainly because she didn't approve of Tilly's lifestyle. But they were still very close, as sisters should be. And if Tilly was prepared to give up her lifestyle and adopt *hers* . . . "There would have to be rules," she said.

"Tell me."

"No sleeping around."

Matilda pouted. "A girl needs her sex."

"Find yourself a steady. He doesn't have to be permanent. But while he's in situ, he's the one."

"Well . . ." Matilda frowned. "Is that what you're going to do?"

"I haven't decided yet. Whatever I do, it's not going to be for a while. I'm pregnant."

"You are what?"

"I'm having it checked out tomorrow. But I'm pretty sure."

"Holy Jesus! What are you going to do?"

"What do you mean?"

"You're not going to have the child?"

"Of course I am. I'm a married woman. It's Howie's child. The eventual heir to Caribee Shipping."

"You really think Caribee Shipping is going to be around in twenty years' time?"

"I have no doubt whatsoever of it. So here are rules numbers two and three. Whatever I tell you, whatever you hear within the company, is strictly confidential. That includes my baby, for the time being."

"But Mums—"

"I will tell Mums when I'm ready. If she finds out before then, you're fired." Matilda joined the gulping club. "Rule number three is total loyalty to me, and to the company, at all times. Got me?" Matilda nodded, brain obviously whirling as she wondered what she had got herself into. "And rule number four," Joanna went on, "is, when I am engaged in any business deals, you don't say a word. And I mean that."

She knew that would be the most difficult of the rules for Matilda to keep. "Is that all?" Matilda asked, somewhat sulkily.

"I'm sure there will be more, but those are all I can think of at the moment."

"What will you pay me? This club I'm at is paying me forty pounds a night."

"That is a hell of a lot of money," Joanna pointed out. "I will pay you thirty a week."

"Oh, come now, Jo! I'm your sister!"

"Which is why you're getting the job. And that is take home pay.

143

Your living, as you will be living with me, will be all found. I think that is a very good deal."

Matilda considered. "Well, I suppose it is," she said at last.

"Right. As of this moment, you're employed. How do you resign from your job?"

Matilda shrugged. "I suppose I just don't turn up."

"Right. You'd better prepare us something to eat."

"Oh. Right." Matilda got up. "What's our plan?"

"For tonight? Eat, and then get drunk, and then go to sleep," Joanna told her.

"Hm," said Dr Alva. "Hm."

Joanna rolled off the examination table and put on her knickers. "Don't worry about it. It's not diabetes. It's pure alcohol. My sister and I tied one on last night. I don't mean to make a practice of it."

Dr Alva sat behind his desk. He was older than she had expected, and wore horn-rimmed spectacles. But his smoothly brushed hair remained jet black, and he had lively eyes – as well as soft hands. "I will have to make a note of it."

"To show whom?" Joanna finished dressing.

"No one, Mrs Edge. But if I am going to be your doctor, I must have a totally accurate record of your health."

"Is anything the matter with it? My health?"

"At the moment, absolutely nothing. You are a very healthy young woman. However, if you consistently maintain a sugar level this high—"

"I've told you, it won't happen again. And if I were to come back and see you again tomorrow, it would all be gone, wouldn't it?"

"I would say so."

"Then there's nothing to worry about, right? Just tell me it hasn't hurt the baby?"

"I doubt very much that one such – ah – overindulgence would have any lasting effects."

"Thank you, doctor. Now tell me how old my baby is."

"Eh?"

"When would you say the baby was conceived?"

"Well, it is impossible to say, exactly. But from the size of the foetus . . . you say you have only missed two periods? And the next would be due next week. Yes. I would say your baby was conceived just under three months ago."

"Which would be early October last year."

"That would be about right."

"Will you make a note of that, please, on my records?"

He raised his eyebrows.

"I like to be exact about these things," she told him.

"What did he say?" Matilda had been forced to remain in the waiting room.

"That we should stick to one bottle a night, at least until the baby is born."

"But there is a baby?"

"I told you there was."

"Four million?" John Andrews scratched the back of his head, where the hair was thinning. "I think we need to consider this very carefully, Mrs Edge." He looked, somewhat apologetically, from Joanna to Matilda, seated in front of his desk. Apart from the introduction, he could tell at a glance that they were sisters, but it was always embarrassing to have to refuse a customer in front of other people, no matter how closely they might be related.

"There is nothing to consider, Mr Andrews," Joanna said. "I am in the process of ordering two new ships, and I will need to make a substantial down payment on them. There are also some other matters that need attending to."

"Don't you think that it would be a wise idea to hold off ordering the ships until after the share issue?" Andrews asked, looking as placatory as he could. "Then you – we – will know exactly how you stand. The fact is, you see, that with the overdraft currently standing at two million . . . you were aware of this?"

"I have been told," Joanna said. "I do not formally take control of the company until the day after tomorrow."

"Yes," Andrews said, getting a world of comment into the single word. "I am not sure that is altogether wise, either, Mrs Edge."

"Please don't start the inexperienced female business, Mr Andrews. I've had that. The present overdraft is secured by our existing ships, is it not?"

"That is so. But frankly, with two of them reaching the end of their useful life—"

"Which is why they have to be replaced."

"—and the last profit and loss statement so disappointing," he went on as if she hadn't interrupted, "we are not sure that our security is adequate. Certainly not for such a large increase in the loan."

"I am prepared to offer you my personal holding in the company. I think we are talking of four million pounds."

"Ah, no, not at this moment. These are early days, of course, but the shares have already been marked down by a considerable amount in view of your husband's death. What will happen over the next few weeks, when the rumour that you are taking over the company yourself becomes fact, well, I don't really know what to say. But I would certainly anticipate a sharp fall in the share price. A considerable fall."

"I see. Then I will have to offer you some other security, Mr Andrews, although I am bound to say that I consider your treatment of an old and valued customer to be disappointing, to say the least."

"Well—" Andrews' face reddened.

"However, I cannot let my personal feelings get in the way of my business," Joanna said, and opened her handbag. "You know Prince Hasim ben Raisul abd Abdullah?"

"Well, not personally."

"However, you may have some estimate of his personal wealth?"

"Well, yes, Mrs Edge. But—"

"He will endorse the loan for me. You may ascertain this by calling him on that number. He will receive your call, I promise you."

Andrews picked up the card and appeared to goggle at it. Matilda was goggling at them both. "The Prince will endorse a personal loan, from us to you, in the amount of four million pounds?" Andrews obviously felt a great need to get his facts straight.

"That is what I have said he will do, yes."

Again Andrews regarded the piece of cardboard rather as if it was a poisoned chalice. "Do you mind if I call him now?"

"I'd appreciate it."

Andrews picked up his private phone, dialled, waited. "Ah," he said. "I would like to speak with Prince Hasim, please. My name is Andrews, and I am calling on behalf of Mrs Joanna Edge." He listened. "I see." He looked at Joanna over the phone, cupping his hand around the mouthpiece. "The Prince is not in at this time." His tone was triumphant.

"Then find out when he will be in, and call him back," Joanna suggested.

He glared at her, but moved his hand. "May I ask when the Prince will be in? Not until tomorrow. Yes. Well then . . . excuse me?" Once again he listened. "Good heavens," he remarked, "will he really? That would be most awfully kind of him. Thank you." He replaced the phone, and gazed at Joanna with the air of a man who has just seen a miracle. "The Prince's secretary says he will call me. Prince Hasim, calling me! Tomorrow."

"Well, then," Joanna said, "I would be obliged if you would let me know the moment you have his consent to the loan. I shall be out in Berkshire tomorrow morning, attending my husband's funeral. But I shall be at Caribee Shipping on Thursday morning. Call me there."

Matilda managed to keep quiet until they reached the Rolls. Then she gasped, "This Prince—"

"You must remember Hasim? He was at that pool party we went to."

"I remember him very well," Matilda said. "He also comes to the club where I dance."

Joanna turned her head, sharply, as the car drove away. "You haven't let him have you?"

"Well . . ." Matilda looked sulky. "He's very rich. As you seem to have found out."

"As I seem to have what's left of every worthwhile man in London," Joanna snapped.

"And now you're letting him have you."

"I have promised to become his mistress," Joanna said, "in return for certain considerations, yes."

"You are a little . . . I can't think of the word."

"I am a woman who is making her way in the world. However, I do not become his mistress until after a decent period of mourning for Howard. Hasim knows and understands this."

"But—"

"Yes," Joanna said. "I think about four months is a decent mourning period. He has agreed to this."

"You'll be showing in four months."

"Absolutely."

"And you think he'll let you off the hook?"

"Of course. Hasim is both a gentleman and constrained by certain religous considerations. I will be unclean."

"And as such all bets will be off. Including his endorsements."

"Not in the least. My promise remains, to become his mistress as soon as possible."

"Which could be several months."

"At the very least. I intend to feed my baby."

Matilda shook her head in wonderment. "My baby sister. But I still think you're gambling for high stakes. He won't wait forever."

"He'll wait for a year or so. Who knows what may have happened by then? Anyway, what's the big deal? What's he like in bed?"

"Different," Matilda said.

They drove out to Berkshire that evening.

"Oh, Mrs Edge." Cummings, the butler, was there to great her. He and all the servants were wearing black armbands.

"I wish I could have been here sooner," Joanna said. "But there was so much to be done. My dear Mrs Partridge." She embraced the housekeeper. "It's so good to be home, even in these circumstances."

"It is good to have you back, Mrs Edge," Mrs Partridge said. "The – ah—" she looked at Cummings.

"The master arrived last night, madam," Cummings said.

"Where is he?"

Cummings led the way as if he himself were the undertaker. Joanna and Matilda followed, and then the servants. The casket was on the billiard table.

"I'm afraid that the undertaker advised us not to open the coffin, madam," Cummings said, as Joanna moved forward. "The journey, and, well—"

"Yes," Joanna said. "I understand."

"Would you care for a drink, madam?"

"A glass of brandy," Joanna said.

He nodded to one of the footmen, who hurried off, and then escorted Joanna to a chair in the winter lounge, Matilda as always following faithfully at her shoulder.

"I took the liberty of having the service orders printed up," he said. Joanna took the sheet of stiff paper and looked at it. "I hope you approve, madam."

"Oh, indeed I do."

The footman appeared with a tray. Joanna took her goblet and held it in both hands, Matilda anxiously following her example. "Would you care to see the dinner menu, madam?"

, "I'm sure it will be fine, Cummings," Joanna said. "How many are we expecting for lunch tomorrow?"

"I'm afraid I cannot say for sure, madam. I am allowing for twenty. But we will be able to squeeze in more if necessary."

"Of course. Thank you, Cummings."

He bowed and withdrew, to be replaced by Mrs Partridge. "Excuse me, madam, but will Miss Grain be staying the night?"

"Miss Grain will be living here from now on, Mrs Partridge. Put her in the room next to mine." Mrs Partridge withdrew.

"I don't have anything to wear tomorrow," Matilda said.

"The service is at eleven. There'll be time for you to run up to town and get something," Joanna said, and drank some brandy.

"You know, you are quite frightfully relaxed," Matilda said. "About everything. I'd be having the screaming heebeejeebies."

"About what?" Joanna asked, getting up and prowling about the room. "Oh, it's all taking a bit of getting used to. I suppose I'm not quite *compos mentis*, at the moment."

"You certainly appear *compos mentis*."

"I figured out what had to be done. That's easy, when you've nothing to lose. It's coming to terms with what you actually are, at the moment; that's difficult, when there's been so much . . ." She whirled to face her sister. "You have no idea what I'm talking about, do you?"

"Not really."

"Well . . ." Joanna finished her brandy, set down the glass, whirled again, pointed at the full-length mirror on the opposite wall. "Howard told me that was a family heirloom. It's worth a thousand pounds."

"I can believe that," Matilda said.

"And now, do you know, I could walk right up to that mirror with a hammer, and hit it as hard as I like."

"Jo," Matilda said uneasily.

Joanna grinned. "I'm not going to. But I could. And nobody could stop me, or criticise me afterwards, at least to my face. And if the insurance refused to pay, well, who cares? You with me? It's to be in such a position. For the first time in my life. But with the knowledge that if I play my cards right, I'll be in that position for the rest of my life."

"It's called megalomania," Matilda muttered.

Joanna sat beside her on the settee, hugged her and kissed her. "Megalomania is when that feeling is uncontrolled. I'm under control, believe me. Whatever I have, whatever I see, whatever I do, is for this little fellow." She rubbed her stomach.

"And the shareholders?"

"The shareholders, darling, don't matter a damn. I have control. Shit!" she remarked, as headlights glowed in the drive. "I really do not want callers tonight."

She got up again, walked towards the door, then changed her mind and sat down again, waiting for it to open. Which it did, a moment later. "Mrs Edge," Cummings said. "Ah . . . Mrs Edge."

Chapter Eight

The Chairman

Remembering the last time she had met Alicia, Matilda gave a squawk and rose from her seat as if stuck with a pin. Joanna as usual remained quite calm; if she had not expected a confrontation quite so soon, she had known it had to happen, and better now than at the funeral. She couldn't invite her rival in, because Alicia was already in, striding towards her, followed at a safe distance by a nanny and the two children. "How nice to see you," Joanna said. "You've met my sister." Alicia gave Matilda a contemptuous glance. "And are these the children? We haven't met." The nurse was looking embarrassed, so Joanna knelt before the little boy. "And who are you?"

"I'm Howie."

"He is Howard junior," Alicia said, getting as much emphasis as she could into her voice.

"Of course. And this is Victoria, I suppose."

It was Alicia's turn to say, "Of course." Then she added, "Where is my husband?"

"Howard is in the billiards room," Joanna said. Alicia stalked out of the lounge. "I'd keep the children here, if I were you," Joanna told the nanny, and followed Alicia. "We are advised not to open the coffin," she said. "I gather the embalming wasn't a complete success."

Alicia turned to glare at her. "Another of your fouls-up, I suppose."

"I had nothing to do with it," Joanna said.

"Are you going to pretend you're not responsible for his death?

152

Taking him into the wilds of that country where you were born, and
watching him drown?"

"I think, at some stage quite soon," Joanna said, "you will have
to apologise for that remark." Alicia flushed. "Now, tell me where
you are staying," Joanna invited.

"Why, here, of course. This is my home."

"I'm afraid you are wrong there," Joanna said. "This is *my* home.
However, you are welcome to stay tonight, if you have made no
other arrangements." She turned to the anxious Cummings. "Have
Mrs Partridge prepare a room for Mrs Edge, Cummings. And one
for the children and the nanny as well. I assume you'll join us for
dinner, Alicia?"

"God almighty," Matilda said, helping herself to brandy. "What *are*
you going to do?"

"About what? And go easy on that stuff."

Matilda, about to add a refill, put down her goblet instead. "She's
here to make trouble."

"Of course she is," Joanna agreed. "But she can make all the
trouble she wants. I'm driving." Alicia appeared in the doorway.

"Brandy?" Joanna asked.

"I'd prefer champagne."

"Then champagne it shall be, and we can all get drunk together.
Cummings!"

"At once, madam." He hurried off.

"I suppose you have twisted them all round your little finger,"
Alicia remarked, crossing the room to straighten a painting on the
far wall.

"I would like to think they are my friends," Joanna said, sitting down.

"Ha!" Alicia sat opposite her. "I really do not wish to have any
quarrel with you, Miss Grain."

"Ah, Cummings, thank you." Joanna accepted a glass of champagne. "I'm sure you have no quarrel with my sister, Alicia."

Alicia glared at her as she took a glass herself. "I was speaking to you."

"But my name is Edge. Mrs Howard Edge. No, that's not right, with Howard dead. Mrs Joanna Edge."

"You can call yourself whatever you like," Alicia remarked. "The fact is that Howard inherited all of this from his father, and he intended all of it to go to his son when he died. Howard Junior."

"But he left it all to me," Joanna pointed out.

"You expect me to believe that?"

"The will is being read tomorrow afternoon. I'm sure you'll be there."

"I shall contest it. How dare you, a so-called wife of less than a fortnight, claim the whole of his estate?"

"I am not *claiming* anything," Joanna said. "I am accepting what I have been given."

"To liquidate the company! To liquidate everything Howard spent his entire life working for."

"Quite the contrary. I intend to build this company into something Howard never even dreamed of."

Alicia snorted. "A twenty-year-old girl?"

"Ahem," Cummings said from the doorway. "Dinner is served."

It was a frosty meal.

People started turning up very early the next morning, by the busload. Joanna had not really expected so many, but it appeared that the crews of all of the ships that were in port were attending; Howard had been a much-loved employer. With them were their wives and children. Joanna, who had herself been up early, went into the pantry in search of Cummings. "We have to feed them," she said.

"What, all of them, madam? That's about two hundred people, all told."

"It'll be a buffet. Use everything you have in the freezers, and send into the village for whatever else you need."

"And drink, madam?"

"Beer or shandy. Lemonade for the kids."

"But . . . where, madam? We can't have it out of doors in winter."

"We'll have it in the house, Mr Cummings. There's space."

"But the mess—"

"Messes can be cleaned up." To his consternation, she gave him a kiss on the cheek. "Don't let me down. You'd be letting Mr Edge down as well."

In the front room she found Howard Junior. "Well, hi," she said. "I hope you and I are going to be friends."

"Oh, yes," he said. "You're very pretty." A chip off the old block, she thought.

Miriam and Ethel arrived, with William, and a host of Edge cousins, some of whom Joanna had met at the wedding. She was conscious that they also felt somewhat askance at this widow of less than a fortnight's marriage being in control of their dead relative's estate, but unlike Alicia they were prepared to accept the situation. Peter Young and Billy Montgomery were there, of course, as well as Captain Heggie and Prince Hasim, who kissed Joanna's hand with great reverence. "I trust everything is working out to your satisfaction?" he murmured.

"Absolutely. I have put you beside me at lunch. We have so much to talk about."

"I look forward to it."

Alicia was last downstairs, with her children, but she insisted not only on driving in the Rolls to the church but also on sitting in the front pew alongside Joanna. Joanna didn't object, she didn't want a scene.

"Detestable woman," Hasim said, as they lunched; he might be a Muslim but he apparently did not include champagne as a wine. "I wonder you put up with her."

"I don't have much choice at the moment," Joanna said. "But things will change."

"My dear girl," Aunt Ethel said, "widowhood becomes you. You look absolutely ravishing."

"It's the black outfit with her yellow hair," Miriam explained.

"I've been hearing all sorts of things," William confided, when at last he managed to get her alone in a corner of the drawing room.

"All true, I'm sure."

"Are you really going to be Chairman of the Board?"

"I hope I shall be Chairwoman, actually."

He blew her a raspberry. "Any hope for, well—"

"When you've got your degree."

"At what?"

"Doesn't matter. Just get a few letters after your name."

"Yeah, Well . . ." he flushed and his shoulders sagged. "The beaks are making pessimistic noises about me getting to university at all."

"You'll just have to work harder."

"But . . . suppose I don't make it?"

"Try. I'll give you a job, regardless, Willie. But if you don't have a degree you'll have to come in at the bottom. Licking stamps."

"You're not serious? I'm your brother."

"And as such, I'm sure you'll work your way up. Now I have to see a man."

Peter Young was making gesticulating signs, mainly with his eyes, on the other side of the room. He had in fact been doing so almost throughout the service. "Have you seen the papers?" he whispered, as she stood alongside him.

"No. I hope they have said some nice things about Howard."

"As a matter of fact, they did. It's the share price. Do you know what it was when you and Howard set off on your honeymoon?"

"Something over six."

"Six pounds, twelve shillings and eleven pence. This morning they're opening at three pounds ten shillings."

"That's a bit of a drop."

"My dear girl, it's freefall. I've had Andrews on the phone. I gather your new loan is endorsed."

"Absolutely. So he doesn't have to lose any sleep."

"The rest of us do."

She squeezed his hand. *"Courage, mon ami.* When the news of the new ships becomes known, and our new trading route—"

"Eh?"

"I'll tell you all about it when I come in tomorrow."

He scratched his head. "Anyway, you can't possibly go ahead with ordering two new ships now."

"What do you suggest I do? Declare bankruptcy? You simply have to find some guts from somewhere, Peter. Or I won't be able to employ you any more." His head jerked as he stared at her. She smiled at him. "But I know you'll bounce back. I'll see you later."

It was time to locate Hasim again. This was the most critical moment since Howard had died. She had never doubted that Hasim would support her, financially, in return for the promise of getting her to bed. Now that promise had to be, at least, postponed. But her instincts told her that to string him along any further would be to risk losing everything – as she was about to do, anyway. "I've been talking with Peter," she said.

He nodded. "It is all gloom and doom in the City."

"But you're still going to back me?"

"Of course. Although selling you, if I may put it that way, to my father and brothers may take a little longer than I had anticipated. But I will do so, never fear."

"I wish the world had more men like you in it. No, I don't, on reflection. They'd be harder to do business with." She took a deep breath. "I would like to see you, alone, for a few minutes before you go."

"Of course. I am yours to command."

"Use the side staircase in half an hour."

She realised that she was intensely nervous. If he decided that he couldn't wait for the four months she had stipulated, which had now become more than a year, there was absolutely nothing she could do about it, having regard to the financial situation. She had set so much store by the fact that he was the ultimate gentleman.

She toyed with the idea of arranging for Matilda to burst in on her after a few minutes, then decided against it. It was she who was betraying Hasim. There was a limit to how far she could go. He even knocked, which was reassuring. "I'm here," she said.

He closed the door behind him, and she realised he was as breathless as she. "Are you afraid?" he asked.

"Of the future? No. Not with your backing. Of you . . . perhaps I am. I do not know what to expect."

He came towards her. "I always keep my bargains. It is as much a religious as an ethical code. But . . . sometimes, when I make a bargain as immense as ours, I need reassurance that there is substance to it."

She held out her hand, and he took it. "There is something I must tell you. Something I found out only yesterday."

"Tell me."

Another deep breath. "I am pregnant. Howard's last gift to me, I suppose."

He did not speak.

"I want you to know that this makes no difference to my bond with you," she said. "If you still wish me, when the baby is born . . . and weaned . . . I shall be yours without reservation." Still no reply, while his face never changed expression. "I'm afraid I really cannot contemplate an abortion," she said. "It is against my principles, anyway. And the child is Howard's. I did love him. I could not destroy his child." What an accomplished liar she had become, so very quickly.

"Do you know that I have never kissed you?" he asked. She slid her hand up his sleeve and round his neck, brought him against her, kissed him on the mouth. He kissed well, deeply and thoughtfully and hotly. She wondered what she had expected? Matilda had said he made love differently to westerners – perhaps she had expected him to kiss differently, too.

Suddenly she felt as randy as he obviously was. But her heart had to be ruled by her head. He could not be either sated or disappointed until her finances were restored. His hand slipped down her shoulder to caress her buttocks, then slid round in front to hold her through her dress. That took her by surprise. "Uh-uh," she whispered.

He stepped back. "I do apologise. When you and I finally get together, it shall be a night you will never forget. Until then . . . I must leave. Will you be all right? It seems to me that quite a few of the people here are after your blood."

"With you in my corner, Hasim, do I have anything to fear?"

This time he kissed her hand. "Absolutely nothing. Remember, I am only a telephone call away from you, at all times." He closed the door on the way out, and Joanna sat down. She felt quite breathless. As for the future . . . but the future was now far away.

Cummings was waiting for her. "There is a telephone call for you, madam. A Mr Richard Orton."

Dick? Reappearing at this moment? Like Andy, no doubt, seeking to grab what he could while he could. "Tell Mr Orton I thank him for his call, Mr Cummings, but I do not wish to speak with him at this time."

Lunch for the two hundred mourners occupied most of the afternoon. It was four o'clock, and with quite a few people still present, before Joanna managed to get herself and Alicia and a few other relatives into the study with Mr Parkins, the solicitor, and close the door. "I'm sure this is something we all wish to get over as rapidly as possible," she said, and seated herself before Howard's desk, presently occupied by the lawyer.

He cleared his throat and opened his briefcase. "This is really very brief," he said, looking somewhat apprehensively over the faces in front of him. "There is a list of small personal bequests . . ." he went through these with some speed. "Those apart, Mr Edge leaves his whole estate, which consists in the main of his control of the shares in Caribee Shipping held in trust and a few other outside investments, as well as his Jaguar car, to his wife, Mrs Joanna Edge, with the proviso that she will continue to make the allowances towards his two children, as agreed at the time of the divorce. These payments will be from her personal income, that is, five hundred pounds a year each until they are aged ten, one thousand pounds a year each until they are aged eighteen, and fifteen hundred pounds a year thereafter – so long as they remain living with, and in the care of, their mother. These payments are to be continued whether or not Mrs Edge marries again, and has issue by that second marriage."

"Just suppose Mr Edge and I had had any children," Joanna said. "Would the will be affected by that?"

"Well, yes . . ." Parkins allowed himself a cautious smile. "Mr Edge was a careful man when it came to money matters, as I am sure you appreciate. Should you have borne him a child, that child would take precedence over those by his previous marriage, and the allowances due to them would be reduced accordingly, by one half. But of course, that is academic."

"Of course," Joanna said.

"That is quite outrageous," Alicia declared. "Do you mean he left nothing to me at all?"

"Ah . . ." Parkins looked embarrassed. But not that embarrassed. He had expected something like this. "You are divorced, Mrs Edge. That means that in the eyes of the law your marriage never was, except in so far as there were, and are, children. Mr Edge has made adequate provision for his children. However, as I am sure you both know . . ." he glanced from face to face. "Mr Edge held very little in his own name. This was of course to avoid death duties. All his shares are held in the trust company in Jersey, administrated by Mr

Montgomery . . ." he glanced at Billy. "Just as his house and his cars are owned by Caribee Shipping. Mrs Edge – Mrs Joanna Edge – has to pay taxes only on the money in Mr Edge's bank account. Thus the trust continues, under Mrs Joanna Edge's control. However, it is Mr Edge's intention, as stated in his will, that when his son comes of age, he shall be a full partner in both the trust and the business, sharing the responsibilities as well as the prerogatives with Mrs Joanna Edge."

"That is ridiculous," Alicia declared. "Howard is only ten years old."

"Then he will have to wait eleven years to become a full partner."

"I shall contest this will," Alicia announced.

"That is your right, madam. However, I must advise you that it will only cost you money. And should you contest the will, Mrs Edge, Mrs Joanna Edge, will be entitled to suspend all payments to the children until the case is settled, which may, of course, take some time."

Alicia opened her mouth and then shut it again. "What nonsense," Joanna said. "You go ahead and contest the will, Alicia. But I will commence my support for the children immediately. In fact, although Mr Parkins may feel the support is adequate, I shall double it, commencing with a thousand a year each now, to be increased when appropriate."

Once again Alicia looked like a fish out of water. "My dear Mrs Edge," Parkins protested. "This is most generous of you. But it is also quite unnecessary."

"I think it is necessary, Mr Parkins," Joanna asaid, allowing a touch of steel to enter her voice.

Alicia fled the room.

"Are you stark staring bonkers?" Matilda demanded, when they reached the privacy of Joanna's bedroom and she could strip off her sweaty clothes and stand in the shower. "There was no need to give away all that money. That bitch won't thank you for it."

"I'm sure she won't. But it'll undermine her case, if she ever brings one." Joanna stepped from the shower, towelled vigorously. "My God! My hair. Get me an appointment first thing tomorrow morning. I've called the board meeting for eleven, so I must be ready for that."

Matilda moved to the phone. "I still don't think—"

"Then don't, darling. Listen. I have given away nothing. By the terms of the will I can, if I choose, have the allowances for the children reduced should I ever have one of my own, by Howard. Now, everyone knows that is impossible . . . save for you and me and my gynaecologist." And Hasim, of course, she thought.

Matilda paused, phone in hand. "Are you really as ruthless as you sound?"

"I don't know. But I'm going to try," Joanna told her.

When she went downstairs the last of the guests had departed, save for Mums and Aunt Ethel and William; Alicia had apparently left with her children, without a word to a soul. Cummings and the staff were still clearing up, but he paused long enough to open a bottle of champagne and ensconce the family in the relative peace and quiet of the winter parlour. "What an experience," Aunt Ethel remarked. "What a lot of people. And that woman—"

"At least there wasn't a scene," William pointed out.

"What are you going to do now, dear?" Miriam asked.

"I am going to run my company," Joanna announced.

They all goggled at her, save for Matilda. "I meant, where are you going to live," Miriam said, keeping her feet firmly on the ground.

"Why, here, of course. It's my home." More goggling. "You are very welcome to come and live with me," Joanna said. "There's bags of room."

"Oh, yes, please," William said.

"Now don't be absurd, William," Aunt Ethel said, severely. "How can you possibly go to school in North London while living in Berkshire?" William looked at his sister for support.

"Of course he can," Joanna said. "I intend to run a business in Westminster from here. William and I will go in by car every morning, and I'll pick him up again in the evening."

"Wow!" William commented.

"What about you, Mums?"

"Well—" Miriam looked embarrassed.

"Oh, do move out too," Ethel said. "It'll be quite like old times, having my house to myself."

"I do think perhaps Joanna needs my support," Miriam ventured.

"I said, it's all right by me," Ethel repeatedly, huffily.

"I'll send the car to pick you up tomorrow," Joanna said. "I'll be out all day, but I'll arrange with Mrs Partridge to settle you in. Well . . ." she smiled brightly at them. "We'll all be together under one roof again. I'm so looking forward to that. And do please come to visit whenever you choose, Aunt Ethel." Aunt Ethel sniffed.

The door opened. "Excuse me, madam," Cummings said, "but there is a telephone call for you."

Joanna raised her eyebrows. "I think you can handle it, Cummings. It's probably someone else offering condolences."

"The gentleman said it was a business matter, and urgent, madam."

"Oh, well . . ." she followed him into the study, picked up the phone. "Yes?"

"Mrs Edge? Mrs Joanna Edge?"

"Yes."

"You don't know me, Mrs Edge, but would I be correct in assuming that you are the widow and sole beneficiary of the late Mr Howard Edge, Chairman and Managing Director of Caribee Shipping?"

"That is correct."

"And that you now own seventy per cent of the shares in the conmpany?"

"I would say that is my business," Joanna pointed out.

"That is," the man went on as if she hadn't spoken, "seven hundred thousand shares. These shares are presently valued at three pounds ten shillings each, but are expected to be marked down again when trading commences tomorrow."

"How very interesting," Joanna remarked.

"Mrs Edge, I have been authorised to offer you four pounds a share for the lot." He paused, waiting for Joanna's reply. But she did not reply; her brain was doing handsprings.

"That is, two million, eight hundred thousand pounds, cash on the barrel, Mrs Edge," the man said. "Think of it. No more trying to keep a sinking company afloat. Two million, eight hundred thousand pounds. Even if you did no more with the money than put it in a savings account at five per cent you would still have an income of one hundred and forty thousand pounds a year. I imagine you can live on that." Again he paused, and again there was no reply.

"Mrs Edge? I know this is a considerable decision for you to make. But the offer is there, and will remain on the table for the next twenty-four hours. All you have to do is ring this number . . ." he gave it to her, "and a meeting will be set up immediately between my principals and yourself." Another pause. "Are you there, Mrs Edge?"

"I'm here," Joanna said.

"Then we'll look forward to hearing from you."

The temptation was enormous. Nearly three million pounds, all for her. Not a worry in her life for the rest of that life. But . . . what about the rest of that life? An empty nothing. She would have failed Howard, and she would have failed the unborn son in her womb; she had no doubts at all that it was a son. Most of all, she would have failed herself.

"Mrs Edge?"

"I'm wondering why, if my company is on the verge of bankruptcy," she said, "you are prepared to pay nearly three million pounds for it."

164

"Well . . . my principal deals in collapsing companies, taking them over, building them up again—"

"So do I," Joanna said. "Tell your principal not to wait for my call, because his hair will go grey before he gets it."

"Now, look here, Mrs Edge—"

"And furthermore," Joanna went on. "Tell your principal I don't like undercover work. It's nearly always underhand. If he wants to make a hostile bid for Caribee Shipping, tell him to put it in writing and send it through the post. I will see that it is laid before my board. Good night to you." She hung up, and remained leaning on the desk for a moment, feeling quite weak. Had that really been Joanna Grain speaking? Then she went back to the lounge.

"Condolences?" William asked.

"In a manner of speaking," Joanna said, and drank some champagne.

She was on a high as she swept into the Caribee Building the next morning at half-past ten, Matilda at her shoulder. "Can I help you, madam?" inquired the receptionist.

"Yes, you can. Direct me to the boardroom, and tell Mr Young to meet me there," Joanna said.

"I'm afraid there is a board meeting this morning, madam. And Mr Young—"

"My name is Joanna Edge," Joanna said. "And yours is . . . ?"

The girl goggled at her. "H-Harriet Newsom," she whispered. "I do apologise, Mrs Edge, I had no idea—"

"You can take us up to the boardroom yourself," Joanna decided.

There was an elevator, but Joanna preferred to use the stairs. That way she passed through all the various departments. There was not a great deal going on; the staff were clearly anticipating redundancy notices as the firm went under or changed hands. The girl showed them into the boardroom, and hovered anxiously. "May I get you anything, Mrs Edge?" She looked at Matilda uncertainly. "A cup of coffee?"

"Thank you. By the way, this is Miss Grain, who is my personal assistant. You may consider anything she says as being said by me."

"Oh, yes, Mrs Edge. I'll get the coffee."

Peter bustled in, carrying a sheaf of papers and folders, and also accompanied by a young woman secretary. They introduced each other, while Peter chafed. "Have you seen the papers?"

"Now you know I do not read the papers, Peter." Joanna sat at the head of the table.

"Three even. They're expected to go down to two ten by tomorrow. Do you realise, Joanna, that the value of this company, and incidentally, your wealth, has been more than halved within a week? The City is saying that we are ready for a takeover."

"They are, are they? Well, some people have been jumping the gun." She told him of her phone call.

"And you refused it?" He was astounded. Matilda, hearing of it for the first time, looked on the verge of a collapse.

"Well, of course I refused it. We are not for sale, at any price. Now, I don't suppose you've heard from the shipyards yet?"

"No, no, there's no possibility of that for several weeks."

"I said one month, Peter."

"Yes, well . . . frankly, I should think they're waiting to see where the money is going to come from, before they bother to tender."

"Have the bank issue guarantees."

"Yes, well, the bank—"

"Peter, everything is under control. Ah, how about some introductions?"

The other shareholders were arriving. There were only three. And Alicia. "Quite a crisis, Mrs Edge," said John Donivan. "Have you seen the share price?"

"There'll be a suspension, I should think," said Clive Toogood.

"There will be a share recovery, you mean, when our plans are publicised, which they will be after this meeting. I intend to hold a press conference as soon as we are finished. Have you arranged that, Peter?"

"Yes, I have, Mrs Edge. Twelve o'clock."

"Well, then, we don't have too much time. Please be seated." She sat down herself. "Would you read the minutes of the last meeting, please, Marica?" she told Peter's secretary.

This was done. "I of course was not in attendance at that meeting," Joanna said. "But I hope you will agree it is a true record?"

They nodded their agreement, and she signed. "Thank you. Now, our business today is to outline and discuss our plans for the future."

"*Our* plans?" Alicia asked.

"You are a shareholder," Joanna said. "I would like from you all a unanimous vote of confidence in the company. Before," she said, as several people looked prepared to speak, "anyone says anything, let me tell you what we are about. Tenders have been put out for two new ships, which will update our fleet. Our two oldest ships, *Caribee Endeavour* and *Caribee Dream*, are up for sale. I'm afraid they are not likely to realise more than scrap value. This means that for the immediate future we will be down to our two existing ships, *Caribee Queen* and *Caribee Future*. However, I am hoping the new ships will be available within a year. This is stipulated in the tenders. These ships will have the latest in refrigeration equipment, and will be intended for operating in the tropical climates. However . . ." she smiled at them, "this does not necessarily mean the Caribbean." Now they were speechless, even Alicia.

"I am in the process of securing a new trade route for our vessels. This will be with the Emirate of Qadir, situated in the Persian Gulf. I will tell you frankly that this new deal has to be accepted by the Qadiri royal family, who own the emirate, but I have received assurances that it *will* be accepted, and that our ships will be welcome there just as soon as they are available. As you may know . . ." another smile, because they obviously did not know, "the Emir's family have a monopoly of all trade with Qadir. This is presently handled by the Ofgood Line. But the Emir, or at least his representatives, are dissatisfied with the service they are getting, and are prepared to give us sixty per cent of their handling. This will substantially improve our profit margins, as we do not intend to give up our Caribbean outlets. Now, are there any questions?"

There were several seconds of silence. Then Alicia asked, "And how are we going to pay for the new ships?"

"Our bankers are prepared to advance us, or I should say, me, the money."

"On what security?"

"The backing of the Emirate."

Another moment of scandalised silence. "Can you trust these people?" Donivan asked.

"Yes."

Alicia stroked her chin, thoughtfully; clearly she was remembering Prince Hasim's presence at the funeral. "Will this endorsement not involve the company in a very heavy loan structure?" someone asked.

"Only in the short term. Our new stock flotation will be launched this summer, and that will actually pay for the ships and liquidate our borrowings."

"It was my impression that the stock flotation would not now go ahead," Toogood remarked.

"Of course it will not go ahead," Alicia snapped.

"It is going ahead," Joanna said quietly. "I have spoken with the brokers, and they are happy. It will be launched this summer."

"Supposing you can find anyone to underwrite it," Alicia sneered.

"I already have. The Emir of Qadir."

"You seem to have this man eating out of your hand," Donivan suggested.

"His son, you mean," Alicia said. "I see it all now. You are, after all, nothing but a whore, Joanna."

"I have witnesses to what you have just said, Alicia," Joanna said.

"Would you care to retract and apologise?" Alicia flushed, while the men looked thoroughly embarrassed. Joanna glanced around their faces. "Prince Hasim is a friend, as he was a friend of my late husband. I assume you were aware of this, Alicia?"

"I did not care for Howard's friends," Alicia said. "I saw as little of them as possible."

"That was your decision. When I returned to England, I visited the Prince and put our situation squarely before him. As a result, he agreed to lend us his financial backing. There will be a profit in it for him and his family, and his state. It was a simple business transaction. Now . . ." once again she looked around their faces. The men were dumbfounded, Alicia was still licking her wounds. "I have outlined, down to the last detail, my plans for resuscitating this company and moving it ahead. I see a very bright future for us all. May I have a unanimous endorsement of these plans?" Everyone looked at Alicia. "Of course," Joanna said, "should any of you retain sufficient doubts about the future of the company as to wish to get out, I am perfectly prepared to buy his or her shares at the current market price."

"Ha!" Alicia commented. "I am not going to sell you my shares. I intend to be here, always, just to make sure you do not ruin the company. And when my son takes over—"

"There is one more thing I should tell you all," Joanna said, and took one of her deep breaths. "I am pregnant."

Part Three

The Phoenix

'Build me straight, O worthy Master!
Staunch and strong, a goodly vessel,
That shall laugh at all disaster,
And with wave and whirlwind wrestle!'
                    Henry Wadsworth Longfellow

Chapter Nine

The Proposal

This time the momentary silence was more scandalised than ever. Predictably, Alicia was the first to recover. "You expect us to believe that?"

"I believe we may share the same gynaecologist," Joanna said. "You have my permission to check with Dr Alva."

"And you're claiming the child is Howard's?"

"The child was conceived in the first half of October 1963," Joanna said, "at which time I was living, with Howard, at Caribee House. Incidentally, Howard is the only man with whom I have ever slept. I would think very carefully before you reply to that, Alicia. Or I will indeed see you in court." Alicia opened her mouth, then closed it again. Then she got up, gathered her papers, and left the room. The men looked more embarrassed than ever.

"Your unanimous acceptance of my plans, please," Joanna said. "I think I am right in saying that, as Mrs Alicia Edge declined to sell her shares, and indeed, made it plain that she plans to remain at the centre of the company's decision-making, she has already exercised her vote in favour."

"Will the announcement of your pregnancy be made at the press conference?" Davison asked.

"Of course," Joanna said.

"If I may say so, Joanna," Peter Young remarked, "you have the knack of living on the edge. Do you intend to continue that?"

"Only as long as it is necessary, Peter. Believe me, I long for a quiet life."

But she was as confident as ever at the press conference, smiled as she answered the most intimate of questions, both as to her financial arrangements and to the parentage of her child.

"As I understand it," said one young woman, "the fact that you are pregnant has no influence on the future of the ownership of the company, unless your child happens to be a boy?"

"That is the situation, yes," Joanna said.

"Would it then be fair to describe your late husband as a male chauvinist pig?"

Joanna continued to smile. "It is the privilege of certain members of the press to insult and diminish the dead, certain that they cannot be sued for libel."

The rest of the questions were more friendly.

"But," Peter said later, "you do realise that should the child be a girl—"

"That possibility is several months off, Peter. And meanwhile, we have a lot to do."

For the moment, everything was on the up. Her press conference, the bold announcement that the company was going ahead with considerable plans for the future, and that a new trade route would soon be announced, had an immediate steadying effect on the shares; her ability to announce that the route would be with the Emirate of Qadir, which she released the moment she received the cable from Hasim, had them moving upwards again. The tenders duly came in, and were given to the yard of Bramell & Hopkins, in the north-east. This brought favourable media reaction, as the north-east was so depressed, and even an invitation to lunch from the Under-Secretary for Trade and Industry. "The Government is very happy that you have decided to place these orders here in Britain," he told her. "I am sure there were some promising tenders from abroad."

"As a matter of fact there were," Joanna agreed.

"But you chose British. We are, as I say, very well pleased."

"Well," Joanna said. "If you felt up to making us a grant, we would be equally pleased."

He smiled. "I shall see what can be done."

The grant, for half the cost of the new ships, duly came though.

Then Prim was on the line. "Great news," he said. "Daley Direct are underwriting twenty per cent of the share issue." He paused, waiting for her reply. "You do know who Daley Direct are?"

"One of our biggest insurance companies," Joanna said.

"Absolutely. Now they have given the lead, others will follow. We may oversubscribe."

"I shall be delighted."

She had not told Prim about the surreptitious offer for her shares. Peter Young had promised to look into the matter, but as he said, there were dozens of potential culprits; nailing one down would be very difficult, especially as she had not heard from the mystery bidder again.

"And none of the other shareholders have been approached," she mused.

"Waste of time. Only your holding matters, because it controls the company."

"Well," she said, "keep looking. Or at least, keep your ears open."

It was three days later, that, as she was dropped before the Caribee Building, Joanna was knocked over. It all happened so fast she was taken entirely by surprise. Charlie the chauffeur had stopped, as he always did, immediately outside the great double doors to the building, and come round the car to open the door for her. As usual she was accompanied by Matilda, but again as usual, Joanna got out first.

As her feet touched the pavement there was a loud shout, and a figure cannoned into Charlie, sending him sprawling. Another body immediately cannoned into Joanna, sending her tumbling to the concrete in a scatter of arms and legs. Matilda, following her out, screamed, and immediately a crowd gathered, quickly dominated by a policeman. "What happened?" he asked.

Joanna lay half in the gutter, hands clasped to her stomach. Matilda knelt beside her. Charlie slowly clambered to his feet. "Two young tearaways, racing along the pavement, not caring who they upset—"

"I saw it all," an elderly lady said. "He's right. They were running along, laughing, pushing people aside—"

"Where'd they go?" the policeman asked.

"Round that corner."

He hesitated. "You all right, ma'am?"

Joanna was beginning to get her breath back. "My baby," she muttered.

"A doctor," Matilda said. "We must get her to a doctor. She's pregnant."

"I'll call an ambulance," the policeman volunteered.

"I'll take Mrs Edge," Charlie said, and swept Joanna into his arms to lay her on the back seat.

By now various people had emerged from the building, and Charlie hastily told them what had happened, so that they could report to Peter Young. Then he got behind the wheel. Matilda had already got into the back beside Joanna. "Are you in pain?"

"Yes," Joanna said. "My baby—"

"We'll be at the doctor in a few minutes," Matilda promised.

As they were. Dr Alva hastily had Joanna carried into a side room, as he already had a patient in his consulting room, but he gave Joanna priority treatment. She lay on the examination bed, gritting her teeth, less in pain than in fear. There was more than the life of her unborn child at stake; there was her entire future. "Hm," Dr Alva said. "Hm."

"For God's sake, doctor," Matilda snapped. "Say something coherent."

"It does not look as if any real damage has been done," Alva said. "No, no, I think, with rest, Mrs Edge will be perfectly all right."

"Oh, thank God," Joanna said.

"But . . . rest. You must go home and go to bed, and stay there for at least the next couple of days. I will come out to see you tomorrow."

Joanna looked at Matilda. "Tell Peter Young, I want to see him, today."

Charlie drove her home to an alarmed Mrs Partridge and Cummings. Mrs Partridge and the upstairs maid put her to bed, made sure she was comfortable, offered her aspirins and tranquillisers. "I don't want anything, until after Mr Young has been," she told them.

Peter arrived two hours later, sat beside her, looking grave. "Are you going to be all right?"

"I am going to be all right," she assured him. "And so is my baby. Although I'd like to see those two young thugs strung up and flogged."

"Yes, well, are you up to talking business?"

"Of course. What's the problem?"

"Well . . ." he cleared his throat. "There is a potentially serious matter which needs to be discussed."

Joanna moved, uncomfortably, in her bed. She was just starting to show. "Yes?"

"It has come to my knowledge that Alicia is having you investigated."

"You mean she's going ahead with contesting the will?"

"No. I think she understands, or has been made to understand by her solicitor, that she would be wasting her time there. No, no, she is having your private life investigated. Her hope is to prove that the child is not Howard's."

"Well, I don't see how she has a hope there," Joanna said. "As I said at the meeting, Howard is the only man I have ever slept with."

"Yes," Peter said, not altogether convincingly. "Sadly, in matters like this, it is often enough merely to muddy the waters, as it were, in order to bring a case. If, of course, we could carry out a blood test, well, the matter would be closed beyond all doubt."

"Are you suggesting we exhume Howard's body?" Joanna demanded, not sure whether she should be amused or angry.

"Well, of course I am not, Mrs Edge. Nor, at this distance of time, do I suppose it would be much good. The fact is . . ." He fiddled with his pen.

"Oh, come on, say it," Joanna invited.

"Well, there remains some doubt in people's minds as to just what – ah – inducement Prince Hasim received to persuade him to back Caribee Shipping so heavily."

"I see," Joanna said, grimly.

"There was also, I believe, a relationship with a young man named Richard Orton—"

"Tell me something," Joanna said, this time pleasantly, "have you been having me investigated too?"

"Of course not, Mrs Edge. What I have been doing is finding out what Mrs Edge – the other Mrs Edge – has turned up."

"I get the message. Well, there is a very simple method of proving that neither Dick Orton nor Prince Hasim can be the father of my child – that blood test you were talking about."

"As a last resort, I agree," Peter said. "The publicity would be unpleasant. Sadly, even if it were proved that neither Mr Orton nor Prince Hasim could be the father, well . . ." he glanced, surreptitiously, at Matilda.

"Jesus wept," Matilda commented, having got the message herself.

"Okay," Joanna said. "Let's have it all hang out, Peter. Alicia is working on the theory that because Matilda has slept around, I must have been doing it too. Right?"

Peter licked his lips nervously. "If it were just a matter of, as you put it, sleeping around, well . . . Mrs Edge has discovered that Miss Grain once worked in a nightclub which was closed down for being a brothel. And that you also frequented this place."

"That woman is clearly designed to be a garbage collector," Joanna snapped. "I went to Tony's once in my life, four years ago. Come to think of it, that was the night I met Howard. I suppose she also has found out that I was once arrested for being in possession of cannabis."

"I'm afraid she has."

"Which was the night I became Howard's mistress," Joanna pointed out.

"Ah, yes," Peter agreed. "She has also discovered that—" he flushed.

"That I was knickerless. But I was also a virgin. And I can prove that."

"Well—" Peter looked more embarrassed than ever.

"Because I lost my virginity that night, to Howard. Alicia can ask Mrs Partridge that – she had to launder the sheets. Anyway, I don't see what any of this can do to help her prove that my baby isn't Howard's. I didn't conceive for more than a year after moving into Caribee House."

"Absolutely," Peter said. "But what Mrs Edge is doing is accumulating a CV, if you like, to prove that you are the sort of woman who might well have had a lover even while living with Mr Edge and anticipating marriage to him."

"But she has to find the lover," Matilda remarked.

"Absolutely," Peter said again. "And if there wasn't one, well . . . you have nothing to worry about. But I thought you should be kept informed."

"I really am most terribly sorry," Matilda said, as they lunched.

"What for?"

"Well . . . if you didn't have a sister like me, your problems wouldn't exist."

"Don't be silly. That woman would have been a pain in the ass anyway. I am going to have to do something about her."

Matilda giggled. "Like hiring a hit man?"

179

Joanna frowned at her, and Matilda's eyebrows shot up. "You wouldn't!"

"Of course I wouldn't," Joanna said, wondering if she was telling the truth; at that moment she was so angry she would cheerfully look at Alicia down the barrel of a gun. "What gets me is her unmitigated gall. Stirring up all this dirt when she doesn't have a shred of evidence. I mean—" she paused with her wine glass on its way to her lips.

"What?" Matilda also stopped eating.

"Shit," Joanna muttered. "That day, my birthday, when I ran into Dick. I'd forgotten about it."

"So you ran into him," Matilda said. "I hope you're not telling me that something happened."

"Of course nothing happened," Joanna snapped. "Not what you're thinking of, anyway. And I was already two months pregnant, even if I didn't know it. But we were alone together. In the car."

"Oh, shit," Matilda said. "For how long?"

"Long enough to . . . well . . ."

"Have it off. But you didn't."

"No, we didn't. But you had put me in such a mood I wanted to. So we kissed and, well, played with each other. But I couldn't bring myself to go through with it. But that chauffeur . . . Wyndham . . ."

"Don't tell me he was there while this canoodling was going on?"

"No, I sent him for a walk. But the mere fact that I did that must have made him suspicious. So I got Howie to change hire firms. Maybe his nose was out of joint, the chauffeur's, I mean . . ." The more she thought about it, the more obvious it became. "Listen, I want you to handle this."

"Me?" Matilda squawked.

"Yes. You want to be my bodyguard. Then be my bodyguard. We have to spike that damned woman's guns. Find Dick, and get him to give a blood sample. That sample we'll store with Dr Alva. It may be possible for him to take blood from the foetus. In any event, the very minute my child is born, we'll know we have proof that Dick couldn't have been the father. But Dick must also be prepared to stand up in court and swear under oath that we did not have sex."

"Okay," Matilda said, slowly. "But if you are so innocent . . . why the agitation?"

"Just get on with it," Joanna told her.

Oh, what a fool she'd been, she thought, as the car stopped outside William's school. But how could one foretell the future? That day in the car she had no more foreseen her pregnancy than Howard's imminent death; she had, she recalled, even been doubting that they would ever get married! Of course, it would be obvious that Dick could not be the father of her child . . . unless it could be proved that they had also met in October. But it would still muddy the waters.

Had Alicia really tracked Dick down, through the chauffeur? Or had he gone to her? But he wouldn't have done that. He could know nothing of the in-fighting which was going on at Caribee Shipping. Or did he? He had no doubt been angry when she had refused to speak with him after the funeral. But what had he expected, that she would jump into bed with him with her husband hardly cold? Or was it much more serious than that, and he had felt that now she was a millionairess all of his troubles might be over?

As for Alicia . . . Joanna found herself frowning, as she remembered herself lying in the back of the Rolls on her way to the doctor, thinking that her entire future rested on the survival of the baby. Alicia knew that too.

My God, she thought. Two young tearaways, running along a crowded London street, pushing people left and right, but just happening to knock *her* down. If her baby had died, Alicia would have been guilty of murder. But her involvement could never be proved, as the police had never caught her two young agents. And she would have secured her own future. "Jesus!" she whispered.

"Hi!" William sat beside her, and the car moved off. She blinked at him, perhaps seeing him for the first time. She supposed that a baby brother is always a baby brother. That he may be growing all the time is hardly noticeable, day by day. But William was now just on six feet tall, with powerful shoulders and legs. He was frowning at her. "You look like a bear with a sore head."

"So life isn't all up."

"Care to tell me about it?"

She glanced at him. "How're things at school?"

"Well . . . not too good, I guess. Old Tommo says I don't have a hope of getting good enough grades for any university, much less Oxbridge. He's muttering about technical colleges and that sort of thing."

"I was really thinking of socially."

"Oh, you mean being picked up by the Rolls? And the beautiful sister." He glanced at her maternity dress. "Even if she is pregnant."

"You are going to get a thick ear in a minute."

"There were a few wiseguys at first, but I soon sorted them out."

Joanna was interested. "How?"

"I walloped them."

"Good lord. Didn't they object?"

"It's hard to object when you're lying on your back seeing stars with a guy's foot on your chest."

"Does Mums know about this?"

"I don't confide in Mums. Do you?"

"I suppose not. Do you *want* to go to a technical college?"

"Not really. I don't want to go to university either, even if I could. But I suppose I'll have to."

"I think one should avoid doing things one doesn't want to," Joanna said, a idea forming at the back of her mind. She needed all the help and support she could get, and where was she going to get it better and more loyally than from her own family? "You once had the idea of working for me."

"Licking stamps, you said, if I didn't have a degree."

"I've changed my mind. You would work for me, but not immediately. You'd have to attend another school, first, for six months."

"You mean some kind of crammer? No way."

"I was thinking of martial arts."

He frowned at her. "Martial arts? Holy hell."

"Don't you think you'd enjoy that?"

"Well . . . yes, sure I would. If I knew what came next."

"You'd come to work for me, as my personal bodyguard."

"Your . . . you need a personal bodyguard?"

"Yes," Joanna said.

William stared at her. "You're serious."

"Yes."

"Would I have to carry a gun?"

"You will not carry a gun. I just want you standing behind me, always."

His tongue came out and slowly licked his lips. "I'd get paid, for doing that?"

"Absolutely," Joanna said. "But, for the time being, this is our secret. Right? Let me down and you can forget it."

Another long stare. "I'm not sure I understand why a woman as tough as you needs a bodyguard at all," he said.

"Because I'm a woman, that's why."

Miriam didn't object to the idea. Miriam had long since given up objecting to anything. She had even gotten over the resentment at being about the last person in the world, it seemed, to know she was about to become a grandmother. She enjoyed gardening, and she had fifteen acres to play with. She spent her days wandering around the estate, usually with one of the gardeners at her shoulder, suggesting this, altering that, ordering this or that plant. Joanna gave her her head. She wanted her mother to be happy. Just as she wanted to be happy. That was difficult right now. She was waiting on so many things. But principally on her baby. By the end of May she was massive, and stopped going into work. Instead she had Peter Young come out to see her every day, with anything that needed signing, and with the latest update on how things were going.

Things were going very well. The new ships were well under

construction, the stock flotation, due in July, was already well subscribed, and the shares had recovered almost their original value. "They'll go higher," he opined.

"As I said they would," she reminded him. "Tell me about Alicia."

"All quiet there. I would say she's licking her wounds."

"Maybe," Joanna said.

She had never told Peter her suspicions regarding her accident, or the steps she had taken to make sure such a thing could never happen again; William was still at his martial arts training school, and she was paying his fees out of her own pocket, not from company funds. What was more disturbing was that Dick had apparently quit his job, and Matilda had been unable to find him. Alicia again? Or pure coincidence? In any event it was worrying.

She was overjoyed to receive a telephone call from Hasim, announcing that he was back in England. "I would like to see you," he said.

"Now? You would go right off me. I look like a house."

"A very lovely house," he assured her. "My house. May I come out?"

"Oh, please," she said.

It had of course been necessary to put William entirely in the picture. "You don't think he means to have it off with you?" he asked.

"No chance. I'm inviolate while I'm pregnant, and while I'm nursing. But he likes to look, and touch. After all, he does virtually own me."

"Ugh!"

"Your racism is showing," she pointed out. "Hasim is a very sweet and gentle man. And when he gets here, you just make yourself scarce."

"I thought I was to be at your side at all times?"

"Not in my bedroom."

She was pleasantly excited, as well as pleasantly reassured. For all the apparent equanimity with which he had taken the news of her pregnancy, she could not help but wonder if he might not have had second thoughts during his visit to his home, and no doubt his chats with his father. But he wanted her as much as ever. Which meant she did not have a care in the world. More than anyone else in the world that she had met, Hasim exuded a tremendous air of omnipotence, of certainty that no problem could arise that he could not handle with the greatest of ease. She needed some of that.

She had given instructions that he was to be shown right up, and a few minutes after his car, a Daimler, swept to a stop before the house he was tapping gently on the door. He wore a blazer and flawlessly pressed grey flannels, with a carnation in his buttonhole. She had forgotten how handsome he was. "Don't get up," he said as he closed the door behind himself. "I'm sure you must not exert yourself."

"I want to get up."

He leaned forward to kiss her. "You are looking very well."

"Considering?"

"No, no, I mean, seriously." He held her hands, sat beside her on the settee. "Now, is all going well?"

"On most fronts."

"You must explain that. Especially in the area where it is not going well. There is no trouble with the ships?"

"No, no. As soon as I'm in better shape, I shall go up to the yards and see how they are coming along."

"I will come with you. And the flotation?"

"Everyone thinks it is going to be a big success. I'm told you have a large part of the action."

"Oh, indeed. And yourself?"

"Well, I, or at any rate the trust company, gets two shares for every one we now hold, so I shall retain control."

"I never thought you would risk losing control, my dearest girl. And the baby?" He looked at her stomach.

She held his hand and placed it on the bulge. "I think he's happy you're here."

"No problems?"

"Well . . ." she told him about the accident. And about her feelings regarding it.

"Then the woman is dangerous," he said.

She rested her hand on his arm. "She's history, Hasim. The baby is fine, so Dr Alva says. And she hasn't tried anything else, since." She grinned. "I have surrounded myself with bodyguards."

"I have not seen any."

"That's because, like all the best bodyguards, they blend with the background. My brother William."

"That boy?"

"He's very capable in a punch-up."

"And he is good with a gun, also?"

"Now, Hasim, really. We do not do that sort of thing in England. It isn't legal."

"It may not be legal, but it is done in England."

"Well, I don't think I actually need that kind of bodyguarding."

"I disagree with you. I shall have to see what we can do."

"Hasim—"

"When you are my wife," he stated, "I must see that you are protected at all times."

Joanna's jaw dropped. "Was that a proposal of marriage?"

"Ah, yes. I am not experienced at these things."

"As Heir of Qadir, you merely tap someone on the shoulder and say, upstairs, tonight."

He kissed her. "Actually, I tap the father on the shoulder."

"You have never tapped me on the shoulder."

"I have wanted to, so very badly. But now—"

"You said you could never marry me, because I am not a Muslim. I am also not a virgin and I am soon to be a mother."

"Yes. We have discussed this, my father and I. The fact is, I *cannot*

186

marry you, as the next Emir of Qadir. As you have just pointed out, it would be against all of my family's principles, and it would offend our people."

"Well, then—"

"However, if I am *not* to be the next Emir of Qadir, I can do what I like."

She stared at him, and again had to bring her jaw up, sharply.

"I have given my position to my brother," he said.

"But why? Not simply to marry me?"

"Yes. Simply to marry you."

"But . . ." Her brain was in a spin. How to tell this large, basically gentle, devoted friend that theirs was simply a business arrangement, that she did not love him, that she had planned not even to honour their agreement, certain that after waiting for more than a year he would simply tire of her and go elsewhere?

"I fell in love with you the moment I saw you, at that pool party, in that bathing suit. You know . . ." he grinned. "One does not have the opportunity of inspecting a woman in Qadir, if she is to be your wife. A concubine, now, that is something different. But a wife must be taken on trust. Most marriages, anyway, are undertaken for political purposes, a repayment of favours from the bride's family, or an anticipation of favours. To look at a beautiful woman, virtually naked, is a compelling business."

"Yes," she said. "But . . . what about all those concubines?" She had to clutch at straws.

"I have pensioned them all off," Hasim declared. "I have given them permission either to retire into private life, or go to the harem of another man, or even to marry, if they wish and can find a husband."

"Oh, Hasim," she said.

"Nor is there anything for you to worry about on the financial front," he said. "I am going to continue as Qadir's representative here in England, with the same income I now possess, and the same powers I now possess. The trading consortium we have agreed will stand, as will Qadir's support for your company, for as long as you need it. Your future is assured."

As indeed it would be, she realised, as Hasim's wife. Hasim's wife! What a fantastic prospect. He was certainly much more wealthy than Howard had ever been, or than she could ever be, she knew. She would never forget the dismissive gesture with which he had greeted her request for a four million pound endorsement. What would she be? A princess, no doubt. The Princess Hasim ben Raisul abd Abdullah. *That* would make Alicia squirm. But she did not love him. She had always intended, once she got things under control, to marry for love. And then, the company! "The Company," she muttered.

"I have said, it will remain secured," Hasim said.

"I meant, my place in it."

"Oh, well . . ." he shrugged. "If it pleases you to continue as Managing Director, I have no objection. It will be something for you to do. Providing . . ." he grinned, "it does not in any way interfere with our love life, or our social life. Or your life as a mother."

"As a mother?" she said, seeking another straw.

"Well, I wish to have many strong, fine sons. I will tell you a little secret. I may never become Emir of Qadir. But one of my sons will. My brother Mutil is, what do you call him in England . . . ? He is actually my half-brother, of course; we have different mothers."

"You're not serious. You mean he doesn't have a harem?"

"Oh, he does, but it is all young boys. So, you see, we have much to work for."

"Much," Joanna agreed feebly. "Hasim, my dearest Hasim, you realise that you have taken me entirely by surprise? I mean, I had never supposed that marriage between us would be at all possible."

"I know. I have sprung it on you."

"Yes," she said severely. "You have. And in my condition. I really cannot think about anything save my baby, at this moment."

"Of course. I am the most inconsiderate and wretched of men. Can you ever forgive me?"

"Of course I will forgive you," she assured him. "If you will promise to keep your proposal of marriage a secret, and not to raise it again until after the birth of my baby."

"Of course I will do that," he agreed. "It would not be right, in any event, for a pregnant woman to announce her engagement to a man who is not the father of her child. But you will allow me to offer you protection?"

"Protection? Oh . . . well, if you must. But it must be unobtrusive."

"You will not even know he is there. All you have to do is taken Wazir on your staff. As an underbutler. He is a very good underbutler."

"As an underbutler," Joanna agreed.

Had she actually said yes? Hasim assumed so, certainly. My God, she thought, what have I done? The first thing she had to do was persuade Cummings and William to accept the situation with Wazir. Cummings was far the less perturbed. "Will this gentleman actually be searching our guests, madam?" he inquired.

"Ah, not at the moment, Cummings," Joanna said, brightly. "We're not having any guests, are we?" Cummings bowed.

William was far less happy. "He's wandering about the place with a bloody great magnum under his armpit," he complained. "A butler! What happens if he shoots someone with it?"

"I'm sure that won't happen," Joanna assured him.

"How does he come to have such a weapon anyway? Is it legal?"

"You'll have to ask Hasim. But I wouldn't, if I were you."

He frowned at her. "What's this character to you, anyway?"

"He's my . . . protector."

"You mean you're his mistress? How can you be, with a bulge like that?"

"Hasim is a man who looks to the future." But then, so did she need to look to the future. A future she refused to contemplate until after her delivery. Yet that was soon enough. She had determined to have the child at home, and when she was about due Dr Alva moved one of his nurses in to be with her, just in case. Hasim also wanted to be present, but she talked him out of it. "You'd shock the neighbours," she said, thinking of Mums and Aunt Ethel. "And you'd be awfully bored. These things take time."

As it happened, the birth took twenty-four hours, and Dr Alva had ample time to be there, and give her a few whiffs of gas, which made it all very easy at the end and compensated for the extreme discomfort earlier. Then he was standing by the bedside, together with Mums and Matilda, smiling at her. "Well done, Mrs Edge," he said. "It was very simple, eh?"

Half drugged as she was, Joanna was only slowly registering. "My baby," she said. The child was placed in her arms.

"Isn't she sweet?" Mums said. "She looks just like her mother."

Chapter Ten

The Mother

Joanna gazed at her mother in consternation, then looked down at the child. She couldn't think, for the moment.

"Do you know," Mums said, "you have never mentioned a name for her? Have you decided one?"

Joanna looked at Matilda, who alone could possibly understand how she felt; she was the only one present who knew the contents of Howard's will. "I think Jo is very tired," Matilda said. "And needs to rest. Don't you, doctor?"

"Of course," Alva agreed. "Nurse!" The nurse hurried forward to lift the babe from Joanna's arms.

"Do not worry," Alva said reassuringly. "She will be well looked after, and returned as soon as you are rested. Your milk will not be in before tomorrow, anyway."

"I'd like Matilda to stay," Joanna whispered.

Mums raised her eyebrows, and left the room. Alva and the nurse did likewise, and Matilda sat in the chair beside the bed. "She's a lovely child," she said. "We were all so worried, after the accident. But she seems absolutely healthy."

"She needn't have bothered," Joanna muttered. "Alicia."

"Now, Jo . . ." Matilda smoothed the sweat-wet hair from her forehead. "You are going to love that little girl?"

"Oh, of course I am," Joanna said, irritably. "It's just that it leaves me with so much to do."

Of which Hasim was only one aspect. But he joined her as soon as he was allowed, held the baby, and then wanted to play with her nipples. "When does the milk start coming out?"

"Tomorrow," she said. "At which time you will have to leave them alone."

"I shall watch," he promised her. "We have so much to talk about, to do."

He didn't know the contents of the will either. But then, if he did, he would merely say, give it all up and just be my wife. She wasn't in the mood to contemplate either of those options.

Peter Young came down the next day, armed as usual with a sheaf of papers and letters for her to sign. Joanna lay propped up in bed, the baby at her breast, and he sat with his gaze carefully turned half away. "I am going to call her Helen," Joanna told him.

"A nice name, Helen. Any family connotations?"

"No. The only name I had considered before the birth was Howard. But Helen . . . wasn't she the face that launched a thousand ships? This Helen will launch at least two."

"Absolutely. Ah . . ." At last he looked directly at her. "I know these are early days, but have you given any thought to, well—"

"The future? I have given a great deal of thought to the future, Peter. But whatever we do must be done very carefully. First thing must be a reconciliation with Alicia."

"Are you serious? When you feel she almost had you killed? Or at least, the baby."

"She happens to be young Howard's mother. I can't get at young Howard except through her."

He stroked his chin. "And you mean to 'get at', as you put it, young Howard."

"There is nothing sinister about that," she pointed out. "If he is going to share the company with me in ten years' time, don't you agree that it would make sense to ensure that we are on the same wavelength?"

"That might be difficult to achieve. Wouldn't you say he has a good number of reasons for disliking you?"

"All planted by his mother. We have ten years to change his attitude, Peter."

"We?" he asked uneasily.

"I." She smiled at him. "But I would like to feel that you are on my side, and that this conversation will remain confidential."

"Absolutely," he said fervently.

As she had hoped, and indeed expected, Joanna received her first prospective breakthrough the next day, when the mail arrived. In the midst of several congratulatory letters was one from Alicia. *So happy for your success. I am sure she will be a lovely child.*

Alicia, of course, must be laughing all the way to her hairdresser, Joanna thought. But it was she who was laying the trap. She telephoned. "Thank you so much for your note." Alicia did not immediately reply, clearly surprised by the approach. "I wondered if you'd care to come here for lunch, whenever is convenient?" Joanna said.

"Me?"

"We have so much to talk about. I suppose Howard is at school."

"Yes. Yes, he is."

"But if you came on a weekend," Joanna pointed out. "You could bring him too."

"Just what are you planning?" Matilda asked. William was equally interested.

"I'm not exactly sure," Joanna said. "But there is no legal way I can beat them, now."

"I'm not sure I like the sound of that," William commented.

"Listen," she told them. "You are my brother and sister. Your business is to support me in everything I do. Don't worry. You are employed by me, not the company. So you cannot lose. Even if I were to lose control of the company, you have nothing to worry about. Hasim will see to that."

"Are you really going to marry him?" Matilda asked.

"It looks like it."

"He'll shake you up a bit."

"Perhaps I could do with some of that."

What *was* she going to do? She really didn't have any idea, save that she had to suborn Howard away from his mother and over to her, some time in the next ten years. She didn't want to contemplate what might be involved – because she found the idea exciting. She was, after all, still only twenty, only ten years his senior. And she knew she was a beautiful woman.

But he was only ten years old. She had to begin by being a most generously friendly older sister. Not for the first time in her life, she wondered if she was really as ruthless as she pretended, even to herself.

Alicia, predictably, was suspicious. But she did bring Howard to lunch, as well as his sister. "You'll be living here again, one day," she told the children, holding their hands as she escorted them into the drawing-room. William made a noise which sounded like a suppressed raspberry.

"Of course they will," Joanna said. "Or Howard will, at any rate. I expect Victoria will have married and set up house by then."

Victoria looked at her mother. "I'm sure she'd rather live here," Alicia said. Joanna signalled Cummings to serve champagne. "Is this all you ever drink?" Alicia asked.

"I'm afraid it was a habit taught me by Howard," Joanna explained. "Willy, be a dear and take the children for a romp in the garden." William made a face, but obeyed, and Matilda also mumbled an excuse and left. Both were under orders.

"Shouldn't your brother be at school or university, or something?" Alicia inquired.

"William has left school, and we have decided against university," Joanna explained. "He works for me. Oh, don't worry, he isn't costing the firm a penny; I pay him out of my personal income."

"Pay him to do what?"

"Why, to be my bodyguard."

"Your bodyguard? You, need a bodyguard?"

"It seems I do. Didn't you hear about my accident, in the spring? I was knocked over by two louts. I could have been badly hurt. And Baby could have been killed in my womb. William is around to make sure nothing like that ever happens again. But actually, I have two bodyguards. Did you notice the large Arab-looking man when you came in?"

"I thought he was a gardener."

"He's my real bodyguard."

"Where on earth did you find him?"

"He's a present."

Alicia's eyebrows shot up.

"From my fiancé, Prince Hasim ben Raisul abd Abdullah."

Alicia's eyebrows seemed totally out of control. "You're going to marry an Arab? So soon after Howard's death?" It was difficult to determine which shocked her the more.

"An Arab prince," Joanna pointed out. "He's very keen. As for when, we certainly intend to wait the full year But as I'm sure you remember, it is the House of Qadir that is backing the firm's expansion. As a matter of fact, that is something I wanted to talk to you about. As soon as I am out and about, which will be in another week or so, I am going up to the shipyard to see how the new ships are coming on. I think it would be a good idea to have Howard come with me."

"What on earth for?"

"They are going to be his ships, in ten years' time."

"Well . . . it'll have to be a time when he's off school."

"I'm sure you can arrange it," Joanna said sweetly.

She reckoned she had won round one. But she had to make certain of it. Three weeks later Alicia telephoned to say that she had arranged for Howard to have a long weekend. "Shall we meet you up there?" she asked.

"Ah . . . why not?"

Joanna summoned William. "I am going up to Newcastle next weekend to look at our new ships. But you won't be coming with me," she said. "Hasim will be doing that, so I shall be perfectly safe. Besides, I have a job for you. I am going up on Friday evening, and I believe Alicia and Howard will be doing the same. On Friday morning, I wish Alicia to have an accident. Nothing serious. I don't want her to be badly hurt. Just sufficient to prevent her travelling."

William gulped. "You mean—"

"Yes," Joanna said. "I do mean."

"Shit!" he muttered. "I could go to jail."

"If you do, I will see that you are well taken care of. But I am sure you won't, if you handle it right. You have a week to find out all about her movements, where and when she does what and with whom. If necessary, you can bring the accident forward to Thursday. But of course, you must remember that the further it is brought forward, the more serious it will have to be. The essential is that she cannot travel on Friday night."

"Do you have any idea what you're risking?"

"I hope I'm risking nothing, because you are my brother and you will never allow me to be involved. If you've a conscience about it, just remember that she tried to have me killed, or at least your baby niece killed, a few months ago."

He swallowed. "I'll see what I can do."

"No, no," Joanna said. "You'll do it. Buy or hire whatever you need in outside help. I just don't want to know about it."

"You frighten me," Hasim said, when he came to dinner. "In more ways than one. It would have been better to let my people handle it."

"I don't agree. William has to earn his spurs some time. And I wouldn't want you to be involved."

"But if he is caught—"

"I shall utterly disown him, and his action. He knows this. That is why he will not be caught out."

He shook his head. "I don't like it." Then he grinned. "But like everything else, I suppose you know what you are doing. This visit to Newcastle, will we share a room?"

The moment of truth, at last. "I am still feeding Helen."

"But she is not coming with us, surely?"

"No, she isn't."

"Then you will not be feeding her on this trip. You will still be carrying milk. I think I like that."

"You are an utterly obscene man."

He kissed her. "When two people are in love, it is quite permissible for them to be obscene together. In fact, it is important that they are. It makes a bond."

Then it was a matter of waiting. William had taken himself off, and Joanna did not hear from him for the rest of the week. But on Thursday night the telephone rang. "Joanna!" Alicia announced.

"Why, hello, Alicia," Joanna said. "When are you leaving for Newcastle?"

"I'm not," Alicia said, crossly. "I've had this stupid accident."

"Accident?"

"Well, you know I go riding every morning?"

"I didn't know."

"Well, I do. I canter my horse through the open ground near where I live. And this morning some absolute lout barged into me."

"On another horse?"

"Well, of course on another horse," Alicia shouted. "Just came out of nowhere, from behind some trees, totally without warning. My little Carrie took fright and reared, and got knocked over herself. Well, I came off, but my foot got stuck in the stirrup, and I've sprained my ankle. My doctor says it's lucky it wasn't broken. In fact, it may be. He's taken X-rays and will let me know tomorrow. But it's gone up like a balloon. And boy, does it hurt. Anyway, I can't travel. So that's it."

"Oh, what a terrible shame," Joanna cried. "But . . . the fellow who did this to you . . . was it someone you knew?"

"Of course it wasn't someone I knew," Alicia snapped. "I told you, it was some lout."

"But . . . what happened to him? Have you had him arrested?"

"Oh, it wasn't anything malicious. He was most apologetic. Seems he was only just learning to ride and completely lost control of his horse. He called an ambulance for me and was as helpful as he could be. Which doesn't mean he isn't a lout. Why any stable let him out on his own defeats me. They're the ones who should be arrested."

"Absolutely," Joanna agreed. "Well, we'll have to sort something out."

"There is nothing to sort out," Alicia said. "There is no way I can travel up to Newcastle."

"But what about Howard?"

"He can't travel on his own."

"He can come with me."

"With you?"

"I'll pick him up and take him up, and show him the ships. I mean, after you've arranged time off school and all—"

"With you," Alicia muttered.

"Doesn't he want to look at the ships?"

"Oh, he does. Very much. But . . . well—"

"I'll look after him," Joanna said. "Promise."

"Wow," Howard said. "I thought we were going by train."

"It's always better to travel by Rolls," Joanna explained. "This is Prince Hasim ben Raisul abd Abdullah of Qadir."

Howard goggled at Hasim. "Are you really a prince?"

"That's what they say," Hasim agreed. "Come and sit here between us."

He had been given his instructions, and the visit to Newcastle continued as it had begun. They had left Alicia's house very early in the morning, Joanna having been allowed into see the invalid, who was looking very pale and wan and obviously in some pain. "It *is* broken," she announced "Can you imagine? I'm going to be here for *weeks*!"

"Perhaps the rest will do you good," Joanna suggested.

They fed Howard on ice cream and crisps all the way up to Newcastle, where they were naturally staying in the best hotel. "Didn't your father ever take you away on business trips?" Joanna asked.

Howard shook his head, staring at the white-gloved waiters and the acres of silver cutlery. "Mine didn't either," Hasim said.

They put Howard to bed at ten o'clock. "Tomorrow is going to be a busy day," Joanna said.

Then she found herself in a bedroom with Hasim. "He seems a nice boy," Hasim said. "Is he really going to be your partner from the moment he's twenty-one?"

"According to Howard's will."

"And you don't think the accident should have happened to him instead of his mother? I mean, permanently."

She gazed at him. "You're not serious, I hope."

Hasim shrugged. "Didn't I once ask you the same thing?"

"What happened to Alicia was no more than what she had happen to me," Joanna pointed out. "Now we're quits."

"But you intend to seduce that boy."

"Just what do you mean by that?"

Hasim shrugged. "I'm easy."

"You mean you wouldn't be jealous?"

He grinned. "Of a ten-year-old boy?"

"He'll grow."

"By the time he does, you'll be my wife. The penalty for adultery is very severe in Muslim countries."

She blew him a raspberry.

"Now," he said. "I would like to make love with you."

It was an ordeal Joanna had dreaded, but which she found the most stimulating experience of her life. Hasim made her strip naked, and then get down on her hands and knees on the carpet. "Don't move," he said.

She made herself keep still, her hair flopping past her face, while he began stroking her, beginning at her neck, coursing down her back, sliding over in front to caress her breasts, all with the most gentle touch. Then he moved down to her calves and ankles and feet, separating each toe to caress it in turn, before coming up to her thighs. By then she was nearly bursting with suppressed emotion, as his hands went between her legs. "Don't move," he said again, and began stroking again. Then he was inside her, but not violently or even over-passionately. Instead the entry was slow and steady and maddeningly titillating. When she fell on her face as he allowed his weight to come down on her, she remained moving and gasping for several seconds.

"Do all Muslim men make love like that?" she gasped.

"There are seventy-eight different positions," he pointed out. "I know them all."

After a night like that, she presumed she had to be pregnant again, but it was Howard she needed to concentrate on. The three of them went to the yard the next morning and were shown over the ships, still in the very early stages of construction. Afterwards they took Howard out to lunch, and then shopping, buying him everything and anything he fancied. Then it was back to the hotel and another bang up meal, and another bang up night with Hasim as well.

For all her initial reluctance, and indeed, a residue of distaste she could not shake off, Joanna had to count it about the most enjoyable weekend she had ever had. But she knew she still didn't love Hasim.

They were married in December. There were two ceremonies, one Christian and one Muslim. There were large crowds at each. Joanna was now on a high, for the stock flotation had been a great success, the new ships were all but finished, and she was the darling of the city. And she was only just twenty-one.

Hasim was as handsome and as dominant as ever. Several of his relatives, but not his father or mother, came over for the occasion. "They don't approve, do they?" Joanna asked.

"I suppose they do not. But they will not stand in my way, now that the constitutional matter has been sorted out."

Amongst those who did come was Hasim's younger brother, Mutil, who was now heir to the emirate. "Be sure that you will always be welcome in Qadir, sister," he told Joanna.

But she didn't think he meant it.

To Joanna's surprise, and relief, she had not yet become pregnant, despite Hasim's vigorous sexual methods. "How many children do you have?" she asked him, while they were honeymooning in the Seychelles.

"None that I know of. Does this concern you?"

"Of course not," she said.

In fact, it was another relief.

"But I shall have children with you," he promised.

And suddenly she *was* pregnant.

But by now she was able to take things in her stride. Hasim's child was much less important than Helen, at least before it arrived. And meanwhile she could continue to run the company as she chose. Peter Young remained a tower of strength, as did Billy Montgomery. She received no more mystery telephone calls, and she could watch her share price climb as the new route came into operation, and Caribee Line ships were to be seen from the Gulf to Panama, while profits grew. Nor was being Hasim's wife as time-consuming as she had feared. Now that he was permanently stationed in London – she gathered it had been intimated that, for all Mutil's invitation, it would be best for the erstwhile heir and his bride to stay out of Qadir – he had his work to attend to, as did she. They met at his London flat in the evenings, during the week, before attending various soirées or going to the opera or the ballet, and spent weekends at Caribee House.

When she began to show, all engagements were cancelled, and as with Helen, she operated entirely from Caribee House. She gave birth to a baby boy in December 1965, very close to her own birthday. His name was Raisul, after Hasim's father. "Because who knows what the future may hold," Hasim said.

That was not the first intimation Joanna had had that he did not entirely count himself, or his family, out of the running as future rulers of Qadir. She found this disturbing. Hasim could do what he liked, but she had no wish for either herself or her son to become embroiled in Middle East politics. However, it all seemed rather remote, looked at from the comforts of Caribee House. She continued to employ both William and Matilda, although they now had very little to do, as Hasim's people took over the job of bodyguarding, although the mere fact that she was now the Princess Hasim protected her. She was therefore hardly surprised when Matilda announced her engagement to Billy Montgomery. If you can't get the best, take the second best, Joanna supposed. But she showered her sister with congratulations, and gave Billy a pay rise.

Her main energy was concentrated on young Howard, as the swinging sixties rose to a crescendo. She saw as much of the boy as was possible, and he always seemed delighted to see her. This entailed seeing a good deal of Alicia as well, but Alicia seemed blissfully unaware, or uncaring, that Joanna might have any ulterior motive than mending fences with both her and her children. Victoria remained somewhat sullen and distant, but Howard continued to be utterly charmed by his stepmother, and often spent weekends at Caribee House when free from school. On these occasions Joanna largely handed him over to William, with strict instructions to entertain his stepbrother to the hilt. She kept a low but very obvious profile, taking Howard for walks, watching television with him in the evening, from time to time letting him sit in on meetings with Peter

Young, being always the gracious, friendly, forward-looking friend and future partner, more than stepmother.

While all the time Howard grew, from a gangling twelve-year-old to a sturdy, good-looking teenager. And she wrestled with her conscience and her ambitions. She was playing a very dangerous game, she knew. But having embarked on it, she was more and more tempted to carry it to its logical conclusion. Amoral and immoral? Certainly. But then so was the entire business world. And so was her marriage. About which she became increasingly concerned. It was not that Hasim proved anything other than a loving and caring husband and father, to both Helen and to his own son. Equally he always seemed to welcome Howard, and even Alicia. But there were things going on that she did not like. Occasionally Arab men would come to Hasim's London flat, and they and Hasim would confer long into the night, while she was politely requested to go to bed. "I would like to know what is going on?" she asked.

"Nothing that need concern you, my darling girl," he assured her. With which she had to be content.

She had other things on her mind, as Mums began to sicken. Joanna reckoned she really didn't have enough to do, as even superintending the garden couldn't occupy her mind. She spent a lot of time just staring into space. Joanna consulted with Matilda, who was in the throes of her first pregnancy. "Make her see a doctor," Matilda recommended. "I'll do it."

But Dr Alva could find nothing actually wrong. "She's mildly diabetic," he said. "But we can keep that under control. She'll probably work it out." Joanna wasn't very happy with that.

It was a fortnight later that she was in her study at Caribee House on a Sunday morning – a weekend when Hasim had decided to stay in London, no doubt for another of his clandestine conferences, she supposed – when Cummings knocked. "There is someone to see you, madam."

"Out here? On a Sunday? Is it someone I know?"

"I cannot say, madam. But he says he knows you."

"Well . . . I think I'd better come down."

She followed the butler down the stairs and into the hall, frowned at the tall man who stood there. He was not much older than herself, she supposed, but very broad-shouldered and heavily tanned . . . "My God!" she exclaimed. Dick Orton.

He flushed. "I hope you don't mind my calling, Mrs . . . ah?"

"Princess Hasim," she said. "Of course I don't mind you calling." She held his hands, drew him forward for a kiss on the cheek. "It is so good to see you. But come in. Cummings, a bottle of Bollinger."

Dick looked uneasy. "At eleven in the morning?"

"I always drink champagne at eleven in the morning," she explained, quoting Howard. "Come in." She led him into the small parlour. "My God, it must be six years."

"Five, actually." He sank on to the settee beside her.

"The car!" But anyone less like the gangling youth she had canoodled with in the back seat of the Rolls all those years ago could hardly be imagined. "And then you disappeared."

"I got fired, for not going to work that afternoon."

"Oh, good lord! But I told you, if anything like that happened, to come to me!"

"I couldn't do that, Your . . . do I call you, Your Highness?"

"You call me Joanna."

Cummings returned with the bottle and two glasses.

"Leave it," she told him, and lifted her own. "Old friends. I should apologise for refusing to talk with you after Howard's funeral. I was a bit cut up."

"Of course you were. It was boorish of me to intrude. I just wanted to say how sorry I was."

"Thank you." There was a brief silence. "Where did you go?" she asked at last. "When you lost your job?"

"I emigrated, worked at various jobs."

"It did you good. Physically, at least."

"Oh, it cleared a lot of cobwebs."

"And now you're back. What are you doing now?"

"Well, nothing, actually."

"Right. So you want a job. You have one. Do you know anything about shipping?"

"Some. But I don't want any charity."

"You're not getting charity. You're getting a job, which I shall expect you to do well."

"Then I shall do well," he said.

"There's just one thing. I do not employ anyone on drugs."

"Oh, that." He flushed as he grinned. "I've never touched them since that night. If you knew how badly I felt about involving you—"

"I wouldn't. But for my arrest that night I wouldn't be here."

"Owning all this."

"In a manner of speaking. You start on Monday."

"Doing what?"

"Just turn up at Caribee Shipping, and you'll be told." She smiled. "Probably licking stamps. But Dick . . ." she rested her hand on his arm. "You'll progress, if you want to. I promise you that."

"Yes, well . . ." he finished his champagne. "I can't tell you how grateful I am . . . do I still call you Joanna?"

"While you're here. In public you'll call me Princess Hasim."

"That sound terribly grand."

"It is terribly grand."

"Well . . ." he stood up, looking awkward.

"Oh, sit down," she said. "There's half a bottle left."

She didn't tell Hasim about Dick's visit, but she didn't consider it necessary to swear the servants to secrecy: they were her servants, not Hasim's. She did, however, allow herself to think about it. She was delighted to see Dick again, for all his misdemeanours in the past. He reminded her of her own past, before she had risen to heights she still found dizzying. She was surprised at how happy a time she found it, in retrospect – she hadn't been particularly happy at the time, she recalled. But to have nothing more serious to decide every day than whether or not to go dancing or to the pictures, and whether or not to allow her escort to get too familiar . . . yet she knew she wouldn't have changed anything.

That was not quite true. Like Miriam. Who did not improve. Dr Alva became grave. "It is a mental problem," he said. "But it is a serious mental problem. I have given her tranquillisers, and stimulants, and nothing works. She just doesn't want to live."

"Why? Why should she feel like that? She doesn't have a care in the world." Joanna was quite angry.

"We have to try a psychiatrist," Alva decided.

But that didn't help either. No matter how hard Mr Hardisty tried, Mirian just wouldn't speak to him.

So there came the morning that Mrs Partridge hurried into Joanna's bedroom, without knocking, for the first time ever, to say, "Princess! Princess! Mrs Grain is dead."

"Why?" Joanna asked the parson. "Tell me why? She didn't have a care in the world."

The Reverend Enderby pulled his ear. "I didn't know your mother very well, of course, Princess Hasim," he said – his way of saying that Miriam had never been a regular church-goer – "but I sometimes wondered if she ever really recovered from your father's tragic death."

"That was eight years ago," Joanna said coldly. Was it only eight years? What a long way she had travelled in that time. But Mother had travelled further.

Hasim came down from London for the funeral, but apart from him and his bodyguards there were not many mourners, just Aunt Ethel, Matilda and Billy, William and the children, and – "Who is that fellow?" Hasim asked, as they left the church.

Joanna turned her head, sharply. Dick was keeping as far back as possible.

206

"A member of my staff," she said. In the commotion of Mums' dying she had quite forgotten Dick.

She found an opportunity to be alone with him during the reception after the funeral. "It was good of you to come," she said. "How did you get off?"

"I asked for time off," he explained. "I told them I was an old friend of your family."

"As you are," she agreed. "But you never met Mother, did you?"

"No. I had hoped to."

He was back to skating on thin ice. "So tell me," she said. "What are you doing?"

He grinned. "Licking stamps. Sort of."

"I'm sorry I've neglected you. Things have been a little fraught."

"Of course. In any event, you're the boss and I'm the office boy."

She felt like slapping his face, but then, she felt like slapping a lot of faces. She just could not believe that Mums had gone and died, without rhyme or reason, was almost inclined to demand a post mortem. Matilda forbade that. "Leave the poor old soul be," she insisted.

No doubt Matilda felt as guilty as she, Joanna realised. They had both followed their own agendas, leaving Mums to trail in their wakes. And now . . .

Two days later she got home from the office – as it was midweek she was staying at Hasim's flat in town – to find the flat unguarded. She unlocked the door, and found Hasim standing at the window, looking down on London with a pensive expression. "What's happened?" she asked.

"My father is dead."

"Oh, my God!" She put her arms round his waist to hug him. "I am so terribly sorry."

"He was pretty old," Hasim said. "Older than your mother."

"Will you have to go to the funeral?"

207

"It has been intimated to me that I should not. I have sent Wazir as my representative."

"I wondered what had happened to him. Oh, my darling." She released him and went to the bar. "Would you like a drink?"

"Yes. A whisky."

She raised her eyebrows. Hasim was not in the least a practicing Muslim, but he very seldom drank spirits. She poured two, gave him one, sat on the settee. "Will this, well . . ."

"Make any difference?" He turned, sat beside her. "Not in the least. All my arrangements, financial and shall we say, political, were made, with Papa's full agreement, to continue after his death."

"But Mutil is now Emir?"

"Yes," he said thoughtfully.

"Hasim . . ." she put down her glass to hold his hand. "You're not going to get mixed up in Qadiri politics, are you?"

"Why should I?" he asked. "I have no interest in Qadir any more. Except in so far as it pays me well." He put his arm round her shoulder to give her a squeeze. "And you, to be sure." Then he grinned. "They say these things always go in threes. I wonder who will be the third?"

Joanna supposed the best bet would be Aunt Ethel, who was several years older than Mums. But Aunt Ethel was in the best of health. Meanwhile she spent an anxious month wondering if Hasim was right that nothing would change, half expecting every morning to find an official letter on her desk informing her that Caribee Shipping's trading concession with the Emirate of Qadir had been terminated. But there never was one.

She found time, and some relief, from the anxieties of the situation by wandering through the vast building, finally discovering Dick on the ground floor, filling out invoices. "Is this what you do?" she asked, while the other clerks waited in hushed and reverential silence.

"I've been promoted, Princess Hasim," Dick said.

208

"How splendid. I have something for you." She placed the envelope on his desk, and returned upstairs to her office. It was an invitation to her twenty-sixth birthday party.

"I want it to be just a small, family affair," she told Hasim. "We are both still in mourning."

"Of course. I entirely agree."

"But you won't mind if I invite that new boy from the office? My old school chum?"

"Invite who you like," Hasim said.

She invited Aunt Ethel, who refused. Matilda and Billy Montgomery came, as did William with a young woman Joanna had not seen before, or even heard of. But she was delighted that William had accumulated a girlfriend. Her name was Norma. Alicia, Howard and Victoria came. And of course Dick.

It was rather a solemn occasion, but the ice slowly began to crack as the second round of champagne was served by Waqar, Wazir's stand-in as butler, even if Joanna did not suppose he would be much good as a bodyguard, for he was small and thin. "Well," she said. "It is so good, having you all here, and being just us. If you follow me."

"You are all the family I have now," Hasim declared. He was still somewhat gloomy.

"But not all you are going to have, eh?" Alicia asked. The two small children were out at Caribee House.

"Well . . ." Hasim actually smiled. "I hope not."

Joanna signalled Waqar to open another bottle. "Now," she said, seating herself beside Norma. "Tell me all about yourself."

"Oh. I . . ." She was tongue-tied with embarrassment. She was a small, dark girl, who looked nervous all the time.

"Norma works in a travel agency," William explained.

"How interesting," Joanna said.

"And she is twenty-two years old," William went on, grinning. "Unmarried, and drives a Mini. Her parents live in Cornwall. My sister," he explained to the still more embarrassed girl, "likes to have everything cut and dried. She'll grow on you."

"Well—" Joanna said, when the flat door opened, surprisingly, as it was locked. But it was Wazir standing there; he had a key. He also had a sub-machine-gun, as did the two men standing behind him.

Chapter Eleven

The Assassin

Joanna stood up, but in common with everyone else in the room, she goggled at the three men. Hasim and Dick were the first to react. Hasim spoke in Arabic, and Wazir turned his sub-machine-gun towards his employer and squeezed the trigger. In the same instant Dick threw himself across the room, catching Joanna round the thighs in a rugby tackle and hurling her right over the settee to the floor beyond with a crash that knocked all the breath from her body. Where her legs went she had no idea, but she suspected one of them caught Norma across the face and tumbled her too to the floor.

Meanwhile the guns continued to chatter, now overlaid by the shrieks of the people being hit as the bullets sprayed the room, while crockery and paintings dissolved, and wood from the walls, torn upholstery, and cascading blood filled the air. The whole thing lasted, Joanna realised in retrospect, a matter of seconds. It seemed an eternity at the time. She kept trying to rise and being held down by Dick's body; he had thrown himself on top of her. The sudden silence as the shooting stopped took them both by surprise, and after a moment he rolled off her and lay on his back, staring at the ceiling. "Are you all right?" Joanna gasped, aware of a weight across her legs.

"Yes," he said.

Joanna sat up, looked at Norma, who was the weight. But Norma was also rolling off her, equally protected by the settee from the flying bullets. "My God!" she whispered. "My God!"

Joanna turned on to her knees. She wasn't prepared to risk standing up, not only because Wazir might still be there, but because she didn't really want to look at the rest of the room, discover who had been hit. But as she knelt, she found herself looking at a stream of blood drifting round the end of the settee. She crawled forward, stared at her husband. She would not have known him save for his suit. The bullets had smashed into his face as well as his chest, shattering them both. She retched, and sank on to her haunches, unaware that the top of her head was now actually above the settee.

Now there was movement, all around her, dominated by a sudden high-pitched scream. Alicia!

Joanna scrambled to her feet, and looked over the settee at the doorway. But the doorway was empty. The three men might never have been, save for what they had accomplished.

William! William had been standing in front of her, joking about Norma. Now he lay on his face, the back of his jacket a mess of blood.

Matilda! Matilda lay against the far wall, screaming, being comforted by Billy; neither of them seemed to have been hit.

Alicia! Alicia sat by the settee, Howard cradled in her arms, while Victoria huddled against her for protection. They were surrounded by blood.

Waqar! Joanna looked at the bar and saw him just emerging from behind it, trembling.

"My God!" Norma kept saying. She had also reached her feet.

"Look after her!" Joanna snapped at Dick, and ran round the settee. "Waqar! Call the police!"

If they were not already on their way; the residents of the other flats had heard the shooting, and there was a great deal of noise and screaming coming from down the stairs and the lift shaft. Joanna knelt beside William, touched his head, realised he was breathing. "And an ambulance," she shouted. "Dial 999." Waqar was already at the phone.

"My son!" Alicia was wailing. "My Howie! Oh, my Howie." Joanna glanced at her, realised that Howard was dead. She couldn't take in what had happened, only that William might also be dying.

"We must stop the bleeding." Dick knelt beside her, ripping William's jacket open to find the wounds. Norma's knees gave way and she sank back to the floor.

"My Howie!" Alicia was screaming. "They've killed my Howie! You killed him, you bitch!"

Joanna merely looked at her. Dick seemed to know what he was doing with William. She turned on her knees, her stockings and dress now stained with blood, and gazed at Hasim. Billy held her shoulders and raised her up. "You should lie down."

"I'm all right," she muttered. "I'm all right."

Waqar stood at her other side with a glass of brandy, and she gulped it. "Will William live?"

"If we get him to a hospital," Dick said.

Sirens wailed, feet pounded on the stairs as the lift whirred. The flat was taken over. White-coated men clustered round William and administered various shots and medication before lifting him on to the stretcher. Hasim was left where he was while blue-coated men photographed and took measurements. Howard was gently extracted from Alicia's arms, and laid on the carpet, while more white-coated men gave her shots as well to calm her down. Victoria appeared to be struck dumb by what had happened.

"You all right, ma'am?" a police officer asked Matilda. Matilda just stared at him.

"She'll be all right," Billy said.

"You being?"

"I'm her husband. William Montgomery."

"Ah!" The inspector realised he had made a mistake and turned to Joanna, who remained kneeling beside Hasim. "Mrs . . . Princess Hasim?"

"Will my brother be all right?" Joanna asked, not looking at him.

"We're doing all we can," said one of the medics who had remained behind. "I think the princess is in a state of shock, Inspector."

"No," Joanna said. "No. It was a political assassination." The inspector pulled his ear. "I know one of the killers," Joanna said. "His name is Wazir, and he was my husband's bodyguard."

"Was? You mean he was sacked?"

"He returned to Qadir to attend the late Emir's funeral. They must have got at him, there."

"Who are 'they', Princess?"

"My husband's brother. His half-brother, anyway. Prince Mutil. I suppose you'd have to call him Emir Mutil, now. He was my husband's younger brother. When he married me, Prince Hasim renounced the throne in Mutil's favour."

"Then why should this Mutil have your husband murdered?"

"Because he feared Hasim might after all claim the throne."

The Inspector was clearly realising this business was a little out of his class. "You don't think this Wazir chap might have just have been disgruntled because he had been fired? Some of these Arabs are pretty hot-tempered. With respect, ma'am," as he recalled that her Arab husband's dead body was lying beside her.

"Inspector," Joanna said. "I told you. Wazir was not fired; he was sent back to Qadir to represent my husband at his father's funeral. And he was not alone; there were two other men with him. And of all the people in this room, only the three men who might have been involved in Hasim's claim on the throne were shot."

The Inspector scratched his head. "This lad," he looked at Howard's body, "was connected with your family?"

"Indirectly. He was my step-son."

"So he had nothing to do with the Qadir side of it."

"No, Inspector. But Wazir and his people did not know that. Their orders were to eliminate any possible claimant to the throne. They must have thought Howard was Hasim's son." But Wazir would have known who Howard was. "My God!" She ran to the phone.

"Who are you calling, ma'am?"

Joanna was punching the numbers. "My home in Berkshire. My son is there. Prince Hasim's son. They'll want him as well."

"We'll take care of it, ma'am." He attempted to take the phone

214

from her fingers, and she jerked away. "Cummings! Listen! I want you to lock all the exterior doors, and windows, bar them, draw the curtains, and let no one into the house. No one, do you understand, until I get to you."

"Madam?" Cummings was clearly mystified.

"Just do it. I'll be there as soon as I can."

"You need to rest, ma'am," the police inspector said, at last managing to relieve her of the phone. He dialled himself, and began giving orders, obviously to the local police, to have Caribee House surrounded. "Yes," he said. "I think some of your people should be armed. I will have permission sent down to you, but do it anyway, now."

He replaced the phone. Joanna had sunk on to the settee. "Do you have any idea who would have given these orders, madam?"

"Prince Mutil, I would say."

"That's a pretty tall accusation, Princess. Like the doctor says, I think maybe you want to lie down for a while. We'll talk again later. Howick, get these bodies out of here."

"Listen," Joanna said. "Catch those men!"

"Oh, we'll do that, Princess," he said confidently. "Now, some of my men will remain here, eh? Just to keep an eye on things. They won't interfere, and they'll make as little noise as possible."

"Thank you," Joanna said. "I must get down to the house."

"The house is under police protection, Princess. No one is going to trouble your son. And you are in a state of shock. Please be sensible about this."

Dick and Billy helped Joanna and Matilda into the master bedroom. Alicia and Victoria had been put to bed in one of the other bedrooms, both having been given tranquillisers. "Norma," Joanna muttered. "What happened to Norma?"

"She went off to the hospital with William," Billy said.

Joanna sat on the side of the bed, her head in her hands, but she looked up as there was a tap on the door. It was Dr Grahame, the police doctor, looking apologetic. "I do feel that you should have some medication, Princess."

"How can I have medication?" Joanna said. "There's so much to be done. I must get home . . . My God! The children."

"You have other children?"

"My daughter and my son."

"Did you tell the police about them?"

"No. Yes. There was so much going on—"

"I'll make sure they have it under control," Dick volunteered, understanding that he was surplus to requirements at the moment. He hurried from the room.

"Believe me, Princess, you'll feel a whole lot better, more able to cope, if you can have a sound sleep," Grahame said.

Joanna sighed. "Oh, very well. You joining me, Tilly?"

"Oh, yes," Matilda said. "My God—"

"Don't start up again," Billy said. "Listen, I'll be in the lounge if you need me. Either of you."

"Should we undress first?" Joanna asked.

Grahame shook his head. "It'll take about ten minutes to work. So you can undress after the shot, go to bed, and have a solid night's sleep."

He injected them each in turn. "I'll stop in tomorrow. Or would you rather have your own doctor?"

"I think Dr Alva should come," Joanna said. She gave him Alva's card.

"I'll see to it." He closed the door behind him.

Matilda was already in the bathroom. Joanna joined her, and they stared at each other in the mirrors as they cleaned their teeth. Matilda's hands were trembling, and her toothbrush kept hitting her teeth. "Weren't you scared at all?" she said. "Don't you ever get scared?"

"I was terrified," Joanna confessed. But her hands weren't shaking.

"I never believed things like that really happened," Matilda said, throwing herself on the bed.

"Only to other people." Joanna lay down beside her. "But I suppose, when I married Hasim, I became one of those other people."

"But you never loved Hasim, did you?"

Joanna sighed. "No. It was always a business transaction. But you don't live with someone for several years without becoming at least fond of him. I'm going to get that bastard, Wazir, if it's the last thing I do."

Matilda giggled. "Some of his Arab blood must have rubbed off on you. And you still have little Raisul."

"Yes," Joanna muttered. Thank God the children had not come up for her party. She fell asleep.

Joanna awoke to a hum of sound, emanating from the lounge. She sat up, for a few moments unable to remember what had happened, looked left and right, expecting to see Hasim lying beside her, and then remembering that it should be Matilda. But Matilda wasn't there, either.

She rolled out of bed, went to the bathroom to splash the sleep from her eyes, looked out of the window. It was daylight. She must have slept for something like twelve hours. While . . . she pulled on a dressing gown and opened the bedroom door, gazed at a scene of ordered chaos, as cleaners removed the bloodstains, helped by Billy and Dick, both unshaven and jacketless, ties pulled down, looking exhausted. Matilda was with them, supervising, while two armed policemen stood about, looking helpless. "You look a whole lot better," Dick said.

Joanna ran back into the bedroom to use the phone there. Now at last her hands were trembling as she punched the numbers. "Cummings! Are you all right?"

"Madam? What has happened?"

"Listen! I'll be with you as quickly as I can. Until I arrive, keep all exterior doors and all the downstairs windows barred. Allow no one near the house."

"Even the police, madam? They are already in the house. But they won't tell us what is happening."

"Oh, thank God!" she shouted. "Well, they should be able to handle it. I'm on my way."

Matilda stood in the doorway. "They were on the spot half an hour after Hasim's death."

"Nobody told me."

"Well, you were asleep. But the children are safe. Believe me. Now, there's someone from the Foreign Office wanting to see you—"

"I'm going out to the house. If anyone wants to see me, they can come there."

She ran into the bathroom, showered, found Matilda still waiting for her. "Won't you have breakfast?"

"I'll have it at the house."

"You want me to come with you?"

"No, stay here. Go to William. Make sure he's all right. I'll be back as soon as I can."

"What about Alicia?"

"What about Alicia?"

"Well . . . she's still here." She gestured towards the other bedrooms.

"Oh, good lord."

"She's had to be sedated again," Matilda explained.

"What about Victoria?"

"She's in there with her. When she wakes up—"

"Give her breakfast. And if necessary, have her tranquillised again."

There was a knock on the door. "Dr Alva is here."

"Oh . . . let him come in." It seemed a waste of time dressing, as he would only want her to undress again.

He peered at her, lifted her eyelids, tested her pulse. "You're all right, Princess."

Am I still a princess? Joanna wondered. She didn't want to be.

"It's Mrs Edge you want to look at," she said. "She's in a hysterical state. Her son was killed."

"Oh dear, oh dear," Alva said. "Do you know that I delivered that boy?"

"See what you can do for her."

Matilda ushered him out, and Joanna dressed. Back to black. She knew that some time soon what had happened was going to get up and hit her straight in the face. But until that happened, she had to hurry, not keep still for a moment, and remarkably, as the medic had promised last night, her brain felt absolutely clear. She just wanted to be with her children, then she wanted to be with William, then . . . she went into the lounge. "Would you like me to come with you?" Dick asked.

She hesitated. "If you promise not to say anything."

He raised his eyebrows, but picked up his jacket.

"About this fellow from the Foreign Office—" Billy ventured.

"I told you, he can come down to Caribee House. Or wait for me to come back up. I'll be doing that this evening. Tilly, I want you to call me the moment you find out about William." Then she was in the back seat of the Rolls, Charlie driving, Dick beside her.

As promised, he didn't say anything, while she tried to get her thinking under control. The firm, the route to Qadir, the presumption that Wazir was still out there . . . had he tried to get at the children, on discovering that they weren't in the London flat? And been beaten to it by the police? But then he would try again. She buried her face in her hands. She had told Matilda that when she had married Hasim she had become one of the Other People. The people to whom things happened, terrible things. Which went on and on and on.

Dick rested his hand on her shoulder. "They'll catch those fellows." She gave him a wan smile.

"Were you very happy?" he asked. "I suppose that's not very tasteful."

"You're entitled to know. No, I wasn't *very* happy. It was a business deal. My body for Hasim's support and protection. Well, I had his support."

"Will this affect the firm?"

"I don't know. I don't know anything, right this minute. You said you wouldn't speak."

"I'm sorry. But you were looking so done up—"

She smiled, and squeezed his hand. "Don't worry about *your* job, anyway. I need friends. Are you my friend, Dick?"

"Always and forever." She lay back with a sigh. She could stand a little more of that sort of loyalty.

Caribee House was like an armed camp, in the midst of which Cummings and Mrs Partridge and the other servants were distraught. Raisul and Helen thought it was all great fun.

"I'm Inspector Garside," the tall thin man told her. "Local police. I was called last night and told to place my men and wait."

"Because those murderers are still at large," Jonna said. "You've heard nothing?"

"Only a confirmation of my original order."

"And no one has tried to get in here?"

"No, ma'am."

She held the children's hands and took them into the winter parlour. Dick was standing around awkwardly, so she beckoned him in as well. "You could do with a bath and a shave," she suggested.

"Where do I go?"

"The house is full of bathrooms," she said. "Just ask Mrs Partridge for one. She'll supply you with a razor and a toothbrush as well."

"What's happening, Mother?" Helen was five.

Raisul was only three. But there was no way either of them could be told the truth, right that moment. "There are some bad men in the neighbourhood," she said, sitting one on each knee, "so

220

the police are going to stay with us until the men have been caught."

"Will they have guns?"

"Baddies always have guns. But so do the police. And the police always win. You've seen it on the telly."

"Why are you wearing black?"

The child was far too intelligent. "Don't you like me in black? It goes with my hair."

"I want to go outside to play," Helen said. "And the policemen won't let me."

"Play, play, play," Raisul chanted.

"You'll be able to go outside soon," Joanna said, and rang for Nanny.

Cummings produced a cup of coffee, and Dick joined her, looking much cleaner even if his clothes might have been slept in. "What do we do now?" he asked. "I suppose I should be getting in to the office."

"My God," she said. "The office. I wonder—" The phone rang. "That'll be Tilly," Joanna cried, as Cummings brought it to her.

But it was Peter Young. "Princess! I've just heard. I can't tell you how upset I am."

"Thank you, Peter."

"Is it . . . will it . . . well . . . ?"

"Business as usual, Peter. Until we hear otherwise."

"Ah . . . right. Will you be coming in?"

"Not today. Tomorrow. Is there anything urgent?"

"Nothing that compares with what has happened."

"Then hold the fort until I see you."

"Right. But by the way, do you know what has happened to young Orton? He's quite disappeared. He didn't come in this morning, and when we rang his digs he hadn't been in all night."

"He's with me," Joanna said. "He was present at the shooting, and he's pretty shaken up. He'll be in tomorrow."

221

"Oh. Right." Peter Young was clearly a puzzled man.

"I'm quite all right, really," Dick said. "I can go home, and change, and get down to the office."

"I want you here," Joanna said.

"I'm not much company."

"I don't want that sort of company. I just want you here. Right?" The phone was ringing again.

"Tilly!" Joanna shouted. "Is he—"

"They've got the bullets out."

"Bullets!"

"There were three. Only one was in a dangerous place. They're using catch phrases: serious but stable. I think he's going to be all right."

"I'll be up to see him in the morning. I just don't feel I can leave the children right now, and I don't want to bring them up to London; they'd be asking where Hasim was."

"Of course. I'll hold the fort. There's just one thing."

"Tell me."

"Alicia."

"Don't tell me she's still at the flat?"

"No. She's gone off. But she's been on television, blaming you for Howard's death. That's slanderous, you know."

"Well, I suppose in a way I am responsible," Joanna said. "For being Hasim's wife."

"You don't understand," Matilda said. "She's suggesting that it was all a plot to stop Howard from taking over, as she puts it, Caribee Shipping."

"You're not serious?"

"She is. I think you have to do something about her."

If you knew how many times I have thought that, Joanna thought.

"I'll have a talk with John Giffard," she said. "Listen, don't worry about it. Tell you what, though, arrange an appointment for me with John for tomorrow morning."

"Will do," Matilda agreed.

"And give William my best love."

Joanna hung up, gazed at Dick.

"You live a fantastically exciting life," he said. And he had only been able to hear her answers.

"Sometimes it gets a bit much," she said. "I want to be with the children. Come with me."

It was about the most domestic day she had spent in a long while. Dick was actually very good with children, and he even managed to make them forget the presence of the policemen. While Joanna could sit in a chair and think. There was so much to be thought about.

Howard! Poor, poor Howard. *Was* she responsible for his death? Legally such a suggestion was absurd. Hysterically it might well attract a few sympathisers. Had she meant to seduce him? She had never been sure about that. She liked to regard herself as an utterly ruthless, determined woman, who would sleep with the devil if it would continue her control of the company, but she knew in her heart that was just dreaming.

Although she had regarded Hasim as the devil when they had first got together. Then he had turned out to be a very ordinary and loving man. Save that he could not forget he had once been the heir to Qadir. That was what had killed him. When she thought of Mutil, smiling, inviting her to visit him in his capital . . . My God, she thought, suppose I had gone?

That didn't alter her ambivalent attitude towards Howard, who was now lying on a slab in a mortuary. Just like his dad, six years ago.

Only Howard senior had never actually lain on a slab. Good God, she thought to herself, you are going round the bend.

"Lunch is served, madam," Cummings said.

The meal over, Nanny took the children away. "I am going upstairs to lie down," Joanna said to Dick.

"Right. Shall I—"

"You will come with me." She went upstairs, closed the door behind them both.

"The servants—" he protested.

"Are my most faithful adherents."

"Your husband—"

"Is barely cold. I do not wish to have sex with you, Dick. I may wish to do so, some time in the future. Some time quite soon. Right now I want to lie down and rest. And I need a man lying beside me. Does that concept hurt your feelings?"

"No," he said. "No. I—"

She unzipped her dress. "Please don't try to explain. You always talked too much. Just be there. Okay?" He gulped, watched her finish undressing. Naked, she crawled beneath the sheets. "Do you think I am a domineering bitch?"

"I think you are the most remarkable woman I ever met. Perhaps who ever lived." He was undressing now, as rapidly as he could.

"Do you know," she said, "this is the first time I have ever seen you naked?"

"Ah—" he checked.

"Oh, I like it," she said. "Very Grecian. But then, this is the first time you have ever seen me naked, isn't it?"

"Yes" he said, and raised the sheet to slide in beside her. "Not at all Grecian."

"Eh?"

"No Greek, including the Venus de Milo, ever looked like you."

"I think she was an Italian copy. No," she said, as his hand slid across to touch her thigh. "Not now. I am mourning my husband, and I don't know how I feel, about anything."

"But you want me to be here?"

"That's right."

The phone was ringing, constantly. Joanna stretched out her hand and picked it up.

"Joanna?"

"Peter?" she asked drowsily.

"I'm afraid things are on the move."

She blinked herself awake. "I take it that means down."

"I'm afraid so. Only a few points, and the market is about to close for the day. But I don't know about tomorrow. Especially . . ." he hesitated.

"Tell me."

"There is a communication from Qadir."

"Terminating?"

"With notice. Oh, very proper and businesslike. No reference to the Prince's death. But none the less—"

"When is it dated?"

"Oh, eight days ago."

"And Hasim was murdered yesterday. There's an admission of guilt."

"They'll claim the two events are unrelated."

"We'll see about that. All right, Peter. As you say, there is nothing more we can do today. I'll be in tomorrow." She hung up, stared at the ceiling.

"Bad news?" Dick asked.

"It wasn't unexpected. Do you know I have no idea where Hasim's body is? Or what funeral arrangements have been made?" She sat up, telephoned Hasim's office.

"Princess," said his male secretary. "We have been looking for you everywhere."

Which obviously wasn't true, as the man had to know exactly where she had to be, if she was no longer at the flat.

"The Prince's body is in a police morgue. They say there has to be an autopsy. But it will be released for cremation tomorrow. I have arranged it."

"And when will the cremation take place?"

"Tomorrow afternoon, after a service at the Qadir mosque."

"Do the police know this?"

"I do not consider that necessary, Highness."

"Well, I do, Nasir. The assassins have not yet been caught. They may well attend the funeral."

"I see. Will Prince Raisul be attending?"

"No, he will not," Joanna told him. "But I shall be."

"Of course, Highness."

She hung up, remained sitting on the edge of the bed. As usual, there was so much to be thought of. The news that the Qadir route was ended would have to be released tomorrow. That would cause another fall in the share price. She could only be grateful that for the moment the company was out of debt and totally viable. But it wouldn't stay viable long trading only with the West Indies. And she had no more strings to her bow. Save . . . she gave a little sigh, and lay down, on her back. Dick was propped on his elbow, watching her.

"Anything I can do?" he asked.

She gazed at him. "Yes," she said. "Cover me. Don't try to get between my legs. Just cover me."

He obeyed with alacrity, looked down into her eyes from a distance of a few inches. "May I kiss you?"

"I would like that."

It was a long kiss. "Do you know how much I love you?" he asked.

"Me? Or Joanna, Princess Hasim?"

"I was thinking of Joanna Grain."

"I know. That's why I want you around. I get so insecure."

"You, Joanna?"

"Me," she said. "Forget the façade. For Christ's sake, I've watched two husbands die, violently. Makes you think."

"So what happens now?"

"Now?" She inflated her lungs, driving her breasts upwards into his chest. "When I get some confidence back, I have a company to save."

Chapter Twelve

The Survivor

Joanna eventually sent Dick home to have a good night's sleep and get to the office the next morning; if she had him around too long they would have sex together, and that was unthinkable while Hasim was still lying on a slab. The trouble was, she was too confused about her emotions, her outrage at what had happened being overlaid by her continuing fear for Raisul, and even Helen, who was always at the side of her baby brother, and by her continuing apprehensions for William. She telephoned the hospital after Dick had left, and was told that her brother was stable but still unconscious following the extensive surgery. How she wanted to be at his side. But she dared not leave the children.

Inspector Garside did his best to be reassuring. "There is no way anyone can get into this house," he said.

"A determined man will always get in somewhere," Joanna insisted.

A car rolled down the drive. Joanna watched it from one of the upstairs windows, but the two men who got out were certainly not Arab. A few minutes later both men were in the house. "A Mr Norton, madam," Cummings explained. "From the Foreign Office."

Joanna had not bothered to dress after Dick had left. She put on a houserobe and slippers and went downstairs, aware that her hair was loose on her shoulders and that she must look as if she had just got out of bed. Which she had. "I'm afraid I was resting," she said, looking from face to face.

"John Norton, Princess, and this is Geoffrey Allan. My card."

She put the card on the table. "Please sit." She did so herself.

227

"You'll forgive us for intruding on your grief, ma'am," Norton said. "But this business, well, it does have ramifications."

"I'm sure it does. My husband was murdered by his half-brother, while living in this country."

"Ah . . . this is what you told the police last night. Have you any proof that Emir Mutil was involved in your husband's death?"

"Well, it's fairly obvious, isn't it? Prince Hasim was negotiating with certain people from his own country—"

"You have proof of this?"

"He was certainly meeting with people from Qadir, exiles like himself."

"But you do not know the subject of their discussions."

"Well, of course I do not."

"They need not have been discussing Qadir at all."

"Oh, for heaven's sake—"

"I wish you to understand the position of Her Majesty's Government, Princess Hasim. Great Britain has very important links with Qadir, both business and defence. It would be a serious matter indeed if those links were to be imperilled. Believe me, we have every possible sympathy with you in the horrible murder of your husband and your stepson, but you must understand that until and unless there is proof that the assassination was carried out on behalf of the present Qadiri government, we would not wish to take the matter any further, nor could we possibly approve of someone in your position throwing out accusations which have no substantiation."

"I had always assumed this was a free country."

"I hope it is. But freedom carries with it a certain responsibility."

"Mr Norton," Joanna said, "I can identify one of the three assassins. He was a man named Wazir, who had been in the employ of my husband—"

"Had been? You mean he had been fired?"

"Oh, God, I went through all this with the police last night. No, he had not been fired. He was highly valued by my husband. When the Emir Raisul died, a few weeks ago, as Hasim had agreed not to

228

return to Qadir, he sent Wazir as his representative at his father's funeral. Something must have happened while Wazir was there. He was suborned, or something. So he came back to murder my husband. And my son."

"But you have no proof of this."

"I do not have any proof," Joanna shouted. "Only that I saw Wazir murder my husband in cold blood."

"I know. Very tragic. It would be unusual indeed if you were thinking clearly this close to such a horrendous event."

Joanna glared at him. "Just what are you trying to say?"

"I am merely trying to put it to you that you, we, all of us, need to think very clearly as to which direction we are going to proceed in this matter. The Arab world is riddled with blood feuds and ancient family rivalries. You say your husband was meeting with various Qadiris. You assume he was discussing politics. But they might have been personal matters, equally important to him, involving this man Wazir."

"Of course," Joanna snapped. "And Jack the Ripper could have been a milkman who just happened to be around when all those women were murdered. Am I to assume, Mr Norton, that you are going to stop looking for Wazir and his accomplices? I wish you to know that I want, and am entitled, to police protection until they are caught."

"We have no intention of ceasing to look for the murderers of your husband, ma'am. They will be caught. And until they are, you will continue to receive protection. And for your son, of course."

"Thank you."

"But in return, I would ask you most earnestly to refrain from making any statements to the press about Qadiri involvement in this matter. It would be far better for all of us, publicly at least, to indicate that this was a personal feud between Prince Hasim and his employee."

Joanna sighed. "I will be careful what I say to the press."

Because that ordeal was now upon her. The press had been besieging the flat and Matilda and the hospital where William was, as well as the Qadiri Embassy in London and even Caribee Shipping. Now at last they had gathered that Joanna was at her home in the country, and they came charging down, to be extremely put out when the police refused them entry to the grounds. Joanna was actually quite in favour of their getting uptight about that, as naturally they floated their own theories as to what was going on, theories which agreed with hers but which could not be related to her. She was, however, upset when she took the children for a walk in the grounds that evening and discovered all the fences lined with snapping photographers, using long-range lenses. It wasn't the photographs that bothered her as much as the thought that amongst those lenses there could be Wazir, armed with a gun.

She hurried the children back inside, had an early dinner. Now she wished she had made Dick stay, but she actually slept very soundly, and was at the office next morning at eight. It had been quite a decision to leave the children, although Inspector Garside swore they would be all right. And for her drive in she had an armed detective sitting in the front of the Rolls beside a highly nervous Charlie. She could see no necessity for his presence; had Wazir wanted her life he could easily have had it in the flat. Peter Young wore his usual long face. "The market isn't actually open yet," he said, "but I've been in touch with Prim, and he tells me the shares will definitely be marked down."

"To what?"

"Well, this time yesterday morning, before the news of the assassination broke, they were eight pounds, twelve shillings and four pence. At the close last night they were seven pounds, eighteen shillings and three pence. That wasn't too bad. But he suggests they may go as low as six this morning. And then, we simply have to release the news that the Qadir link is now broken. Irrevocably?"

"Yes," Joanna said.

"Well . . . we could be looking at five, even. Worse if we don't come up with a new route." He peered at her over the tops of his glasses.

"No new route, at the moment," Joanna said. "I shall have to work on it."

"You understand that this could be a most serious matter," Peter said.

"We've faced serious matters before."

"Indeed we have. But . . . well . . ." he looked embarrassed.

She knew what he was thinking; before she had had Prince Hasim waiting in the wings. "The ships need a refit, anyway," she said.

"Which will cost money we do not have."

"It is still necessary. And then put them on the Caribbean route. Advertise the extra sailings. We should attract some passengers. And contact our manufacturers and tell them we shall be placing additional space at their disposal."

"You do realise that there is a limit to how many washing machines and dishwashers one can sell in an area like the West Indies? It's geared to tourism more than anywhere else. A few live very well, and they have all the household appliances they require, and the rest live rather poorly, and they can't afford the latest models, or any models at all."

"I understand that, Peter. But we can at least ship more rice and sugar, can't we?"

"If they can grow more. I hate to be a merchant of doom and gloom, Joanna, but—"

"Listen," Joanna said. "Just do all the things I have told you, and let me worry about what happens next."

He looked as if he would have spoken again, then shrugged. "And the news from Qadir?"

"Oh, as you say, that must be released this morning, certainly the moment trading begins. Now I have a couple of funerals to attend."

First she went to the hospital to see William. He remained in intensive care, and with his oxygen mask and the mass of bandages she couldn't

231

really identify him, until their hands touched and he squeezed her fingers. "We anticipate your brother will make a full recovery," Dr Alva told her.

Which was at least a crumb of comfort.

Billy and Matilda accompanied her to Hasim's funeral. They were not the only English people to attend, but the others were all very obviously plainclothes policemen, not only protecting her but looking out for Wazir. As if he would be foolish enough to turn up.

"You going back to the office?" Billy asked, when all the prayers had been said and chanted, the body had disappeared, and they stood on the steps of the mosque.

"No. I've had enough doom and gloom for the moment. And I need to brace myself for this afternoon."

"The funeral, or the share price?"

"Both."

"Well, if you want to have a chat about the shares—"

"I'll be in touch. Are you going to Howard's funeral this afternoon?"

"I think we should," Matilda said.

"Then will you pick me up?

"Two o'clock," Matilda promised.

Joanna had Charlie drive her to her own flat. Her ivory tower. There were, as always, several bottles of champagne in the fridge. She took one out, gazed at it for several seconds, then put it back again. Becoming an alcoholic was not going to help her situation.

She kicked off her shoes, lay on on the bed, stared at the ceiling. She was so tired. Mentally more than physically. She had thought the fighting was over, history. She had fought, and she had won. But her victory had been built on a mound of shifting clay. It was very easy for her to appear confident and commanding to Peter Young; she had a lot of experience at that. But the fact was, she had the strongest temptation to cut and run. Once the news from Qadir was released, and it should already have been released, no one could accuse her of insider dealing if she now placed her shares on the market. She almost felt that Billy had been hinting that might be the best thing to do. But that would drive the price through the floor. It would bankrupt the company. With no guarantee that she would clear anything worthwhile.

How considerations change, she thought. Nine years ago she had landed in England without a penny to her name. Now she was disgruntled because she might only clear a couple of million rather than the six she was presently worth. As for the company, who was she now working for? Young Howard was dead. Would Raisul be interested? That was a long time in the future. Helen? Could she possibly wish on Helen all the stress she had undergone over the past few years?

The phone was ringing. She let it go through to the ansaphone; she had no desire to speak with anyone at the moment. Then she played it back. "Joanna! Andy Gosling. I really would like to get together with you. Just for a chat. Give me a ring."

God almighty! What a pain. Quite apart from the lack of taste. But he had been as tasteless after Howard's death. But suddenly she didn't want to be alone any more. She telephoned Caribee Shipping, was put through to the downstairs desk. "Lunch with me," she told Dick.

"Ah . . . yes, ma'am. Where?" She gave him the address of the flat.

There was a supermarket on the corner. Joanna went down and bought a couple of steaks and a bottle of red wine. She was cooking when Dick arrived. "Who owns this?" he asked, looking around him.

"I do. Or, I suppose, the Company. It's my *pied-à-terre*."

"You know how to live."

"There's champagne in the fridge. Open a bottle and pour."

He obeyed. "Is this a wake?"

"Perhaps. But I'm not quite sure for whom."

He gave her a glass. "There's all kind of chat at the office."

233

"I believe it."

"So, what are you going to do?"

"Would you believe that I don't have a clue, Dick? I am teetering on the edge of financial collapse. Which could mean that you're teetering on the edge of losing your job."

"It's happened before. But you—"

"It's happened to me before. Nearly. This time . . ."

She served their meal while he opened the bottle of wine. "I'm sorry, I should have done that before."

He looked at the label. "Ten minutes breathing will do. We can finish our champagne." He sat opposite her. "Obviously now is not the time, and you're still the boss, but . . . when you've sorted all this out and finished mourning Hasim, would you marry me?" Joanna choked on a piece of steak, and he had to come round and pat her on the back. "Is that such a horrendous prospect?" he asked.

Joanna drank some wine and wiped the tears from her eyes. Horrendous, she thought. Dick worshipped her. And he was someone she could love. Perhaps. But . . . he wasn't in her league. He was basically a drifter. He had been as terrified as everyone else when Wazir had started shooting. Oh, he was kind and gentle, and she had thoroughly enjoyed the previous afternoon. But everything that had happened, or more importantly, had not happened, had been at her behest. He had obeyed her utterly and without question. Did she want, could she, risk a husband that subservient? There was no way she could have allowed either Howard or Hasim to lie naked on her body without having sex with them. Dick had just lain there, happy to accept that crumb from her table. "Of course it isn't horrendous," she said. "It's very flattering. But a little surprising. I assume you are not marrying me for my money?"

"It's your money."

"What's left of it. I think, as you say, that I have rather a lot on my plate right now, Dick. I need a little time."

"Of course." He grinned. "I just felt I should get my proposal in before all those other guys."

234

"What other guys?"

"The guys who'll be queueing up to get their hands on you once the fact of Hasim's death sinks in."

"Chance would be a fine thing."

He finished his meal, looked at his watch. "Do you wish me to stay?"

"No. I have to go to Howard's funeral. But . . . come back tonight."

"Here?"

"Here. We'll have supper together. I may be more settled in my mind by then."

"May I kiss you?"

"I'd like that."

Joanna wondered why all the decent, hard-working, gentle people in the world were failures. Simply because not one of those qualities worked in the real world. She telephoned the house, was reassured by Cummings. "Everything is under control here, madam."

"Are the police still with you?"

"Oh, yes, madam."

"And the children are okay?"

"Oh, yes, madam."

"Right. Well, Cummings, I'm going to spend tonight in town. But I'll try to get down there first thing tomorrow."

"Of course, madam."

There was no business news available on television at that hour, and she did not feel like speaking with Peter Young. Whatever was going to happen would already have started happening. She made up her face carefully while she waited for Billy and Matilda to collect her, checked her stockings. When this funeral was over, she thought, she was going to burn this entire outfit.

Then she telephoned John Giffard, her solicitor. "I know Alicia has been making slanderous statements," he said. "But in my opinion your best course is to ignore them. Everyone knows they're the ramblings of a hysterical woman. I'm sure you can do without a court case right now."

Joanna knew he was right, and accepted his advice. But she had barely hung up when the phone rang again. She regarded it for a few seconds before picking it up as the ansaphone cut in. "Joanna! I've been trying to get hold of you all day."

"I'm sorry, Andy, I just haven't felt like being got hold of. And right now I have to rush—"

"Listen! I want to have a meeting with you."

"I'm not in the mood."

"Do you know what's happening in the City?"

"I don't want to know, right now."

"Are you having a breakdown?"

"Possibly. Now I simply have to go."

"Jo—"

She hung up.

"You don't look too good," Matilda said, as they sat together in the back of the Rolls.

"I think I have every reason for not looking too good," Joanna pointed out.

"Absolutely. Therefore no one could possibly blame you for giving this one a miss," Matilda pointed out. "I can represent you."

"No," Joanna said. "He was my stepson. I am more than partly responsible for his death."

"Jo—"

"I am going," Joanna said fiercely.

But she accepted Matilda and Billy's suggestion that they remain at the back of the church, well away from the group of Alicia's family. Alicia herself, in black with a black veil, was a birdlike figure, flitting from group to group, up to the very moment the coffin was brought into the church. Predictably, she had refused cremation, and after the service there was a line of cars leading to the cemetery. Once again Matilda and Billy kept Joanna at the very back while the last words were spoken, then they would have hurried her away. But they had not reached the car when Alicia caught up with them, Victoria at her heels. "Murderess!" she hissed. "Whore! Husband-stealer!"

Joanna just stared at her, not certain what to say. Matilda stepped in front of her. "That is quite uncalled for," she said. "Our own brother was caught up in that attack."

"Your brother is *alive*," Alicia ground out.

"And my brother is dead!" Victoria shrilled.

"Get into the car," Billy muttered, urgently, at Joanna's shoulder.

"Bitch!" Alicia shrieked, and lunged forward. By now a considerable crowd had gathered, mostly mourners, while the road behind had suddenly become equally crowded with cars. Joanna could not stop herself stepping forward. It was quite against her character to back away from any crisis, and she could not believe that Alicia meant her any actual harm.

"Behave yourself," she snapped, and was utterly surprised when Alicia's body cannoned into hers. She stumbled backwards, her high heels caught in the gravel, and she went down with a thump that knocked all the breath from her body.

"Bitch!" Alicia screamed again, and hurled herself onto her, red-painted nails turning into claws. Gasping, Joanna got her hands up to catch the searing blows. She caught Alicia's wrists, even as Alicia's body again thumped into hers. As they were both wearing heavy coats the impact was less severe than it might have been, but Joanna's returning breath was again driven from her lungs. Desperately she forced her strength upwards, and in the same movement drove her assailant over on to her back.

Now it was Alicia's turn to gasp as she rolled in the mud, her hat coming off to expose her hair. Joanna gazed into the handsome, distorted face, and knew an almost killer urge, but was then struck a savage blow between the shoulder-blades, and went down herself, face into the mud. Yet again she lost her breath, but by now Billy had run forward and seized Victoria by the shoulders to stop her hitting Joanna again. Matilda was grasping Alicia, while other people crowded round to help.

Slowly Joanna pushed herself to her hands and knees, scraping mud from her face; mud clung to her mink, and there was mud in her hair. She was desperately angry, turned to find Alicia, blood pounding through her arteries. But she had her arm grasped as she was turned away from the shouting people. "You want to get out of here," a voice said, and before she knew what was happening she was bundled into the back of a Rolls-Royce that had drawn up alongside her own Rolls.

She fell on to the back seat, scattering mud, pushed herself up as the car drove away, blinked at Andy Gosling. He grinned at her. "You sure do make it hard for a guy to get hold of you," he said.

"Listen," she said. "Put me down."

"On the street? Do you have any idea what you look like?"

She blew mudstained hair from her face. "You are kidnapping me."

"I would say I am rescuing you from an embarrassing situation."

"All right," she said. "You have rescued me. I'm grateful. Now take me home."

"Which home?"

"My London flat will do. I assume you know where that is, as you keep telephoning."

He smiled at her. "You certainly need a bath." He tapped on the glass partition separating them from the driver. Who nodded. "He knows the address," Andy said.

"Thank you." Joanna gathered her mink around herself, suppressed a shiver. She was really quite shaken up. She knew Alicia was a fairly unstable character, but to be attacked like that . . . she had experienced more in the last couple of days than she could reasonably stand. "That woman needs to be locked up."

"I entirely agree with you," Andy said. She shot him a suspicious glance. "Do you know she's been making all manner of utterances to the press?" he asked. "She actually held a press conference this

238

morning, just an hour before her son's funeral, mind you, to say that it was her inside knowledge that Caribee Shipping is effectively bankrupt? That the true facts are being disguised?"

"That's not true," Joanna snapped. "We have no financial difficulties until . . . well, until and unless I manage to find a new route for our ships."

"Of course," Andy agreed. "I know that. You know that. I hope your bankers also know that. But the press are always hungry for a story."

"Such as suggesting that I, and Caribee Shipping, are on our way out. They've tried that before."

"Indeed they have." The car was stopping outside the flat. "Mind if I come up?"

"Andy, I have today buried my husband and my stepson. If you make a pass, I shall break a bottle over your head." Because, she thought, I intend to have sex tonight, although you won't ever know that, with a man I could really love.

"I'm not going to make a pass. Word of honour. I wish to talk to you. And you need to talk to me."

"Tell me why."

"I will, upstairs."

She shrugged, got out of the car. They rode up in the elevator gazing at each other, but not speaking. She unlocked the flat, walked straight through to the bedroom to look at herself in the full-length mirror. There was mud everywhere, even on her face. "Minks can be cleaned," Andy said, from the doorway.

"So can human bodies. I intend to have a shower. Would you mind closing the door? There is champagne in the fridge."

"At three-thirty in the afternoon?" He grinned. "Don't tell me, Howard always drank champagne at three-thirty in the afternoon." He closed the door.

Mud had even managed to get under the mink, on her stockings. Even her knickers had mud on them, which must have meant that at some time during her fight with Alicia her dress had ridden up.

239

What a show for the public. And at the funeral of their son! Damn that woman.

She threw all of her clothes on the floor together with the coat, stood beneath the hot jet for several minutes, then washed her hair, which was also thick with mud. It was half an hour before she emerged, wearing a dressing gown, with her hair wrapped in a towel even after five minutes with the blower.

Andy sat on the settee, a glass in his hand. As soon as she appeared, he got up and poured her one too. "You look magnificent."

She made a face, sat beside him. "My idea is to have several of these, and then go to bed for a nap. I have a dinner engagement."

"Lucky chap. Are you able to concentrate?"

"I am always able to concentrate."

"I once made you an offer for your shares." She stared at him. "Oh, it was through an intermediary."

"You? You bastard."

"Why so? It was a straightforward offer. And more than the shares were worth, at that moment."

"You were a bastard for not coming straight out and telling me who you were. And for trying to get control of the company. So now you're back. What are you offering this time?"

"I have already bought out John Donivan. Only seven thousand shares, to be sure, but it gives me a stake in the company."

"When did this happen?" Surely she would have known.

"An hour ago."

"You really are a bastard. So, your speciality is buying up collapsing companies and restructuring them. Where do you get your money?"

"Have you never worked out that all of Howard's friends were millionaires? And he was at the bottom of the list, just about."

"You claim to be a millionaire?"

"I'm afraid I am one. I'm not quite in Hasim's class, but I am several times more wealthy than Howard ever was. Or than you are now."

"And now you reckon you have me across a barrel."

"I would love to have you across a barrel, Joanna. But as you said, you're not in the mood right now. But what's more important is that over the last few years I have developed a considerable admiration for you. I think you were magnificent when Howard died. I'm not going to pretend that I approved of your marriage to Hasim. Oh, he was a nice enough chap, and I knew you weren't going to be ill-treated in any way, but I know quite a lot about Qadiri politics, and it seemed to me that you were getting in over your head. As I am sure you realise by now."

"Yes," she muttered.

"All of which has persuaded me that you deserve to keep control of Caribee Shipping. But you do need help. We can work together."

"Oh, yes? With you employing me, is that it?"

"Not at all. You have something like seventy per cent of the company in that trust company of yours. I already have three per cent of the remainder. I would like you to sell me forty-four per cent of your shares at a mutually agreed price. But I do promise you it will be considerably over the current market value."

"And you will then virtually own the company. No deal."

"Hear me out, Joanna. If I am going to invest money, a lot of money, in your company, I need to have ultimate control, if only to be able to persuade my partners that the investment would be viable."

"You have partners?"

"Doesn't everyone?"

"I am not giving away my company, Andy."

"You still haven't let me finish. You will keep your company. There will be a clause written into the contract between us that as long as you retain a twenty-five per cent share holding, you are entitled to remain as Managing Director and Chairman."

She glanced at him, suspiciously. "And you will immediately take steps to have my share holding reduced below twenty-five per cent."

"I have never got the impression that you are a woman who can be persuaded to do anything she doesn't wish to. As it happens, I want you to remain Chairman. You know the firm, you know the ships, you know the men who sail them. They all worship you. No, no, there can be no change at the top."

"But you will tell me what to do."

"My God but you are a suspicious woman. I will not tell you what to do, Joanna. I shall merely control the finances."

"And you'll lose your shirt. Reduced to the Caribbean run, we are bound to lose money."

"I have a new route for you."

Her head jerked.

"Australia. There is a hole waiting to be filled. It is a small hole, but small holes often grow into big ones. There is a contract awaiting you for the shipment of dry goods in and sugar out of Darwin."

She gazed at him. "Suppose I tell you, no thanks, and take up that offer myself?"

He grinned. "Were you going to do that, Joanna, you would not have told me. But in any event, I control this contract as well. It's a company I acquired a couple of years ago. I've just let it tick over, waiting to see what was going to happen with your Qadiri connection. But I always knew it was right for Caribee Shipping."

"You're quite a guy, Andy Gosling," she said. "Talk about still waters."

"Then will you accept?"

"I'd need my head examined if I didn't. Providing everything you've suggested and offered is on the up."

"In my business, one has to be on the up." He refilled their glasses. "Well, here's to us."

"Partners," she said. "Business partners, Andy."

"Business partners, Joanna. For as long as you wish that."

He did not even kiss her. Odd. She couldn't believe a man like Andy Gosling could regard her simply as a business partner. But if that was how he was willing to play it, she was happy, because she couldn't play it any other way. She put on a pair of jeans and a shirt, so that she could go out to buy something for supper. But she had the wit to look out of the window first, and changed her mind. The paparazzi was gathering, and a few minutes later her doorbell was ringing. She ignored it, called Caribee Shipping. "Oh, Princess," gushed the telephone girl. "Mr Young was about to ring you."

"I'll speak to him in a moment," Joanna said. "Put me through to Richard Orton."

"Richard Orton. Right." If the girl was surprised at her boss's order of priorities, she concealed it well.

"Dick," Joanna said. "Listen, I have a problem."

"You mean dinner is off."

"Dinner is not off. But my flat is besieged by media people and I really don't want to face them. So I'd like you to go to the supermarket on your way here and buy whatever it is you feel like eating; I'll cook it. You'd better get some wine as well. Then go to the street behind mine, and find the interior fire door. Come in there and up the stairs. That way they won't see you."

"But surely that fire door is kept locked? Or at least, barred from the inside."

"Yes, it is. What time are you aiming to get here?"

"Well . . . sevenish."

"Make it six-thirty. We have a lot to do. I shall go downstairs by the fire staircase at six-twenty and hook back the bars, so the door can be opened from the outside. Be sure you put them back into place before you come up."

"Right. I'll see you then. Listen, did I ever tell you that I love you?"

"Could be. Hang up. I'll speak with Mr Young now," she told the switchboard, wondering if the girl had been listening in.

"Joanna! The roof's caving in."

"Tell me."

"We're down to five pounds fifteen, and there can be no doubt the slide is going to continue tomorrow."

"Perhaps. But the day after we'll be back on top."

"Eh? Don't tell me—"

"That I've found another sugar daddy? Not really, Peter, but we're back in business, with adequate financing and a new route."

"How in the name of God did you manage that?"

"I'll tell you tomorrow. And listen, call a board meeting for eleven, so I can put the facts before them all. Did you know John Donivan had sold his shares?"

"I had a call from Prim."

"And you never told me?"

"I couldn't get hold of you. Anyway, it's a symptom, rats and sinking ships and that kind of thing."

"He'll be sorry. Have a good night, Peter. I'll be in early tomorrow."

The bell had stopped ringing, but when she looked out of the window she saw there were still quite a few reporters there. They knew she was inside. Well, they were welcome to wait. She considered having some more champagne and decided against it; that could wait until Dick got there. She turned on the television, and sure enough on the local London news there was an item about a fight at the funeral, between the Princess Hasim and Mrs Alicia Edge. Thank God there had been no cameras about.

She switched off the set and moved restlessly about the room. She really was behaving very badly, she knew, so soon after Hasim's death. But she so wanted to begin a new life, with someone she genuinely liked, perhaps even loved, rather than someone who just happened to have accumulated her for her looks. And now that Andy Gosling had so strangely given her the opportunity to look to the future . . . She picked up the phone, called the house. "Everything here is fine, madam," Cummings assured her.

"The police still there?"

"Oh, yes, madam. I believe they intend to remain until those men have been caught. I shouldn't think it'll be long now."

"God, I hope not. Give them my love, Cummings. I can't come down first thing in the morning, but I'll be there tomorrow afternoon. Right?"

"Of course, madam."

She hung up, went to the window. It was quite dark now, but she could still see the cluster of people in the street, smoking cigarettes, gossiping. As it promised to be a cold night, they would surely push off, eventually. She looked at her watch: six-fifteen. He'd be on his way now, from the supermarket, laden with goodies, she hoped. She would have to pay him for them.

She made herself sit down. She was as nervous as . . . the first time she had gone out with Dick, she realised. That was stupid. He was a friend, not a stranger. They were going to make love. Have sex. But it would be loving sex. And then . . .

Her head jerked as there was a soft tap on the door. Again she looked at her watch. Six twenty-five. Where had the ten minutes gone?

She got up, made herself walk to the door rather than run. She drew the bolts and the safety catch, pulled it in, and Wazir placed his hand on her chest and pushed.

Joanna stumbled backwards, taken utterly by surprise. Her legs struck a chair and she fell over, missing the chair and sitting very heavily on the carpet. Wazir stepped inside and closed the door behind him.

Joanna gasped and got her breath back. "You bastard," she said.

He grinned. "And you are very beautiful, Princess."

Oh, my God, Joanna thought. The idea of rape had not entered her mind. But he couldn't have come here, with all the attendant risk, just to rape her. Anyway . . . "How did you get in?"

"I followed the man. Your lover. He opened the fire door for me. Very generous."

"You made him open the door?"

Oh, Dick, she thought, how could you?

"No, no, Princess. I waited for him to open the door, then I came in."

"Where is he?"

She was slowly pushing herself to her feet.

Wazir grinned again, and drew his finger across his throat. "He did not put up a fight. He was taken by surprise, and his arms were full of groceries."

"You killed him? Bastard!" she shrieked, and having reached his feet, hurled herself at him.

But Wazir was a big man, and caught her flailing arms without difficulty, forcing her back across the room and on to the settee, sitting beside her as he held her there. "You stop fighting," he said, "or I will hit you."

Joanna panted, but subsided. She needed to think. But she could only think, Dick is dead. This thug has killed him. As he killed Hasim and Howie, and nearly killed poor William. And thus I am alone, in my flat, with a killer. There was nobody else coming to see her tonight. There was nobody even going to telephone her. But there were those reporters in the street, waiting to see her. If she could reach the window . . .

Wazir released her arms, and she rubbed where his fingers had bitten into her flesh. "Now, you see," he said. "If you do not resist me, I will not hurt you. If you resist me—" he reached inside his jacket – he was, as always, wearing European clothes – and produced a knife, with a blade several inches long, "I will cut you. In my country, when a woman misbehaves, her husband has the right to mutilate her. I could cut off your nose, or take out one of your eyes, or cut off a breast. Perhaps both breasts."

Joanna found herself panting; he spoke so casually. "I am not your wife."

"You are my enemy. That is the same thing."

She looked past him, at the door. He had not replaced the bolts. If she could get to the door. But the window was a safer bet. "Now I will tell you what I wish you to do," Wazir said.

She got her eyes back to gaze at his. "My mission is to destroy the male house of Prince Hasim," he said. "To complete this, I must kill Prince Raisul. But I cannot get to him, in the house in Berkshire, because of all the police. You must get him out of there for me."

"You expect me to deliver my son to you, to be murdered?"

His left hand shot out so quickly she didn't have time to move. It closed on her throat, while his right hand thrust forward with the knife. For a moment she supposed he was going to stab her, but he merely slit her blouse, parting it to each side to expose her body: she was not wearing a bra. "You will do that," he said, his face close to hers, "or you will die, here, slowly and in great agony."

Joanna's brain seemed to have gone dead; there could be no doubt he meant what he said. So, play along with him and pray that something would turn up between here and Caribee House. But she couldn't give in too quickly, or he'd know she was planning something. "Here is what you must do," he said. "You must telephone your home, and tell your people there that the danger is now over, and that you would like your son brought to you here. You understand that?"

Joanna licked her lips. "I'll see you damned first."

He peered at her for a few seconds, then grinned, released her, and stood up. "Get up," he said. Joanna stood up in turn. "Take off that shirt," he said.

"Are you a rapist as well as a murderer?" he said.

He continued to smile. "I need to see what I am cutting, Princess." Joanna took off the shirt and threw it on the floor. "Very beautiful," Wazir said. "And you are twice a mother. Women who are twice mothers in my country are often fat."

He seemed absorbed. Joanna glanced at the window again. He would of course catch up with her. But if she could just open it and shout. "Go into the kitchen," he commanded.

Joanna turned as if to obey him, then turned back again, ducked under his arm, and ran to the window, fingers fumbling at the catch, other hand seizing the frame to throw it up . . . and Wazir caught her shoulder, pulling her back and swinging her round with a force that sent her scattering across the room. She stumbled into the settee and fell right over it, crashing to the floor beyond. While she lay there, breathless, he knelt above her, and slapped her face several times, sending her head to and fro. She thought she was choking, as she could not breathe. "You play games with me, eh?" Wazir growled.

Joanna blinked at him even as she tasted blood. "Well," he said, "I fix you good." Still kneeling above her, he began to unfasten her jeans.

And the door opened.

Both Joanna's and Wazir's heads turned together, staring in consternation at the apparition which stood there, a bloody mask of a face, into which blood still dribbled from the cut on his head; the blood had also stained his jacket and shirt and even his pants, and there was blood on his hands. But he was moving forward with a quite terrifying determination. Wazir muttered something in Arabic, and got off Joanna, drawing his knife as he did so.

"Dick!" Joanna screamed, both in relief and as a warning.

But Dick was already kicking, the toe of his shoe slamming into Wazir's wrist and sending the knife flying across the room. He immediately kicked with the other foot, catching Wazir on the side of the head and knocking him back to the floor. Joanna rolled away from him and reached her feet; pulling up her zip she scrambled over the settee and found the knife.

Wazir was attempting to get up, but Dick was on him again. They were much of a size, but Wazir was the heavier. For a moment they wrestled, Wazir trying to close his hands on Dick's neck, Dick slamming short-arm punches into Wazir's body, both men grasping and grunting. Their heaving took them against the settee, and it and they fell over together, the two men landing almost at Joanna's feet. She had the knife poised, but dared not use it at the moment, even if she could bring herself to use it at all, as the bodies beneath her were constantly changing position.

Then Wazir managed to thrust Dick away from him, and stagger across the room, back against the window. Panting, he thrust his right arm into the left side of his jacket, and drew an automatic pistol. It hadn't occurred to Joanna that he might have a gun as well as the knife. Now she stared in horror as Wazir levelled the gun at Dick, who was slowly getting to his feet. "No!" Joanna screamed, and hurled the knife.

She had never thrown a knife before, and it turned several times in the air. But the sight of it distracted Wazir, and his shot was wide. He tried to turn away from it, and struck the window heavily. The glass shattered, and he half fell through, desperately clutching at the frame to stop himself. From below there came shouts of alarm and excitement.

Dick hurled himself forward, seized Wazir by the belt, and jerked him back into the room. The pistol fell from Wazir's hand, and Joanna picked that up as well. "Oh, Dick," she said. "He told me you were dead."

"Well," he said. "He certainly hit me hard enough."

"Oh, Dick," she said again. "I thought—" she bit off the words. She could never tell him that she had always considered him a bit of a wimp. Because after all, he wasn't, and he had saved her life.

He grinned through his blood-caked lips. "Seems to me our evening together is ruined. Shall I let those characters up for their story?"

"I think they're entitled to it."

He pressed the street door switch. "Come on up, you guys," he said. Then he turned back to Joanna. "Give me the gun, and you'd better put something on."

Joanna hesitated, looking at Wazir, who was rolling to and fro on the floor, moaning, blood streaming from cuts on his face and neck and hands where he had shattered the glass.

"He's not going anywhere," Dick assured her.

Aunt Ethel's sniff could be heard throughout the church, quiet as the parson pronounced them man and wife. But she'd said it all already. 'Marrying one of her own clerks,' she had declared at large.

Joanna presumed there were a few people in Caribee Shipping who felt the same way, Peter Young amongst them. But she was the woman with the golden touch, even if none of them understood quite where the touch came from. She could marry whomever she chose. They moved slowly down the aisle, because William, although strong enough to act as Dick's best man, was still not fully fit. Joanna concentrated on walking straight; she didn't want to consider that at the age of not yet thirty she was on her third husband.

But she smiled at Andy Gosling. Andy had taken the news that she was not going to marry him with his usual insouciance. She had an idea that he was waiting, with seemingly endless patience, for her, the company, everything to fall into his lap.

Andy was perhaps a problem for the future. Her only problem for the present was Raisul. But the police had captured both of Wazir's accomplices, and felt sure there would be no further attempts on the boy's life for the foreseeable future, the more so as the Foreign Office had discreetly let Emir Mutil know they knew what he was about.

She had to believe that, just as she had to make sure Raisul grew up as an Englishman and the heir to Caribee Shipping, with never a thought about Qadir. She also had, she knew, to cope with Alicia's hysterical machinations. But she felt she could do those things. Thanks to Dick and Andy, to be sure, but most of all, herself. For the first time in her life, she was her own woman.

She had learned how to survive.